THE COLLECTED STORIES
—SEASON THREE—
VOLUME I

THE SHERLOCK HOLMES AND LUCY JAMES MYSTERIES

The Last Moriarty
The Wilhelm Conspiracy
Remember, Remember
The Crown Jewel Mystery
The Jubilee Problem
Death at the Diogenes Club
The Return of the Ripper
Die Again, Mr. Holmes
Watson on the Orient Express

THE SHERLOCK AND LUCY SHORT STORIES

Flynn's Christmas
The Clown on the High Wire
The Cobra in the Monkey Cage
A Fancy-Dress Death
The Sons of Helios
The Vanishing Medium
Christmas at Baskerville Hall
Kidnapped at the Tower
Five Pink Ladies
The Solitary Witness
The Body in the Bookseller's
The Curse of Cleopatra's Needle
The Coded Blue Envelope
Christmas on the Nile
The Missing Mariner
Powder Island
Murder at the Royal Observatory
The Bloomsbury Guru
Holmes Takes a Holiday
Holmes Picks a Winner

The series page at Amazon:
amzn.to/3GNiahd

Sign up at SherlockAndLucy.com
to stay up-to-date on Lucy and Sherlock adventures

THE **SHERLOCK HOLMES/
LUCY JAMES** MYSTERIES

THE COLLECTED STORIES
— SEASON THREE —
VOLUME I

BY **ANNA ELLIOTT**
AND **CHARLES VELEY**

This is a work of fiction. Names, characters, organizations, places, events, and incidents are either products of the author's imagination or are used fictitiously.

Text copyright © 2021 by Charles Veley and Anna Elliott
All rights reserved

No part of this book may be reproduced, or stored in a retrieval system, or transmitted in any form or by any means, electronic, mechanical, photocopying, recording, or otherwise, without express written permission of the author.

Typesetting by FormattingExperts.com
Cover design by Todd A. Johnson

Stories

The Missing Mariner 1
Powder Island 87
Murder at the Royal Observatory 217

THE MISSING MARINER

Chapter 1: Watson

"Double Murder in Mayfair?" I asked, reading from the headline in the *Times*.

Holmes waved the suggestion away.

It was just before nine o'clock on the morning of Wednesday, January 18. Snow had fallen the day before, accompanied by a harsh wind that had now given way to fog. Barely a week had elapsed since our return from Egypt and, still softened by our previous month in that more temperate clime, I was grateful for the radiant warmth of fresh coals from our fireplace at 221B Baker Street. Holmes sat in his usual chair on one side of the blaze, and I on the other side, both of us well sheltered from the dank cold that pervaded the streets of London. I had been further warmed by a hot breakfast of bacon and eggs from Mrs. Hudson, followed by hot coffee. The plate, cup and silverware that Holmes might have used for his own breakfast remained clean and untouched on our table.

Regrettably, Holmes was not in the mood to appreciate our creature comforts. Indeed, he was not in a mood to appreciate much of anything at all. Since we had come home to London, Holmes had resisted all my attempts to promote the only safe remedy that I knew of for his currently despondent state: namely, a new investigation.

Nothing I had suggested thus far could rise to a level of complexity or novelty high enough to interest him.

"Not outré enough for you?" I asked, hoping to at least prompt a reply.

"The facts of the Mayfair case clearly indicate the guilt of the second footman. I have already communicated as much to Lestrade."

I studied the paper in search of another headline.

"Robbery of rare masterpiece from Hampton Court Palace," I read aloud.

Silence ensued.

I scanned the first paragraph of the article. I must confess that I had an interest of my own in the case, since I had always wanted to visit the palace and see the wonderful paintings it contained, not to mention the spectacular public state rooms and the stupendous kitchen built for the massive scale of entertainment demanded by King Henry VIII. I gathered my thoughts for a moment. If I could persuade Holmes to take the case, I thought, a visit would be required.

I looked up. "This might be promising, Holmes. According to the newspaper report, the painting disappeared yesterday in broad daylight at the height of visiting hours and under full view of the warders. The Lord Chamberlain's spokesman refuses to comment on the identity of the painting except to say that it is rare and irreplaceable and that every effort is being made to find the responsible parties."

Holmes, though, remained slouched in his chair. "If the warders at Hampton Court are foolish enough to allow themselves to be duped or distracted, I fail to see that it is any business of mine—unless, as will probably happen, the police throw up their hands and come to me begging for assistance. Until then, however, I have little interest in a stolen painting, irreplaceable or otherwise."

I studied my old friend's lean, hawk-like countenance. In truth, I thought I knew what had produced this troubling descent into ennui. Once upon a time, I would have been consumed with the further worry that boredom would lead Holmes to resort to the stimulus of the cocaine bottle. That was not my fear in the present instance—although my habit of worry was nearly as difficult to break as any addiction to drink or drug.

No, what troubled me now was that I feared there was little remedy for what ailed Holmes. A few short weeks ago, a villain whose pursuit had consumed the whole of Holmes's energy for nearly an entire year had at long last been defeated. It was only natural, perhaps, that coming on the heels of that victory there should follow a certain feeling of emptiness. Not unlike a soldier who returns home after his time at war, Holmes now faced a gaping hole where once had been the desperate, defining purpose of our lives.

Even more than that, though—and here, I thought, lay the incurable aspect of Holmes's malady, if malady it could be termed—Zoe Rosario had returned to her career as violinist at La Scala Opera House in Milan. Roughly eight hundred miles away from London, Baker Street, and Sherlock Holmes.

I opened my mouth, feeling as if I had to say something to prod my friend into action. What I would have said I am not sure, since Holmes avoided all talk of personal matters in general and Zoe in particular as he would the proverbial plague. However, I was perhaps fortunately prevented from making any clumsy attempts at commiseration, for at that moment there came from below the sound of a ring at the front door.

"Well, Holmes," I said instead. "Perhaps this indicates the arrival of a new client with a problem knotty enough for your liking."

***

Our visitor was indeed a would-be client. However, I very much feared that Holmes would consider her problem as drab as any that had appeared in the paper.

Mrs. Athena Spenlow, as she introduced herself, was a very pretty woman, although no longer in her first youth, being somewhere about thirty or thirty-five years old. She had a touch of the Spanish beauty about her: black hair that curled around a heart-shaped, vivid face, with high cheekbones, a pert, pointed chin, and flashing dark eyes.

Those eyes were fixed imploringly on Holmes's face as she laid out the background to her case.

"It's my brother, you see, Mr. Holmes. Ronald. I haven't seen him in … it must be twenty years, now. He quarrelled with my father when we were young and ran away to sea to become a merchant sailor. We had no word from him in all the years that followed, and our mother feared—indeed, we all feared—that he had died in some accident at sea." Her eyes fell to her gloved hands, which lay clasped in her lap. "Our parents are deceased now, and I am quite alone in the world, my husband having died several years ago."

"My condolences, madam," Holmes said.

"Thank you." She bowed her head. "But I did not come here to speak of my own bereavements. Ordinarily, I reside in East Molesey, and lead a very quiet life. However, three days ago, I came up to London to do some shopping. I was in a carriage, driving along Cotton Street, when I saw him. My brother, Ronald, in a dark blue seaman's coat and cap. He was just boarding an omnibus that was travelling in the opposite direction from mine, and by the time I could make my driver understand that

I wished to halt and turn around, the omnibus was long gone. But it was my brother."

Holmes said nothing, but Mrs. Spenlow hurried on as though he had spoken. "I know what you will say—how could I possibly have recognised him, after so many years? You will point out that I may have been fooled by a mere passing resemblance. I can only say, Mr. Holmes, that I know—know absolutely—that the man I saw was Ronald Stiles, my brother. He had in fact changed very little since last I saw him and … it was he. Of that I am perfectly certain."

She spoke with complete assurance, her hands clasped and her voice quivering with emotion.

Holmes studied her a moment, then said, "I will not argue with your conviction. I would merely ask why you have come to me?"

Mrs. Spenlow's eyes opened a trifle wider. "Why, because I am hoping—praying—that you may be able to help me find Ronald again, of course. I am not without resources—I will be happy to pay any fee that you name, if you will only help me find my brother."

Holmes seemed to watch her a moment more from under half-lowered lids, then said, "I have no wish to cause you pain, but has it occurred to you that your brother may have no desire to be found? If the man you saw was indeed he, then he is clearly back in England. And yet he has made no attempt to contact you."

"Yes, but … but matters are not quite so simple. Ronald swore when he left our house after his quarrel with our father that he would never darken the family doorstep again. He would not know of our parents' deaths. And I—Ronald is several years older than I am, I was just a young girl when he left. He would not know my married name, or where I had settled after my marriage.

Mr. Holmes"—she clasped her hands more tightly—"I implore you, please, will you help me find the only family I have left in all the world?"

Holmes was silent a moment. Even a man who prided himself on being unmoved by emotion would have found it difficult to remain immune to Mrs. Spenlow's appeal. However, I truly had no idea whether he would accede to the lady's plea for help or no. It was not at all the sort of case he usually accepted—and very far from the innovative or unique crime he had been demanding a mere twenty minutes earlier.

However, after a moment's silence, Holmes stood up with one of those sudden bursts of activity which characterised his movements, crossed to the hearth and tapped the ashes from his pipe into the grate.

"If I am to assist you, Mrs. Spenlow, I will need some particulars about your brother. You say that his name is Ronald Stiles?"

Mrs. Spenlow bit her lip and nodded. "Yes. But … that is, there may be a difficulty. My father disinherited Ronald. At the time of their quarrel, he swore that Ronald was entitled to nothing from him. And Ronald replied that he would accept nothing from our father, not even his name. So it may be possible that he is going by another name, other than Stiles."

"I see. And have you any idea of what other name he might have chosen?"

"I don't know. It's possible … he might have decided to call himself Ronald Benson. Benson was my—our mother's—maiden name."

"Ronald Benson," Holmes repeated. "I see. Watson, would you kindly make a note?"

I belatedly drew out a notebook and pencil and complied.

"Cotton Street is near the docks," I said. "That makes it sound likely that your brother is still pursuing his career as a sailor. Perhaps he may have recently come in on a ship and be on shore-leave?"

"Perhaps," Mrs. Spenlow agreed. "So far as I know, he has no other trade, but of course there is much of my brother's life these past twenty years of which I must be unaware."

"Just so. However, inquiries among the dock workers and sailors are at least a place to begin our search," Holmes said. "I suppose it is too much to hope for that you might have a photograph or some other likeness of your brother?"

"I do, actually." Mrs. Spenlow opened her reticule and drew out a faded daguerreotype. "This was taken just a few months before my brother left home."

She passed the sheet across to Holmes, who studied it, then handed it to me.

The image showed a handsome young man, clean-shaven but for a well-trimmed moustache, of somewhere around twenty years of age, dressed formally in frock coat and pinstriped trousers. I had unconsciously expected that Ronald would resemble his sister, but in fact so far as I could tell from the black-and-white image, his colouring was fair: light hair, combed straight back from his forehead and eyes that I would wager were blue.

His head was thrown a little back, and he was smiling out from the photograph with all the unthinking arrogance of youth. Not, perhaps, a face with great strength of character, I thought, but he looked both engaging and good-humoured. An adventurer, seeing the world as a stage on which to enact his own daring adventures and schemes.

I turned the photograph over, noting as I did that one side of the sheet was a little ragged, and that the image was narrower than the usual portraits I was used to seeing.

Mrs. Spenlow saw my glance fall on the tattered edge and smiled sadly. "It was originally a portrait of our whole family. My father tried to rip Ronald's picture out of the group and throw it away. But my mother salvaged the piece and saved it without my father's being aware. I am glad that she did, for what you hold now is the only likeness of my brother I have."

Holmes took the daguerreotype back from me, studied it a moment, then laid it down on the mantle.

"I will accept your commission, Mrs. Spenlow. Where may I contact you to report any progress?"

Mrs. Spenlow released a breath of relief, sinking back in her chair. "Mr. Holmes, I cannot thank you enough. I have decided to stay here in town for a few days—at Fenton's Hotel in St. James's Street. Once more, I thank you again and again for your willingness to help."

Holmes accepted her thanks in what I felt was, even for him, a more than usually abstracted manner, and Mrs. Spenlow departed. I waited until I had heard the front door close down below before saying, "Hardly the sort of case I should have expected you to choose, Holmes. Do you think it possible that Ronald Stiles—or whatever name he is calling himself now—is involved in some sort of criminal activity?"

It had occurred to me that the suspicion might have been at the root of Holmes's warning comment about Mrs. Spenlow's brother possibly having an aversion to being found.

Holmes's gaze had returned once again to the photograph of Ronald which Mrs. Spenlow had left, and at my question he seemed to pull back from whatever complicated train of thought his mind was following.

"I believe there are several points of unexpected interest about Mrs. Spenlow's trouble," he said. "At a bare minimum, I think it well worth dispatching Flynn to make inquiries at the docks about any seaman answering to the name of either Ronald Stiles or Ronald Benson."

CHAPTER 2: FLYNN

Someone was following him.

Or at the very least, someone was watching him. Flynn wasn't used to that feeling of prickling awareness at the back of his neck. Usually no one on the London Streets gave him a second glance, especially in a neighbourhood like this one. Down here near the docks, the streets were full of shabby, slatternly tenements, gaudy public-houses and beer-shops—and every place packed with half-naked children, miserable-looking women, and drunken men either quarrelling or slumped in doorways to sleep if off.

Mixed in amongst that lot, Flynn was usually about as noticeable as one extra flea on a dog.

Not today, though.

He risked a quick look over his shoulder, but he couldn't tell who it was that was giving him the uncomfortable feeling of being stared at.

It was still early morning. Carts carrying vegetables, milk, fish, eggs, and bones for family dogs rumbled towards the market. An old, white-bearded man in a checked coat and incredibly ancient top hat was rapping his bamboo pole on the windows of each house along the street—because of course no one would have money to buy an alarm clock in a neighbourhood like this one—to let people know it was time for them to get up and dress for work.

Flynn turned up the collar of his coat, quickening his steps as he approached the corner of a narrow alley-way.

This didn't make any sense. Today's job for Mr. Holmes had started out just like any other. Actually, compared to a lot of jobs he'd done for Mr. Holmes, this one was simple.

Go down to the docks and ask around about a man who might be called either Ronald Stiles or Ronald Benson. Either a walk in Hyde Park or dead boring, depending on which way you looked at it.

Flynn rounded the corner and broke into a run—almost tripping on old bed springs and splintered packing crates and all the other assorted rubbish that collected in filthy back alleys like this one.

A couple of kids were playing kick the can at the entrance to the next street over, and they gave Flynn a dirty look as he tore past, scattering the cans for their game.

The street he came out on ran directly alongside the river. The air was filled with the familiar smell of mud and fish, and there weren't as many crowds about here. The other people on the street with him were mostly coal porters on their way to work and sailors reeling back to ships after a night of drinking in one of the gin palaces or public houses.

Flynn slowed down, trying to decide whether he'd lost whoever had been following or not.

If there really had been anyone there?

No. Flynn could count on the fingers of just one hand the number of people or things he trusted in this world—but one of those things he believed in was his own gut instincts. He'd stayed alive in a lot of dangerous situations before by trusting his gut. The fact that he was sensing trouble now meant that there was something wrong.

Further up the road, an old lady selling gimcrack jewellery

from a tray was competing with a missionary preacher for the attention of everybody passing by.

Neither was having much luck, as far as Flynn could tell. A coloured lantern show with pictures of famous murderers through the ages was drawing a much bigger crowd.

Hands in his pockets, Flynn approached the crowd who were pushing and shoving to pay their halfpennies and get a look through the slide-show peepholes at all the murderers. He wondered for a second or two how many of the pictured killers Mr. Holmes might have been responsible for putting behind bars.

But mostly he was trying to work things out in his own mind, because none of this made any sense.

For a start, it wasn't as if he'd found out anything important.

He'd asked around among the sailors and labourers at Saint Katharine's Docks, the London Docks, and the West-India Docks. He'd been prepared to spend all day and maybe even longer on this job, because if ever a task sounded like hunting for a needle in a haystack, this was it. London's docklands had hundreds of warehouses and space to moor thousands of ships—any one of which could have brought Mr. Ronald Stiles in on it.

After the West-India Docks, he'd have moved on to the East-India Docks, the Victoria Docks, and then the Grand Surrey Docks and the Commercial Docks.

But as it had turned out, at the West-India Docks, he'd run across someone who claimed to know a man called Ronald Stiles.

Whether it was the same Ronald Stiles that Mr. Holmes was looking for, Flynn didn't know. The fellow he'd talked to had been an old porter with a bent back and a mouthful of broken, yellowed teeth. Flynn would have bet more than the price of a hot meal that the man did a brisk side business in lumping—or helping himself to the shipping goods he was supposed to be helping unload. But he'd told Flynn he knew a sailor called Stiles, though he hadn't seen him in a year or more, not since he took up with a girl—a fancy piece, the old porter had called her—who thought she was too good for the likes of a lowly tar. Ronald Stiles had gone off to look for other sorts of work, but when the old porter had known him, Ronald had been renting a room in a lodging house on Cable Street. The old porter hadn't remembered the number, but he thought Ronald's rooms might have been over a fish shop.

Not much of a lead, considering that Ronald Stiles could have easily moved to new lodgings in the past year. But it was all Flynn had, so he'd set off for Cable Street.

That was when he'd got the feeling he was being followed—soon after he'd left the West India Docks, although he didn't know exactly when the feeling had started, so he didn't know if whoever it was had somehow overheard him asking questions about Stiles.

It seemed like a solid bet that they must have. Flynn couldn't think of anything else he'd done that would attract anyone's notice—not lately, anyway.

Now here he was, at the end of Cable Street, trying to figure out a plan that would let him identify who'd want to bother following him to an east end fish shop that might or might not be a place where a common sailor had lived.

Well, the obvious answer to that one was that Ronald Stiles *wasn't* just a common sailor.

He'd got himself mixed up in something dangerous or illegal or both.

Flynn could see a fish shop, now, halfway up on the other side of the road.

He thought, then took out a scrap of paper and a pencil from his pocket, pushing his way further into the crowd around the lantern show.

Then he ducked down out of sight behind the big painted box that held the coloured lanterns and slides, scribbled a quick note, and wrapped it around a sixpence he'd dug out of his pocket.

"Here—you."

He poked the arm of a small boy who—while the owner's back was turned—was standing on tip-toes trying to get a look into the lantern-show peep-holes without paying.

"Want to make a tanner?"

"What for?" The boy gave him a suspicious look.

"Just take this note to—" Flynn stopped. He'd been about to say, "Baker Street," but they were actually closer to the house where Becky lived with Lucy and Jack. More likely the kid would go there than tramp halfway across London. Even then it was a long shot, since he could just as easily pocket the coin and toss the note in the gutter. But it was the best Flynn could do.

He gave the boy Becky's address along with the note.

"They'll give you another sixpence when you get there, but only if you hurry."

The boy nodded and ran off, whether to spend his newfound riches or to actually deliver the message Flynn couldn't say.

But he couldn't go straight to Mr. Holmes or to Lucy and Jack himself, at least not yet—that might lose him the chance of finding out who else was trying to find Ronald Stiles.

Hands in his pockets, Flynn walked casually up the street a bit to a vendor's cart, where a fat, red-faced man was selling household brushes of all sorts.

Flynn forked over the money for a horsehair clothes brush,

then kept walking until he came to the brick building with the words *Boules' Fish Shop* printed in gold letters over the door.

Again, no guarantees that this was the right fish shop, but it was a place to start.

He walked up—not to the fish shop, but to the house next door, and knocked.

An old woman with a sharp nose and grey hair answered his knock, took one look at the brush in Flynn's hand, and started to slam the door in his face.

"Oh, please, don't go back inside yet." Flynn wished he were as good at pretending to cry as Becky, but he tried to let his lower lip tremble a bit. "My old dad's watching me." He jerked his head in the direction of the original brush seller down the street. "Business is slow, so he sent me to go door to door, like. He's watching me, and if you go right back in, he'll say I wasn't trying hard enough and give me a beating. You don't have to buy anything," he added. "Just let me stand here a little longer?"

The grey-haired woman sniffed, but maybe she wasn't as bad-tempered as she looked, because she said, "All right. But only for a minute, mind. I've got calves-foot jelly cooking on the stove, and I can't go a-lettin' it burn."

It sounded proper nasty to Flynn, and from the smell filtering through to him from the open doorway, the stuff wouldn't be any worse if it caught on fire.

But he gave her his most soppy-looking smile and said, "Oh, thank you ma'am! You've got true Christian spirit." He pushed his cap to the back of his head, then asked, making his voice sound hopeful, "What about next door—the place over the fish shop? Do you think it's any good my trying there?"

"I shouldn't think so." The woman sniffed disapproval. "I'd

lay odds the man who lives there has never cleaned anything in his life. He's a bad lot—comes in at all hours, roaring drunk. Why, just last night he was a-bashing and clanging up there fit to wake the dead. Had to get my husband to shout out the window, tell him to stow it."

The back of Flynn's neck prickled. "Some kind of a row, d' you think?"

"Who knows? He shut up soon after, that's all I cared about."

"What's his name, do you know?" Flynn asked. "I've got a friend whose uncle lives around here," he added by way of explanation.

"Harold? Ronald?" The woman shrugged. "Something of that sort. Don't know his other name and don't care to." She craned her neck to look up at the windows above the fish shop. "Either he's not awake yet or he's gone out again. The windows is all dark, and I haven't heard a peep out of him since last night."

Flynn nodded. "Well, thanks very much, ma'am." He touched the brim of his cap. "Think of me if you ever do want to buy any brushes."

The woman went back inside, and Flynn turned to survey the street, trying to decide if he was still being followed, or if the uneasy feeling crawling all over his skin was just left over from before.

Carts and wagons rumbled past ... A blond woman with a shopping basket ... A dark-haired woman pushing a baby's pram.

Flynn shook his head. Nothing out of the ordinary that he could see, but it never hurt to be careful.

There was a narrow side street branching off from the main road a few doors up. Flynn ambled slowly towards it, but no one followed or paid him any notice that he could tell. He stopped as soon as he rounded the corner and was hidden from view of the rest of Cable Street.

There were a couple of starving alley cats fighting over a scrap of rotten fish, but otherwise the street was empty for now. Flynn could hear loud, quarrelling voices coming from the house on the end, and a crying baby from one of the windows on his right, but nothing else.

He breathed out.

He'd got a promising lead on Ronald Stiles, now. He could go back to Mr. Holmes and make his report—

A crashing blow struck him on the back of his head, and the world vanished in a shower of exploding yellow sparks.

Chapter 3: Lucy

The front door rattled and shook with the force of a heavy blow. But not for nothing had our locks been chosen by Sherlock Holmes. The bolts held.

Prince whined beside me, his ears flattened back and his tail tucked down.

"It's all right—" I started to murmur to him.

But I didn't get the chance to finish.

Our intruder had moved on to lock picks, and was easily as skilled with them as I was, because after a bare handful of seconds, the door swung open, revealing the tall, broad-shouldered figure of a man wearing a dark mask and carrying a club in one hand.

His head turned, surveying the room, taking in the table in the centre, where a small patent-leather shoe was just barely visible from under the edge of the table cloth.

Slowly, the masked intruder approached the table—and Becky exploded out from behind the door, where she'd been braced in the corner, hidden from sight when it opened.

She aimed a hard kick at the back of our invader's knee that made him stumble forwards. Then, while he was off-balance, she aimed a blow to his head, using the cricket bat she had clutched in one hand.

Our attacker fell to the ground, rolled over, and pulled off the mask.

"Well done," Jack said. He nodded at the bat. "And thanks for not actually hitting me with that."

Becky was grinning, her small freckled face triumphant. "I tricked you! You thought I was under the table!"

Jack sat up. "Nice touch with the shoe." It was hard not to smile back at Becky, but he was trying to stay serious as he placed a hand on his younger sister's shoulder. "That's exactly what you do if someone ever tries to break in, but *only* if—"

"Only if I've already discovered that the house is surrounded and I can't get out through a window or the back door and run away," Becky recited obediently. "And *only* after I've tried to telephone for help."

"Exactly."

"I still tricked you!" Becky grinned again. "That means that I get to choose tonight's desert, and I pick ..." she furrowed her brow in thought. "Eclairs from the bakery on Oxford Street. You can pick them up on your way home from work."

"Oh, I can, can I?" Jack rumpled his sister's hair. "All right. A bargain's a bargain. But you'd better go up and finish your arithmetic now, you and Flynn have a tutoring session this afternoon."

Becky made a face. "Next time I'm going to wager that you have to do my lessons for me if I win. No—wait, never mind. I'll do my lessons, but if I trick you next time, you have to buy me my own set of handcuffs!"

She started up the stairs to her room.

Jack dropped onto the sofa beside me.

"Does it ever strike you that our family is slightly unusual?" I asked him.

"Why, because we're raising an eleven-year-old who dreams

of owning her own set of handcuffs?" Jack was smiling, but sobered. "At least she'll be prepared."

I studied his face. Even at rest, there was a contained energy about Jack, and the kind of hard edge that most policemen acquired, the edge that comes from having seen and faced down the ugliest sides of life and human nature. But I thought now that there was an unusually grim undertone to his voice. "Do you mean prepared in the general sense, or prepared for something in particular?"

Jack opened his mouth to answer, but the telephone rang, cutting off whatever he'd been about to say.

He went to answer it, and when he came back, the grimness that etched his lean, chiselled face was even more pronounced.

"What's wrong?" I asked. My pulse had already sped up.

"A police sergeant was killed this morning. Sergeant O'Hara, from the Holborn Station."

"Holborn?" That had been Jack's first posting in the metropolitan police service, the station where he'd been assigned as a constable when I first met him. "Did you know him?"

Jack nodded. "We went through training together. I hadn't seen him in the last year or two, though."

"And Scotland Yard has been called in to investigate … I'm assuming that he was murdered?"

I worked to keep my voice level.

Jack and all of the policeman who patrolled what Watson had famously described as the Great Cesspool of London had a dangerous job. I knew it and accepted it—and it didn't do any good to dwell on the fact that Sergeant O'Hara could easily have been the one getting the same sort of telephone call about Jack's having been killed in the line of duty.

"It looks that way," Jack said. "I don't know any details yet. But I have to go in."

"Of course. Becky and I can walk over to Oxford Street and visit the bakery ourselves if you're not back in time for supper. She'll understand."

Like anyone who lived with an officer of the law, Becky was perfectly accustomed to plans needing to be changed. Criminals unfortunately didn't take holidays.

"Thanks." Jack gave me a brief smile and went to the front rack in the hall to shrug into his blue uniform tunic. "I'll try to send word if I'm going to be late," he said over his shoulder.

"You don't have to worry about being late. Just let me know if there's anything I can do."

"Thanks," Jack said again.

He kissed me lightly on his way out the door, but it was an abstracted kiss—and then he was gone.

I dropped back down onto the couch, absently scratching Prince's ears when the big dog bumped his nose against my palm.

The murder of a member of the police force always occasioned the most serious of responses from their fellow officers. And the fact that Jack had actually known Sergeant O'Hara, trained with him, could certainly explain the shadow at the back of Jack's gaze.

And yet—

Becky's head appeared at the top of the stairs.

"What's the matter with Jack?" she asked.

There was no point in trying to keep anything from Becky, since she inevitably made it her business to dig out the truth anyway.

"A police officer he used to know at Holborn Station was killed."

"I know—I heard," Becky said. "I meant other than that."

I sighed. Becky was, in addition to her lessons in arithmetic, taking private training sessions in the art of observation from Sherlock Holmes. It would be too much to hope for that she wouldn't have reached the same conclusion I had done.

"I don't know," I told her honestly.

We might be in the same profession of criminal investigation—Holmes and myself in the private sector, Jack in the official, public one. But there were still private matters concerning Scotland Yard that Jack couldn't speak of, not even to me.

And Jack had been on his own for most of his life, since he was younger than Becky. Even now, he didn't share troubles or worries easily.

"Why don't we—" I started to say to Becky.

A knock at the door interrupted me, making my heart try to leap up into my throat.

But when I looked out through the peep-hole that had been another of Holmes's installations, the figure standing on the front mat was a small, ragged boy, no more than six or seven years old.

"You owe me a tanner," he said, as soon as I opened the door.

My eyebrows edged up. "I see. And why would that be?"

"Because I brought you this note, didn't I, just like the other boy said."

He thrust out a grubby, crumpled sheet of brown paper that looked like it had once been used to wrap up fish and chips.

"Boy?" Becky appeared beside me, ducking under my arm to stand in the doorway, as well. "What boy?"

"How do I know?" The child shrugged. "Now what about my tanner?"

"Here you are." I added a half crown and another sixpence to the boy's payment—all the spare change I had ready to hand—which earned me a look of deep suspicion and a muttered, *Thanks*, before the boy darted off.

Becky unfolded the grubby note and caught her breath.

"What is it?"

"It's from Flynn!" She looked up at me, her face gone pale. "He's in some sort of trouble—look."

She held out the note.

Flynn hadn't written much—probably because he hadn't had time. The writing on the paper was hurried and untidy even for Flynn, and the pencil had gone straight through the paper in a couple of spots, suggesting that he hadn't been able to find a proper surface to write on.

SOS. Urgent, the note said.

And then on the last line was a scribbled address: *46 Cable Street.*

CHAPTER 4: FLYNN

Flynn was adrift in a dark sea. His body rose and fell with the throbbing in his head.

No, he was *actually* moving. Something rattled underneath him, and there was a steady clop-clop he ought to recognise.

But when he tried to grasp hold of the memory, the pain swelled up, tangling his thoughts. He sank down into darkness once again.

Chapter 5: Watson

"Now, Lestrade," Holmes said, "why did you not come to me yesterday, when the crime was fresh?"

Lestrade had perched on our settee, his dark, ferrety features pinched with tension, his knuckles white as he clutched the bowler hat on his lap.

"Because we thought we had our man."

"Indeed?" Holmes's brow lifted. "That was not in the newspaper account."

"We did not want to alert the suspect. Nor did we want to alert the public."

"So, what has changed?"

"We were watching the suspect's home, certain that he would return. He had left all his belongings behind."

"Who was the man?"

"A warder at Hampton Court Castle. He was on duty at the time of the theft."

"And he did not report afterwards? Or go home?"

"He lived in a boarding house. His landlady said he hadn't been there since Monday night, but that he hadn't removed any of his things."

"And now?"

Lestrade shifted uncomfortably. "There's been another death reported."

"Another? I had not known of a first death."

"It's been kept out of the papers. Two warders were assigned to guard the missing painting. One was found in the gallery, murdered. The other warder was our suspect."

"And now his body has been found?"

"Possibly. We were hoping you and Dr. Watson could have a look?"

"Where?"

"An inn in Hampton Wick called The Three Pines. They let rooms. On the second floor."

"How far from the man's boarding house?"

"That's in the same town. About ten minutes' walk."

"Time of death?"

"Difficult to determine. You see, the window had been left open, and the cold air—"

"When was the room rented at the inn?"

"Monday night, for a week."

"The night before the theft."

"Yes. Now will you come? It's only an hour on the train."

Holmes held up one finger. "First, please describe the stolen painting."

"Why, that's not information available to the public. The loss of it is quite an embarrassment to the government. It's a symbolic affair, you see, very political."

Holmes looked steadily at Lestrade, pointedly drumming his fingers on the arm of his chair.

"All right. There are portraits of these twelve women, you see, from the time of King Charles II—"

Holmes shook his head. "What are its dimensions and how was it framed?"

Lestrade fumbled in his coat pocket and withdrew a small notebook. He read from it, "About 3 feet by 4 feet. Gilded wood frame."

"The frame was missing?"

"Yes,"

"And a search for it was made at the Palace?"

Lestrade nodded. "You have no idea what an ordeal that was. There are these private apartments in the Palace, you see, free of rent to dozens of important toffs currently in favour—"

Holmes stood. "You can tell us more on the train."

We took the first train to Hampton Wick.

CHAPTER 6: LUCY

The address Flynn had given proved to be the small set of rented lodgings over a fish shop.

Becky and I approached cautiously, standing on the opposite side of the road to watch the place before moving any closer.

"I don't see Flynn anywhere," Becky murmured.

"No. But at least I don't see any sign of trouble, either."

Everything about the scene looked perfectly ordinary for a London street in the middle of winter and at mid-morning: housewives doing their shopping—the fish shop was doing a brisk trade in oysters and haddock—porters hurrying up and down with loads carried from the nearby docks.

"What was Flynn doing this morning, do you know?"

Before leaving home, I had tried telephoning to Baker Street to ask Holmes about whatever job Flynn had been on, but there had been no answer. Holmes and Watson were out, and Mrs. Hudson would be doing her weekly marketing on this Monday morning.

"I don't know exactly," Becky said. "When I saw him yesterday, he said that Mr. Holmes had given him an easy task this time—just to go down to visit the docks and ask around about a sailor. Flynn said the man's sister came to Mr. Holmes and wanted help in finding him, because they'd lost touch."

"That doesn't sound as though it should have turned dangerous."

"I know." Becky bit her lip. "I don't know why he would have sent us to this address, either—if he found out that's where this woman's brother is living, why not just go and tell Mr. Holmes?"

I considered the building in front of us. "I think we need to get inside number 46," I said.

Becky looked up at me quickly. "You mean that we're going to break in?"

"Only if no one answers the door. Come along—and try to look as though we've every right to be here."

I had learned that confidence and an attitude of complete unconcern were the best way to avoid attracting attention.

A rickety flight of wooden stairs at the back of the fish shop led to the entrance of the rooms above. Taking Becky's hand, I led the way up and knocked on a door that was badly in need of a new coat of paint.

There was no answer.

I knocked again and waited. When my third knock failed to get any kind of answer from inside, I took out the lock picks I always carried in the inner pocket of my cloak.

"You keep watch," I told Becky. "Let me know if anyone is coming."

But as it turned out, I didn't need the lock picks after all.

I inserted the first of them and found the door already unlocked. The knob turned easily in my hand and the door swung open.

Becky and I looked at each other. The threads of uneasiness that had been slowly tightening inside me now solidified into a solid knot under my rib cage.

"Flynn?" Becky called out softly. "Flynn, are you there?"

No one answered.

I stepped through the doorway cautiously, but a glance around was enough to assure me that the place was deserted. There was only one small, square room, sparsely furnished—and what furniture there was had been flung about as though this had been the site of a small hurricane or tornado.

Two rickety wooden chairs were toppled over near the door, and a table was overturned in the centre of the room, with the kerosene lamp that had plainly stood atop it likewise now lying on the floor. The cushions in a worn and shabby-looking sofa had all been slashed, and stuffing spilled out. Dishes and cups from a cupboard over in the corner were scattered as though someone had tossed them off the shelves one by one.

Becky followed me inside and gave a shocked exclamation. "What happened here? It looks like someone was searching for something. Or—" She gasped. "No, it wasn't a search, there must have been a fight, Lucy look!"

She pointed to a scarlet stain on the floorboards, just visible behind the torn sofa. "That looks like blood! We need to go and tell the police—or Mr. Holmes—" She turned, starting for the door, but I stopped her, catching hold of her arm.

"Not yet."

"But Flynn—" she started.

"I know you're worried about him," I said gently. "I am, too. But this place is the only clue we have at the moment to whatever happened to him, and something about all of this"—I gestured to the wreckage all around us—"isn't quite right. Now, stand right here and see if you can tell me what it is."

Becky blew out a breath but did as I asked, standing with me and obediently surveying the room.

"That lamp," she said after a moment. Her brows were knitted together, her anxious look replaced by a puzzled frown. "If the table was tipped over during a fight, and the lamp was on it, it should have broken when it fell on the floor. But it's *not* broken. There's not even a crack in it."

"Very good. Anything else?"

"Those dishes." She pointed to the corner. "They ought to be broken, too, if someone threw them out of the cupboard."

And yet every one of the cups and dishes was perfectly intact. "Exactly," I told Becky. "Conclusion?"

"Someone wanted to make it *look* as though there had been a fight here." Becky looked up at me. "Why would they do that? And what does any of this have to do with Flynn?"

"I don't know. But I can tell you that I don't think that stain on the floor is actually blood." I stooped and sniffed at the dark red stain. "No, it's not. It's red paint."

"So whoever did all this wasn't very well prepared," Becky said slowly. "Otherwise they would have used animals' blood from a butcher's shop or something more believable."

"They cared about not damaging any of the furnishings here, too," I said. "Which makes me think that whoever set this all up is the man who actually lives here, and who didn't want all of his things smashed."

"Man?" Becky repeated.

I pointed to a shaving brush, strop, and razor that sat on an untouched wooden shelf.

"The sofa, though," Becky said. She was still frowning, surveying the stuffing that sprouted like dingy mushrooms from the ruined cushions. "That couldn't have been done in a fight—and it *did* cause damage."

"True. So, what do you think happened?"

"Someone really did come here to search—after the man who lives here staged the fight. Someone he was afraid of," Becky went on. "That's why he wanted it to look as though he'd been in a fight and either been killed or dragged off."

"It certainly looks that way," I agreed. "Now, I think it's time to find out as much as we can about the both of them—the man who lives here, and whoever he was so afraid of."

Chapter 7: Watson

On the train to Hampton Wick, Lestrade told us the warder slain during the theft had been found with a warder's ceremonial Tudor dagger protruding from his chest in the region of the heart, near the spot where the missing painting had hung. Presumably the other warder on duty, a man named Olson, had done the murder and the theft. The constabulary had been unable to determine how the painting had been taken from the building or where Olson had gone. The snow from Tuesday afternoon had obscured what might have been helpful footprints.

"How was the body discovered?"

"A tour group, led by one of the docents, came in and found the body. There was a general commotion, and a doctor was sent for."

"What time was the tour?"

"It was the noon tour. The second of the day."

"Where was the previous tour group?"

"They had gone ahead to their next destination on the tour."

"Which was?"

"The private bedchamber of King William."

"How much time elapsed between the departure of the first tour and the arrival of the second?"

"Fifteen minutes."

"How many people in each group?"

Lestrade consulted his pocket notebook. "Ten. The tours are limited in size. And before you ask, yes, all ten persons in the two groups have been interviewed, along with the two docents guiding the tours, and none of them saw anything suspicious or unusual, other than, of course, the loss of the painting. The empty spot was observed by the second group and not the first."

"All might be lying, of course," I said. "Though that is unlikely."

"Were any of the other paintings to be moved that day?"

"No. Several had been moved for cleaning the day before. Mondays are the regular day for that, since the public tours are limited on Mondays."

Holmes was silent. Beneath our carriage, the clatter of the steel wheels on the steel rails beat on in its regular rhythm.

"Perhaps we ought to see for ourselves," I offered. "A tour might shed some light on the circumstances surrounding the theft."

"Perhaps," said Holmes.

"Perhaps we could arrive in time for the two o'clock tour," I said. "I have heard of the beauty of the paintings and the furnishings—"

"But we must begin at the Three Pines Inn," said Holmes. "An unidentified body awaits us."

***

Not long afterwards, we arrived in Hampton Wick, a small village between the Thames and the great open park that adjoins Hampton Court Palace. It was only a minute's walk from the railway station to the Three Pines Inn.

Lestrade gave a meaningful glance at the upper story of the inn. The building had been constructed recently, in a contemporary version of the Tudor style so fashionable in the area.

Beneath one of the eaves of the steeply sloping roof, a window on the second floor was partially open. "We left everything as it was," Lestrade said.

"Has the body been identified as Olson, the missing warder?" Holmes asked.

"Not yet. Identification may be difficult."

"Who discovered the body?"

"Crows," Lestrade said. "People on the street saw 'em at the window, going in and out."

***

There were three closed doors at the top of two flights of stairs inside the inn, clustered around a narrow central hallway. All were painted to match the woodwork and the whitewashed plaster. A uniformed constable stood guard at the centre door.

Lestrade asked, "Have you spoken with the other tenants?"

"Yes, Inspector. No one saw or heard anything."

"Or won't admit it." Lestrade pushed open the door, holding it open for us to enter. I felt the rush of cold air from the room, and detected an all-too-familiar scent. "It's a right mess in there," Lestrade went on. "I had them close the curtains to keep out—"

"Understood," Holmes said. He was bending over the body of a Caucasian man. Face up on a single bed, the man might have looked peaceful if he had retained his face. As it was, the forehead had been caved in, the skin broken by the force of the blow, and the birds had compounded the disfigurement.

"The quantity of blood that issued from the wound was sufficient to attract the crows," Holmes said. "The outside air also caused the body to cool rapidly, and then freeze, making it difficult to determine the time of death."

"You think the killer deliberately raised the window?"

"Someone did, after the murder. The lack of bloodstains at the bottom of the frame is conclusive on that point, given that there are bloodstains on the sides, and the sill."

Holmes bent over the body once more. "Dr. Watson, would you please examine this wound and tell me your impression?"

I did so. Looking closely beneath the massive fracture that covered the front of the wound, I saw a smaller, darker area. I looked up. "The man has been shot in the forehead. The fracture was done to conceal the entry of the bullet."

"Likely the blow was struck using this table lamp." Holmes pulled a brass lamp from beneath the bed and placed it on the bedside table.

"Bloodstains on the base," said Lestrade.

Holmes had opened the empty drawers of an oak dresser, and now was examining the contents of a matching wardrobe that served as the clothes closet for the little room. "We have the man's overcoat here, and nothing else. He is dressed in an ordinary suit. The label inside proclaims it to be a ready-made affair. The shirt and tie, aside from their damaged and stained condition, appear to be perfectly ordinary. However, I do believe he can now be identified as a warder from Hampton Park Castle, if not the warder Olsen."

"How?"

"His shoes." Holmes pointed to the shiny leather black shoes worn by the dead man. They had odd-looking toes, bulbous and blunt.

Lestrade slapped his head. "Of course. I ought to have noticed myself. The warders wear Tudor doublets and breeches and all, and their shoes are this old-fashioned duckbill variety."

"They appear quite new," Holmes said. "An inspection at the mortuary will show whether they fit."

"We can also bring Olson's landlady in to identify him," said Lestrade. He brightened considerably as he went on, "Well, I'm getting a clear picture here. This man is Olsen, the warder. He needs money. He is in the castle every day, surrounded by priceless paintings. Maybe he has a grudge against the other warder who guards them. He decides to do the deed. According to his landlady, he went out the night before the robbery. We can assume that was when he meets with an accomplice, probably the man who would sell the painting for him. The two stay up all night working out the details. He goes straight in to work the next day, puts on his Tudor costume, and when the opportunity arises, he stabs the other warder. He takes the painting, meets his accomplice here, they have a falling out over the share of the swag or how to fence it or whatever. The accomplice shoots him, leaves the body here with the window open, and makes off with the painting. I'll put my men onto asking around the neighbourhood. Someone must have seen the accomplice leave the inn."

"Particularly memorable, if he were carrying a painting in a three-foot by four-foot gilded frame," Holmes said.

Lestrade gave Holmes a suspicious glance. "You don't agree?"

Holmes shrugged. "And if the thief carried the painting here, from Hampton Court, a distance of nearly a mile and a half, that would also be an event likely to have been observed and remembered by passers-by in the park. Particularly if he were wearing his full Tudor costume rather than only his Tudor shoes."

Lestrade's jaw muscles tightened. "He obviously would have left his Tudor costume behind, so as to be less conspicuous. Or he might have taken a cab."

"Indeed, he might have done. If so, your interviews with cab drivers are likely to prove fruitful."

Lestrade said, "All right, Mr. Holmes. What is wrong with my theory?"

"Nothing at all, though it does require the assumption that the murderer of this man was an unusually considerate and respectful chap, judging from the condition of the shoes and the lower part of the bed spread here."

"I see nothing wrong with either the shoes or the bed spread."

"Quite so. Both are perfectly dry, other than the bloodstained area above the pillow. Therefore, since we know that there was snow on Tuesday at the time of the theft, the murderer must have been considerate enough to wipe his victim's shoes and polish them before positioning the body on the bed. As we both observed, the shoes still appear quite new."

"Are you patronising me, Mr. Holmes?"

"Far from it, Lestrade. However, you may wish to devote your resources to exploring another possibility."

"Name it."

"That this murder was done the night before the robbery. That the victim was lured here, killed, and left inside this room, so that his costume might be used by an accomplice who would impersonate him the next day. You might ask his landlady whether he had visitors in the days leading to the robbery, or if she could shed any light on his habitual activity after his daily shift as a warder."

Lestrade looked thoughtful. "Yes, that would fit. Kill him for his uniform, eh? And it would set us haring off after the wrong man, wouldn't it?" He rubbed his hands together in anticipation. "Now we are getting somewhere." He paused. "But the man who impersonated Olson. How did he get the painting out of Hampton Court? You yourself noted how conspicuous it would be, to go walking across the park with an object that large."

Holmes nodded. "But if packing crates were available from the cleaning activity scheduled the day before, they might be used to conceal and transport the painting. And it would not require a very long walk from the palace to reach the Hampton Court river docks, would it?"

Lestrade's beady eyes sparkled. "Ah! Motor launches! Always some of them around. Now we really are getting somewhere. We shall ask the Thames riverboat pilots. Someone must have seen something."

"You might also ask Olson's landlady if she recalls his purchasing new shoes," Holmes said. "He may have been wearing them Monday night, so as to break them in before his shift began on Tuesday."

Lestrade scribbled furiously in his notebook.

"Shall we walk across the park to the Palace?" I asked.

To my disappointment, Holmes said, "But now, Lestrade, Watson and I must be getting back to Baker Street. There is another case of ours that is somewhat pressing."

Chapter 8: Lucy

"Lucy—wait!" Becky stopped and froze with her foot on the bottom step of the Hansom cab. "We need to go back upstairs to number 46!"

"What is it?"

Questioning Mr. Boules, the fishmonger who kept the shop downstairs, had elicited the information that the room was rented to a man by the name of Ronald Stiles. Although we had learned precious little else. The fishmonger was a large, flabby man with a perpetually flushed face and a suggestive network of broken veins under the skin. He'd assured us—slurring his words and breathing out profoundly alcoholic gusts of breath—that Ronald Stiles was, "a good shhhhhort," who paid his rent on time and gave no trouble.

But he couldn't give us any further details about Mr. Stiles' life, and he certainly had no idea where his missing tenant might have gone.

He hadn't seen anyone answering to Flynn's description, either, although that didn't necessarily signify. I doubted that that Mr. Boules ever contemplated the outside world much, unless it was through the glass bottom of his latest pint of beer.

Now Becky hopped down from the cab step. I waved the driver on.

"Have you remembered something?" I asked her.

We hadn't questioned any of the other neighbours, since

without knowing more about the case, I hadn't wanted to draw undue attention to our reason for being in the neighbourhood. But we had made ourselves as conspicuous as possible, walking up one side of the street and down the other.

If Flynn was hidden anywhere nearby and watching, he would have seen us. But he hadn't emerged from any of the leaning tenement doorways or entrances to dirty back alleys.

"I think so," Becky said. Her eyes were screwed up with concentration. "The floor—over by the shelf with the razor and things on it. But it will be quicker if I show you, come on."

She led the way, racing two steps at a time back up the stairs to Ronald Stiles' rented lodgings, and then straight to the back corner of the room.

"I knew it!" she said. "Look—there, those marks on the floor." Crouching, she pointed to some scuff marks on the wooden boards where something heavy had plainly been dragged away from the wall. "I think that cupboard—the one with the dishes on it—used to stand here," she said. "It would just fit, see? And it must have been Ronald Stiles who moved it, because he took the trouble to unload all the dishes without breaking it first. Whoever came afterwards to search and then tore up the couch wouldn't have bothered with that."

"You're right—that was very well spotted," I told her. "So, the question is, why did Ronald Stiles feel the need to move the cupboard away from this particular patch of wall?"

I knelt down beside Becky and ran my hand experimentally across the faded and water-stained floral paper that covered the wall. "I don't feel anything … wait a moment."

One of the floorboards had moved, squeaking under the pressure of our combined weight.

I took out the knife I always carried in the top of my boot and used the blade to pry up the loose board. It came up easily, revealing a shallow hiding spot, about ten inches long and five inches deep.

Becky peered inside excitedly, then let out a breath of disappointment.

"It's empty!"

"Well, it stands to reason that if Mr. Stiles took the trouble to uncover this hiding spot, he must have wanted to retrieve what was in here and bring it along with him. But it's not completely empty—look."

A small scrap of paper had caught on a nail at the side of the loose board. I detached it carefully, smoothing it out on the palm of my hand.

"What is it?" Becky peered down at the tattered scrap, then frowned, her shoulders drooping with discouragement. "Oh—it's just the corner of a pawn shop claims ticket. The kind the pawnbroker gives people so that they can buy back the things they've sold him, if they get the money. That's not much help, is it?"

"It might be." I put the slip of paper into my pocket. "For now, though, I think we'd better get back to Baker Street."

I hadn't any concrete reason for feeling uneasy, but the back of my neck was prickling unpleasantly. At a minimum, whoever had slashed the cushions of the sofa might come back to see whether Ronald Stiles had returned home.

Becky nodded, stood up, and started for the door—just as it flew open to reveal a large man framed in the doorway, armed with a knife.

Chapter 9: Lucy

The man didn't so much as glance at Becky—perhaps he didn't even see her; she was partly behind him, over by the door, and his entire focus was on me and the still-open hole in the floorboards.

He was medium height, muscular, dressed in dirty blue trousers and a worn pea coat. Only a few wisps of hair clung to his otherwise bald head, but as though to make up for that, the lower half of his face was covered by a dirty blond beard whose bushiness I'd only seen rivalled by one of Holmes's disguises.

Unfortunately, that didn't make him any less of a threat, particularly in a closely confined space like this one, where speed and agility didn't count as much as sheer brute strength.

He probably outweighed me by a solid seventy or eighty pounds.

"Who are you?" he growled. "And where's old Ronny boy? Got himself a new fancy piece, has he?" His eyes narrowed as he looked me up and down. "His old lady's not going to like that much, I can tell you."

I shifted, wishing that I hadn't set my own knife down a few feet away when I pried up the loose floorboard.

"Don't move!" the stranger barked.

Even that small motion drew him a step nearer, brandishing the knife.

"Not unless you want me to carve up that pretty face of yours! Now, tell me: where is Ronald Stiles?"

I had learned that the next best thing to having an actual weapon in hand was to let your opponent to underestimate you. I held my hands up, trying to look frightened. "I don't know where he is—I swear it!"

Actually, it wasn't hard to inject a quaver of fear into my voice. My attention had been suddenly caught by Becky, who was still standing unnoticed several feet behind the stranger.

Completely by chance, she was in exactly the same position as she'd been for attacking Jack in his intruder's guise.

I could see her eyes flick to the stranger's broad back, calculating the distance between them.

My heart hammered as I gave a barely perceptible shake of my head, hoping to catch her gaze. If I was unlikely to win in a physical confrontation with the intruder, then Becky's pitting herself against him would be like a kitten trying to attack a rampaging bull. Her best option was to try to slip out the door and hope that there was a policeman nearby—

I was so focused on Becky that I missed the first part of the stranger's reply.

"—don't believe you!" he was saying. He brandished the knife again. "Thought he could double-cross me, but he'll be sorry when I catch him. Now where's old Ronny hidden himself, eh?"

"I don't know," I said again. "I—"

Behind the stranger, Becky charged, running full-tilt and diving to strike the back of the big man's leg with her joined fists.

My pulse skittered to a standstill. Although at least she'd had the sense to aim for a vulnerable point of attack.

The man stumbled forwards, but didn't entirely lose his balance. Cursing, he recovered and rounded on Becky—which gave me the chance to snatch up the loose piece of floorboard and bring it down in a smashing blow on the back of his head.

He still didn't go down. Instead, he spun back, flailing wildly with his knife. The blade caught the side of my arm, opening up a stinging cut.

I brought the board up again, smashing it into his face.

This time, he collapsed backwards, keeling over like a fallen tree and nearly crushing Becky, who jumped out of the way just in time.

She stared at me, her eyes huge.

"Lucy, you're bleeding!"

"It's all right." I examined the damage to my arm. "It's not much more than a deep scratch, really. I won't even have to trouble Dr. Watson for stitches."

Becky wasn't to be so easily reassured, though. She looked from me to the stranger, who was lying unconscious on the floor.

"I'm sorry!" Becky said. "I know you wanted me to run, but I couldn't leave you alone with him, I just couldn't!"

I sighed and put my good arm around her, after wrapping the bleeding one in a fold of my cloak.

Becky always had been a law unto herself—and if I were honest, I hoped that she always would be. Difficult as that frequently made it to keep her safe.

"You did very well," I told her. "Now, thanks to you, we have an excellent lead on finding out exactly what Ronald Stiles has got himself mixed up in." I nodded at the unconscious man. His nose, I noticed with grim satisfaction, was bleeding freely and probably broken. "We can bring him back to Baker Street for questioning."

Chapter 10: Flynn

Flynn came awake slowly. His head hurt, but not as much as before. Not so much that he couldn't think.

He still couldn't remember *why* he'd got a pounding headache, though. Had he got into a fight? Fallen off a carriage when he'd tried to hitch a free ride?

Both those things had happened to him before, but he didn't think that either of them was the answer now.

His eyes felt weighted, but he managed to pry them open—then felt his heart slam against his rib cage as he wondered in a panic whether he'd gone blind.

Blows to the head could do that, couldn't they? He thought he remembered Mr. Holmes saying it could happen.

It took a second for his pulse to stop pounding and for his head to clear enough to realise that he could still see, it was just that it was pitch dark where he was. But there was a thin seam of daylight right over his head, like there was a crack in the surface above him.

So, where the dickens was he?

He tried to pull himself up and realised he couldn't move. His hands were tied behind him and his legs were bound together, too.

And as the rest of his senses filtered back, he realised he'd got a rag or some other bit of cloth stuffed into his mouth to stop him making any noise.

No wonder his tongue felt dry as a cobblestone street on the hottest day of summer.

Not good. Not good at all.

Flynn strained against the ropes around his wrists, and got nowhere but to make his shoulders ache.

Right. He took a breath through his nose, trying to squash down another wave of panic. What would Mr. Holmes do?

Find out where he was, probably. Maybe he couldn't see, but he could still feel. Flynn wriggled around a bit, moving as much as his bonds and the tight space would let him. He seemed to be in some kind of a trunk. A steamer trunk, maybe? He could feel hard wooden slats underneath a cardboard covering. And—

Flynn jolted, his heart starting to race. Because just beside him, his fingers had connected with the hard metal point of a nail that must have not been hammered in straight and had popped through the trunk's lining.

A nail. A *sharp* nail.

It took him a solid ten minutes and he was sweating with effort by the time he managed it, but at last Flynn got himself into a position where he could rub the rope that tied his hands together against the point of the nail.

Chapter 11: Watson

"And so we found a policeman to help us get him into a cab, and brought him here," Lucy said, concluding her narrative.

Holmes and I had returned from Hampton Wick to find Lucy and Becky waiting in our sitting room, along with her scruffy blond-bearded prisoner, who had remained unconscious.

Holmes said, "An interesting development. Now, Becky, will you please join Mrs. Hudson in the kitchen. I will need to interrogate this man, and I believe he will talk more freely if he does not see you here."

"But—" Her lips pursed, and she looked as though she were about to launch a mighty protest.

"I shall accompany you now," Holmes said. "I shall use the telephone downstairs. Then, later, I will have a task for you."

"I want to know anything he says about Flynn."

"That I promise," Holmes said.

While they were out, I took the opportunity to clean and bandage the cut on Lucy's arm.

"That feels much better, Uncle John," she added, with a smile at me. "Thank you."

Upon Holmes's return, he studied the bearded man, who lay sprawled in an armchair with his hands and ankles tightly bound. The man's dissolute face still bore the evidence of his encounter with Lucy: his nose was swollen, blood smeared his upper lip and stained his beard, and he had the beginnings of what promised to be two very impressive black eyes.

"And now I believe it is time that we had a conversation with our friend here," Holmes said. "Watson, if you would be so good as to pass me that vial from my chemistry table—yes, that one, beside the Bunsen burner."

I passed him the small, stoppered glass vial he had requested. Holmes uncorked it, and instantly an eye-watering odour filled the air.

"A little preparation of my own invention," Holmes said. "Fully as effective as smelling salts, though slightly less pleasant."

He passed the vial underneath the unconscious man's nostrils.

Whatever chemical derivative was contained in the vial, there was certainly no doubt as to its efficacy.

The bearded man snorted, coughed, choked, and came awake with a violent start that brought the back of his head into painful-sounding contact with the wooden frame of the back of the chair.

"Wh—what?" He glared blearily around the room.

Holmes wasted no time with preamble. "My name is Sherlock Holmes. Earlier today you visited Mr. Ronald Stiles' place of residence. I wish to know why."

The man gave another look around the room—this time, I thought, taking in the fact of Lucy's presence, then returned to Holmes with a look of calculation. "What's it worth to yer?"

Holmes returned his gaze with a calm look. "One should only attempt to bargain from a position of strength—which, in case it has escaped your notice, is a description that in no way fits your current circumstances, Mr.—?" he paused in question.

"Jones," the man muttered.

"Jones." Holmes's eyebrows edged up in a way that suggested he shared my doubt that the name was genuine. But he appeared willing to let the matter pass. "Very well, then, Mr. Jones. Your reason for seeking out Ronald Stiles." His voice grew clipped on the final words. "Now."

Jones made a motion as though to try to rub his swollen and doubtless painful nose, then abandoned it as he realised that his hands were bound.

"Well, you see it was this way. Ronny Stiles is a mate of mine." He tried to raise his hands again. "Here—any chance you could untie these?"

"No. Go on."

Mr. Jones sighed. "All right. But this is all just a misunderstanding, see?"

"Indeed." Holmes brows lifted again. "I look forward to your enlightening us as to the nature of that misunderstanding."

"Well." Jones licked chapped lips. "Ronny Stiles is a mate of mine, just like I said. Only I hadn't heard from him in a while, and I got to worrying about him, like. I thought as how maybe something had happened to him—or he might have taken ill."

"I see. Truly, such concern for your friend does you credit," Holmes said.

A more perceptive man would have been put off by the dryness of his tone. Mr. Jones gave him a slightly doubtful glance, but then went on.

"Well, I got to old Ronny's place—and I saw the … ah, the young lady there." He nodded towards Lucy. "Well, how was I to know what business she had being in Ronny's rooms? I thought as how maybe she was a burglar as had broken in to rob poor old Ronny of his valuables. I was just trying to scare her off, see?"

"As any good friend would." The irony in Holmes tone was now strong enough to penetrate even Mr. Jones' awareness.

He swallowed nervously, but didn't answer.

Holmes eyed him a long moment, during which Jones attempted to squirm but was restrained by his bonds.

"Mr. Jones," he said at last. "It is fortunate for you that you are an abysmal liar."

The man shifted uncomfortably again. "What d'you mean?"

"I mean that if I thought there was any truth in your absurd story, I would simply hand you over to the police, who would arrest you and charge you with assault."

Mr. Jones' face blanched as he looked at Lucy, who as yet hadn't spoken. The strip of white bandage on her arm, however, was a graphic reminder that Mr. Jones would have difficulty in persuading any policeman that he had intended no harm.

"However," Holmes went on, then stopped. "Ah." He tilted his head, listening. "That, if I am not much mistaken, is Ronald Stiles' sister, Mrs. Spenlow, arriving downstairs."

"Sister?" Mr. Jones startled.

"Yes. You have met her, perhaps? As a friend of Mr. Stiles?"

"I … no, never heard of her," Jones growled.

Holmes's gaze lingered another moment on Mr. Jones' face, then he went on, "I telephoned to her at her hotel shortly after your arrival, asking her to join us. Lucy, would you be so good as to go and let her in? Explain the situation here, and ask her whether she would be willing to sit in on the remainder of our conversation with Mr. Jones?"

Chapter 12: Lucy

Mrs. Spenlow looked nothing at all like the woman I had expected.

Ever since coming face to face with Mr. Jones in Ronald Stiles' room, I had been attempting to dispel the feeling that had so far pursued me through this case: of having entered a play halfway through the second act, or having opened a book in the middle of the story.

As yet, Holmes hadn't even had the time to fill me in on the full background of Ronald Stiles. I knew nothing beyond the bare fact that his estranged sister wished to find him.

And, of course, that Flynn had must have encountered trouble finding Stiles, since he was now missing.

Mrs. Spenlow listened in silence to my account of what had so far happened in our search for her brother.

After introducing myself, I had brought her into the parlour of 221A, the flat below 221B up above, so that we could speak in private, and her eyes grew progressively wider as I talked.

"That poor boy!" She put a hand to her throat when I had finished. "Missing, you say? That is truly terrible! Do you believe it may be the … this *person* upstairs who has … has harmed him in some way?"

Ordinarily, I despised euphemisms that sought to cover up an ugly truth. But in this case, I couldn't entirely blame her for flinching away from the fact that Flynn might have been hurt—or worse, killed.

I had been ruthlessly shoving the thought to the back of my own mind. But it would explain why Becky and I had found no trace of him, and why we had heard nothing from him since the note that had brought us to Cable Street.

"And now Mr. Holmes wishes me to see the man whom you captured in Ronald's room?" Mrs. Spenlow went on without waiting for me to answer. "Of course, I am willing, if he believes that it will help. But I cannot see what assistance I may give. I haven't seen my brother in over twenty years, and so naturally any of his acquaintances would be complete strangers to me."

"I'm not sure what Holmes has in mind," I told her.

That was the unadorned truth. I had no idea of Holmes's plan—beyond the certainty that he had one. Holmes never did anything without calculation.

"It may be that he's hoping your presence will have some effect on Mr. Jones in inducing him to tell us what he knows," I said.

Although my experience with Holmes's plans suggested that his current one was unlikely to be as simple as that.

Mrs. Spenlow bit her lip, her brows furrowed and her expression anxious. "I suppose he is a very … rough individual?"

"Very."

I watched her as I said it. I hadn't quite taken Athena Spenlow's measure yet. I had unconsciously expected that the sister of a merchant sailor would be middle-aged, motherly, and plain, instead of the vibrant, mature beauty who faced me now. She seemed at least at first glance the type of woman who might very well wish to avoid a confrontation with a known violent offender.

Not that I could blame her for it if that were the case. Most sane women would wish to avoid meeting a man of Mr. Jones's disposition.

The cut on my arm wasn't overly painful—I'd had worse—but it was certainly a strong argument against underestimating the man now tied up in Holmes's sitting room.

I had apparently misjudged Mrs. Spenlow, though, because she straightened her shoulders and lifted her chin.

"Then of course I will come," she said. "Anything I can do to help; you and Mr. Holmes have only to ask."

* * *

The interlude did not appear to have improved Mr. Jones' temper. He was sitting with his head sunk on his chest and his still blood-smeared face set in a sullen glower, lips tight within the frame of his beard and brows drawn.

He didn't look up as we entered the room. Mrs. Spenlow trailed along behind me, her hands twisting nervously.

I had thought perhaps Holmes wanted to watch Jones' face when he was confronted with Ronald Stiles' sister. But instead he rose to greet us, taking Mrs. Spenlow by the hand.

"Ah, thank you for coming. I promise you that had I not thought it necessary, I would not have subjected you to this unpleasantness."

"You need not thank me, Mr. Holmes. It was I asked that you find my brother—I who bear the responsibility for what has since occurred. But I don't understand." Mrs. Spenlow's voice wavered slightly as she looked past Holmes to Mr. Jones' hunched and scowling figure. "Do you believe that Ronald has gone missing because he was involved in something—something of questionable legal standing?"

"Do you think that likely?" Holmes asked.

Mrs. Spenlow twisted a ring around one finger of her hand. "Twenty years ago, I would have said no. Ronald was high-spirited—impulsive. But not vicious or dishonest. Now, though ..." she raised one hand and let it fall. "How can I say? I do not know what sort of trials he has endured over the years, or how they may have embittered him. I only know that whatever he has done, he is still my brother, and I still wish to find him. If he is in trouble—danger of some kind—perhaps I may be able to help." She drew a breath, seeming to brace herself, then took a step forward, towards Mr. Jones. "I implore you, sir, if you know anything at all about my brother's whereabouts, please tell it now."

I should have thought Mr. Jones was somewhat less likely to be moved by an appeal to emotion than he was to put on a green beard and start singing vaudeville show tunes.

But he gave Holmes a quick glance and muttered, "I don't want to go to prison."

"That, Mr. Jones, is what one might term stating the obvious," Holmes said. "However, if you prove yourself able to tell us something useful, I might be persuaded to forgo any police involvement in this matter and simply forget that this afternoon's unpleasantness ever occurred."

"Well—all right." Mr. Jones licked his lips, then said, "Stiles owed me money, see? But now he's done a bunk so's not to have to pay me back. That's why I went to his place this afternoon—hoping to find someone as could tell me where Ronny'd hidden himself. Or else find something of his that I could take in payment of the debt, like."

"So you have no idea where Ronald Stiles is now?" Holmes asked.

Mr. Jones' lips pulled in a scowl. "If I had, I'd have found him, wouldn't I, and made him pay back the money wot he owes me—not gone messing about with you lot!"

Holmes regarded him for a moment from under half-lowered lids. Then, at last, he gave a short nod.

"Very well. Watson, take Mr. Jones downstairs and hand him over to the police constables who are waiting in the street outside. I telephoned to summon them at the same time that I invited Mrs. Spenlow to join us here. They will be expecting you."

"*What?*" Mr. Jones' twin blackened eyes opened so wide that they looked almost ready to start out of his head. "You're handing me over to the coppers? But you said—you said—"

Holmes gave him a calm look, faintly tinged with distaste. "I said that I *might* be persuaded to forgo bringing in the police—not that I would in fact do so. And your story, Mr. Jones, has not been at all persuasive."

Chapter 13: Watson

I led the still spluttering and protesting Mr. Jones downstairs, depositing him into the charge of the two police constables, who were waiting just as Holmes had said.

When I returned, Mrs. Spenlow was addressing Holmes.

"What will happen to him, Mr. Holmes?"

"Mr. Jones will be charged, questioned, and then escorted to Holloway Prison, where he will await his trial before a magistrate."

"Oh, but surely—" Mrs. Spenlow bit her lip. "That is, if he has any information about my brother, we shall lose the chance to question him if he is in prison!"

"True. But I have every confidence that Mr. Jones quite genuinely has nothing of value to tell us about your brother or his current whereabouts."

"But—" Mrs. Spenlow's voice was filled with distress. "But if that is the case, we are no nearer to finding Ronald than before!"

"The situation may not be quite so hopeless as that. But first—" Holmes turned to Lucy. "If young Becky is not listening at the door by now in hopes of hearing news of Flynn, she soon will be. Would you mind fetching her from the kitchen?"

It seemed to me that a look, brief, but nonetheless of some significance, passed between Holmes and Lucy—although what the look signified, I was unable to say. Perhaps he wished Lucy to contact the mortuary nearest to Cable Street and ask whether a body answering Ronald Stiles' description had been found?

If he disbelieved Mr. Jones' story, and suspected that the man had already made away with Ronald Stiles, Holmes might have been unwilling to speak of it before Stiles' sister.

Long though I had known Holmes, I had come to accept that there were moments when his own and Lucy's kinship meant that they shared a way of thinking and communicating that was beyond me.

"Of course," Lucy said.

The speed with which she and Becky returned confirmed Holmes's theory that Becky would not have waited much longer to be included in the conversation.

"Now," Holmes said, when they were seated opposite from Mrs. Spenlow on the sofa. "I believe you mentioned finding a scrap of paper in the hiding spot uncovered in Ronald's Stiles' room? A fragment from a pawn shop ticket?"

"That's right!" Becky sat up straighter. "You put it in your pocket, Lucy, just before that man broke in."

"That's right, I did."

Lucy drew out the fragment and handed it across to Holmes, who took it between his thumb and forefinger.

"A pawnbroker's ticket?" Mrs. Spenlow repeated. "But of what use is that in finding Ronald?"

"Ah, but you see, this is not just any pawnbroker's ticket." Holmes took up his magnifying glass from where it had lain on the mantle and used it to examine the small paper fragment. "Do you see this design here? The Greek key motif on the edge of the paper?" He held the paper and magnifying glass out to Mrs. Spenlow. "I happen to know that particular pattern is unique to the tickets issued by a pawn shop in Mitre Street, Whitechapel. That is not far from Mr. Stiles' room at 46 Cable Street."

"Really?" Mrs. Spenlow's eyes had gone wide with surprise.

I shared her surprise—although I should not have done. Holmes could identify the mud and gravel particular to every square inch of London. Was it so unbelievable that he would also be familiar with the city pawnbrokers and their tickets?

"The establishment is run by a man named Mr. Jibbit," he said.

Becky still looked discouraged, the corners of her mouth turned down. "This doesn't really get us any closer to finding Flynn, though," she said.

"Perhaps not." Holmes spoke with unaccustomed gentleness. "But it does possibly put us one step nearer to finding Ronald Stiles—and that is the first step in the road to us finding Flynn."

Becky nodded again, though shakily. "All right. Are we going to see this Mr. Jibbit now?"

"We shall. Although I have a different assignment for you, Becky," Holmes said.

"What is it?"

"I wish you to remain here, and to keep Mrs. Spenlow company. That is"—he addressed Mrs. Spenlow—"if you do not object to remaining here?"

"I have no objection," Mrs. Spenlow said slowly. "But why—"

"Your brother appears to have attracted the attention of at least one dangerous individual—and it is entirely possible that others besides Mr. Jones may be searching for him," Holmes said. "Until we know more, I believe that it would be safer for you to remain here."

"Of course." Mrs. Spenlow's cheeks had lost a little of their vibrant colour, and her dark eyes were anxious. "Of course, Mr. Holmes, if you think it advisable, then I will stay."

CHAPTER 14: FLYNN

Flynn sawed away at the rope around his wrists, rubbing it as hard as he could against the nail. How long had he been at this?

It felt like hours. The muscles of his arms and shoulders felt like they were on fire from the effort it took to hold them in the right position so that he could reach the nail.

And the rope still hadn't given way. He couldn't even tell for sure if he was making any progress. Although surely the rope had to break eventually?

Unless whoever'd nabbed him came back for him first.

Flynn tried to stomp on that thought. But as if he'd made it happen just by thinking about it, he suddenly heard footsteps.

He jerked his hands away from the nail and lay still, his heart hammering so hard in his ears that he felt sick.

Should he pretend to be still knocked unconscious? Or try to jump out and attack whoever came to check on him?

Fat lot of damage he'd be able to do, trussed up like a turkey for the market. Unless his kidnapper died laughing.

Flynn didn't move, holding his breath. But the footsteps didn't come any closer. Instead, the trunk he was in wobbled a bit—as though the surface it was standing on had just moved. And then he heard about the last sounds he'd been expecting: the clop of hooves, and a horse's neigh.

Chapter 15: Watson

Jibbit's pawn shop proved to be a squalid little storefront along Mitre Street, less than fifty paces from Mitre Square, made infamous by the discovery of one of the victims of Jack the Ripper more than a decade earlier. The neighbourhood had not improved since. The narrow street was clogged with trash and debris. The sallow, careworn faces of the passers-by gave no impression that they wanted anything more at this moment in their weary lives than to get away from their fellow-creatures and reach some shelter. The storefront window glass of the shop was woefully neglected. The dust on the panes obscured the few articles of clothing and cheap jewellery on display, and the sign proclaiming that cash might be advanced for similar items was virtually illegible through the accumulated grime.

Inside the shop, a tidy, round-faced bespectacled clerk stood behind a high counter, sifting through a pile of tarnished cutlery laid out on a yellowing pillowcase, watched closely and hopefully by a bedraggled young woman. Behind her several similarly hopeful women stood in a line, each holding cloth bundles, waiting for their turn for the attention of the clerk behind the counter.

"Mr. Jibbit!" Holmes shouted.

All customers present turned to look at Holmes, and at Lucy and me behind Holmes just inside the entry door.

The clerk, too, glanced up from his pile of cutlery. "He's in the back," he said. "Couldn't help hearin' you. Be out in a moment, I expect."

And in a moment, indeed, a tall, cadaverous looking grey-moustached man emerged from the shadowy doorway at the rear of the shop. He brightened when he recognised Holmes. "Ah. Mr. Holmes," he said. "How can I help?"

Holmes took the torn photograph of Ronald Stiles from his inside coat pocket and showed it to Jibbit along with the ticket fragment. "Has this man been here recently?"

Jibbit pursed his lips thoughtfully. "Don't recall him. But we get so many, and I don't see them all—"

Then came Lucy's voice. "Look sharp."

Behind us the door opened, and a surly, loud voice said, "'Ere now! Are you Jibbit? I'm lookin' for Ronald Stiles!"

The shop owner and the clerk both stared, eyes widening in shock. I saw that the newcomer, a burly, thuggish man in a dirty black jacket and flat cap, was brandishing a gun. The women waiting in line shrank back, gaping in fear, clutching their cloth-wrapped bundles tight against their chests as if they were holding their own infant children.

Holmes stepped to one side. The thug pushed forward, thrusting out his gun at Mr. Jibbit. "What's Stiles pawned, now? I want it! Bring it 'ere, or—"

But before the thug could complete his threat, three things happened.

Holmes, on the man's right side, swept one hand up beneath the thug's outstretched arm, grasping the man's right wrist, and then turning the man sideways, bringing the thug's elbow down hard on his own upraised knee. There was a loud crack and a roar of pain as the ligaments of the elbow tore. The gun clattered onto the counter.

I jumped for the thug's gun and gripped it in my hand.

At the same time, Lucy, on the other side, stepped forwards and kicked hard at the side of the thug's left knee. The leg buckled. The man staggered, trying to support himself.

I pressed the barrel of the gun under the thug's chin.

"If you wish to avoid more permanent injury—" I began.

"—you will leave at once," Holmes finished, rather to my surprise, for I thought Holmes wanted to interrogate the thug.

The man glared at the two of us, and made a move with his one good hand to grab the gun from me. But Holmes shoved him away. The thug staggered in the direction of the front entry door, which Lucy held open with a gesture of mock politeness.

The thug lunged at her, and I believe he would have borne her to the ground beneath his weight, if she had not stepped nimbly aside and, grasping his dangling broken right arm, pulled him onwards, through the door, and then across the narrow pavement of the street, using his momentum and lack of control to sling him against the brick wall. The man struck his head and slid part way to the ground.

Lucy crouched beside him, reached into his pocket, and pulled out a wicked-looking knife.

She slapped him across the face. He stared at her.

"Spoils of war," Lucy said, holding up the knife. "We'll keep the gun as well. Unless you'd like to dispute that?"

The man got to his feet. He looked at the gun in my hand, and at the knife in Lucy's.

Then he shambled away.

"Let him go," Holmes said from the entry doorway.

Mr. Jibbit had come out from behind the counter. "Thank you so much, Mr. Holmes," he said. "I have no idea what that man was trying to obtain, but I do know that I am in your debt!"

"Not a bit of it, good sir," said Holmes. "Only too happy to help. But we would be grateful if you would allow Dr. Watson the use of your telephone?"

The shop owner nodded assent. Acting on Holmes's instructions I telephoned to Baker Street, leaving a request for Mrs. Spenlow to meet us in Ronald Stiles' room at 46 Cable Street.

Chapter 16: Flynn

Flynn tried to think in the midst of the bouncing and jolting of the trunk. He was clearly strapped to the back of a carriage—the way people did with pieces of luggage. But he couldn't even guess where he was being driven.

Mr. Holmes probably would have been able to tell exactly what street he was on, just going by the noise of the carriage wheels as they rolled over the cobblestones. But all Flynn could say for certain was that being bumped around inside a moving steamer trunk hurt. Every time the carriage went over a bump, he'd smack his head or bang his knee or elbow.

He heard the clop of more horses' hooves, shouts from other drivers, and the occasional rumble of an omnibus, so they were on busy streets. But with the gag still firmly in place in his mouth, he couldn't shout to attract attention. And all the bouncing and jolting meant that he couldn't stay in position long enough to keep sawing away at his bonds.

Just when Flynn felt like his head was going to roll off his shoulders if he banged it one more time, the carriage stopped. He blinked hard, trying to stop his senses from swimming, then felt around for the nail, ready to start trying to break the rope around his wrists again.

But before he could get to work, he heard a click from up

above—someone must have unlocked the latch on the trunk. Flynn froze, the breath in his lungs turning to stone as, slowly, the lid of the trunk started to lift.

Chapter 17: Lucy

Mrs. Spenlow shivered a little as she stepped through the doorway into Ronald Stiles' room. I didn't blame her. The air felt damp and chilly, the furniture was still in disarray, and drops of dried blood—both mine and Mr. Jones'—splattered the floor from our fight.

"This is where my brother has been living?" She turned her head, taking in the sparse, shabby furnishings. "Poor Ronald! But why have you asked me to come here? Do you know where my brother is?"

"I shall come to that in a moment, Mrs. Spenlow," Holmes said.

A commotion seemed to be taking place in the street down below: shouts and angry yelling filtered up to us. I crossed to the window and looked out.

Below, I could see the carriage Mrs. Spenlow must have come in: a handsome black affair with an emblem in gold blazoned on the side.

In the street beyond, a rather unkept-looking man was scuffling with a pair of men in blue uniforms.

"Lucy?" Holmes glanced at me questioningly.

"It's all right. It looks as though a police constable has arrested a man for being drunk and disorderly, that's all."

I crossed to pick up one of the fallen chairs and sat down.

Holmes nodded. "In that case, Mrs. Spenlow, I beg you to

sit down and allow me to trespass on your patience for a few moments in order that we may return to the beginning of this case."

Mrs. Spenlow sat down on the second rickety chair Holmes indicated, but looked at him in confusion. "The beginning of the case? Do you mean when I came to see you yesterday?"

"Not quite. To return to the start of this affair, we must go back a trifle further—two days further, to be exact—to the day when a priceless masterpiece was stolen from Hampton Court Palace, and one of the warders there was found killed."

Mrs. Spenlow drew in a quick, sharp breath. "Are you suggesting—do you mean that my brother Ronald was somehow involved—"

Holmes held up a hand, stopping her. "As I said, I will explain fully, in due time. That was the beginning of this affair. We have reason to believe that there were at least three members of the gang of thieves. One who distracted and murdered the dead warder at the time of the theft, and who, the night before the theft, may have murdered Olson, the warder who was to have been on duty the next day, so that a second thief could take Olson's place. And then a third accomplice, who piloted the river launch on which the thieves escaped with the stolen painting. Unfortunately, the phrase *honour among thieves* has little or no meaning to actual members of London's criminal underworld. As frequently happens in such affairs, the gang members had a falling out in which the pilot of the launch double-crossed the other two. I have no way to know for certain, but I suspect that he may have been prepared to commit robbery, but not murder—and that when he learned of the death of two Hampton Court Warders, he rebelled against his partners in crime, made away with the portrait, and vanished. The other two hunted for him in vain—going so far as to come here in order to ransack this room." Holmes extended a hand, indicating the chaos and the torn sofa cushions around us.

Mrs. Spenlow pressed the back of her hand to her mouth. "Then … then you do believe that Ronald—" she broke off. "I implore you, Mr. Holmes, speak plainly. If you know where my brother is now, please, please tell me!"

Holmes put the tips of his fingers together. "That, Mrs. Spenlow, is a somewhat more complicated request than it might first appear. If you are inquiring as to the whereabouts of a man born to your own father and mother, then I must confess that I have absolutely no idea where such a one might be found. However—" He raised his voice a little, speaking over the small, incoherent sound of protest that Mrs. Spenlow made. "However, if you are asking about the man who goes by the name of Ronald Stiles—or occasionally Ronald Benson—then you know that as well as I do. He was arrested this afternoon at my flat and brought to prison."

Mrs. Spenlow stared at him for what must have been a full ten seconds before she gave an uncertain little laugh.

"I—but Mr. Holmes, is this some sort of strange jest? What do you mean? That man Mr. Jones … are you suggesting that I would not know my own brother—"

"What I am suggesting, Mrs. Spenlow, is that Ronald Stiles is not and has never been any relation of yours." Holmes's voice was silky-smooth, and yet held an underlying note of steel. "No blood relation, that is. He is, however, related to you by marriage. That photograph of a young Ronald Stiles which you so conveniently produced—that was an error on your part, for it was that which first led me to suspect that you were not quite what you appeared. The pose, dress, and the size and placement of Ronald Stiles' figure in the photograph you gave me were entirely wrong for a family grouping. Had there been an entire family photographed with him, his likeness would have appeared much smaller in order to accommodate the greater number of people in the frame. The picture was, however, precisely right for half of a wedding photograph. *Your* wedding photograph, with your own image by necessity cropped out to prevent recognition. Ronald Stiles is your husband. Or perhaps he was your husband. The evidence would suggest that you have been separated—whether legally or otherwise—for some years, but that you approached him on the pretense of attempting a reconciliation when you sought to make him a co-conspirator in your plan. A plan that involved the theft of a priceless masterpiece from Hampton Court."

Mrs. Spenlow's face had gone very flushed, unhealthy red colour suffusing her cheeks. She sprang up in outrage, crossing to the window before spinning back to face Holmes. "Really, Mr. Holmes, what you are suggesting is not only outrageously insulting—"

Holmes ignored her entirely and went on as though she had not spoken, drawing out the photograph of the young Ronald Stiles from an inner pocket. "You assumed that your husband would shave his beard in an attempt to disguise himself, and that this image would present enough of a likeness to his current appearance to enable recognition. As we know, he did *not* remove his beard, and thus bears very little resemblance to this image from twenty or more years ago. However, certain features do not change with time: the shape of the ears, for example. Likewise, the shape of a man's hands. If you examine the photograph of Mr. Stiles closely, both of those features are identical to those of Mr. Jones."

Mrs. Spenlow opened and closed her mouth, but no sound emerged.

Holmes went on. "As I mentioned before, Stiles became uneasy—or perhaps developed a conscience—after the robbery, when he learned of the murder of the two warders. He absconded with the painting, leaving you and your other co-conspirator, whom we had the pleasure of meeting earlier today in Whitechapel—not only to face murder charges if you were caught, but without even the ill-gotten gains from your crime to fund an escape to a new city—perhaps even a new country. Unable to locate Stiles yourself, you thought to enlist an expert's skill at finding a missing individual—namely, mine. You or your co-conspirator followed my agent as he made inquiries about Stiles, ultimately following him to this neighbourhood, where you discovered the room where Ronald Stiles had been living. You found, however, that he had already fled. And even venting your frustration by slashing the cushions of this sofa did not yield a single clue as to where he might have gone."

Mrs. Spenlow had recovered enough to draw in her breath and straighten, her posture one of rigid indignation. "Mr. Holmes, I have nothing to say, save that you appear to have taken leave of your senses. This wild tale would be better suited to the pages of one of Mister Dickens's works of fiction. You have not a shred of proof—"

"Ah, but that is just what I do, in fact, have." Holmes said. "You unexpectedly came face to face with your husband Ronald Stiles in my sitting room, while he was pretending that his name was 'Mr. Jones.' It must have been quite maddening to be so near to him, and yet unable to demand that he return the stolen portrait. No wonder that you spoke out against his going to prison; you hoped that you and your other confederate might capture him as soon as he departed from Baker Street and force him to reveal the painting's location. I, however, thought that prison would be the safest place for Ronald Stiles, since it would place him out of your reach. Now, as you recall, I identified the fragment of a pawnbroker's ticket as having come from a particular pawn shop in Whitechapel. I lied. It is unlikely in the extreme that Ronald Stiles ever set foot near the pawn shop I mentioned." He spoke the words entirely calmly. "Indeed, there is nothing whatsoever to connect the scrap of ticket with Mr. Jibbit's establishment—nothing, save the fact that I spoke of Mr. Jibbit's shop in your hearing. You alone outside of ourselves knew that Mr. Jibbit's shop was our destination. You alone knew of the fictitious connection between the pawn shop and Ronald Stiles—and somehow we were ambushed there by a man. Not, you will note, demanding to know Stiles' current location, since you already knew that quite well. No, the intruder demanded to know about Ronald Stiles' supposed visit to the place, and whether he had left anything there to be redeemed or sold. A question no one but an associate of yours, informed by you of our plans, would have known to ask."

Mrs. Spenlow's face had gone slack with shock. She drew back as though trying to retreat, pressing against the window behind her. She clutched her reticule to her waist.

"It was a trap, Mrs. Spenlow," Holmes said. "And you walked straight into it. Lucy?"

Taking Holmes's lead, I took a step forwards and knocked the reticule from her grasp. It landed at Watson's feet. There was a metallic thud as it hit the floor.

Watson bent down, retrieved the reticule, and withdrew a small revolver.

"You used this at the Three Pines Inn, didn't you?" Holmes asked.

Mrs. Spenlow drew a harsh, rattling breath. Her face had changed, twisting, so that she looked no longer lovely but more like a rat caught in the trap Holmes had mentioned.

"I wouldn't be acting too high and mighty, Mr. Holmes." Her voice, too, had lost its cultured accents. "You don't know what aces I might have up my sleeve."

"Ah." Holmes gave her another level look, although his face hardened in a way that had frightened more vicious criminals than Mrs. Spenlow. "I assume that you are referring to Flynn, whom you and your confederate abducted. I suppose I must pay you the compliment of not underestimating my powers of deduction as badly as some have done, in that you had the foresight to take Flynn as a potential hostage in case we should happen to discover your real identity."

Mrs. Spenlow gaped at Holmes another moment, then turned to look out the window, raising her hand.

I smiled. "I assume that you're trying to signal your confederate, who drove the carriage that brought you here. Do you really think we would have overlooked him? He was the man I described as drunk and disorderly when you first came. The man the police arrested—"

I got no further, though. With an incoherent cry, Mrs. Spenlow made a wild run for the door, wrenching it open and lunging through.

Watson looked about to pursue her, but Holmes held up a hand. "It's all right."

The sound of a high scream came from the staircase just outside, followed by a loud series of thumps and crashes.

Flynn appeared in the open doorway.

"Tripped her on the stairs," he said with satisfaction. He looked even dirtier and more rumpled than usual, but otherwise none the worse for his experience. "Silly twit didn't even look where she was going. Staggered and stumbled, right into the copper's arms at the bottom."

Holmes bestowed one of his rare smiles on both Flynn and Becky, who followed close behind him. "Well done. I take it Mrs. Spenlow made an excuse to use the telephone at Baker Street, as expected?"

"Yes, just as you and Lucy said she would. She said she'd something she needed to tell her maid back at the hotel—but I managed to listen under the door while she was talking, and she was giving someone the address of Mr. Jibbit's shop in Whitechapel. So, when your telephone call came, asking her to meet you here, I pretended that I would stay behind in Baker Street. But I hung onto the back of the carriage the way you told me to, and found Flynn."

"Well done," Holmes said again. "And now, I believe it is time to reclaim the painting that has been the cause of all this tumult."

Watson startled. "You mean that the painting is actually here, Holmes? That it was here all of this time?"

"Mr. Stiles' action in returning here—only to be met with Lucy—would suggest that there was something of value hidden in the place," Holmes said. His grey eyes were flicking rapidly around the room, considering potential hiding places and discarding them. "The staged ransacking of this space was a bluff, intended to make it plain that there was nothing of value here. However, Stiles did return, and when confronted by a stranger—one who plainly didn't recognise him—thought it prudent to pretend to be merely another ruffian hunting for Stiles rather than the man himself."

"I wish we had recognised him then," Becky said with a dissatisfied frown.

"Yes, well, in your defence, you had never seen the photograph of Ronald Stiles—" Holmes broke off as his gaze fell upon the empty cupboard that had been moved aside to reveal the hidden recess in the floor boards.

"I wonder … another bluff?" Holmes spoke meditatively. "This time, perhaps, a double one? Flynn, if you would be so good as to take hold of the cupboard and turn it round?"

The cupboard, like everything else in the room, was of rickety build and not heavy to lift. Flynn did as Holmes asked, turning it around so that the front faced away from us.

A drab woollen blanket had been nailed over the back.

"Ah." Holmes gave a murmur of satisfaction, and the rest of us drew in our breath as he pulled away the blanket and we saw the gilded frame of a painting.

The frame had also been nailed to the back of the cupboard, which would probably cause the Hampton Court custodians severe anguish. But the painting itself was entirely unharmed. Even in the dim, shabby little room, the colours glowed softly with all the vibrancy of a masterful artist, and I could easily recognise the woman in the portrait. She was Frances Stuart, Duchess of Richmond. During my school days at Miss Porter's School, she had been much discussed among the girls and the instructors alike, both as the lady of exemplary principles who had refused the romantic advances of King Charles II, and as the duchess whose image, now costumed as Britannica, appeared on coins throughout the realm.

Watson also recognised the painting. "No wonder they hushed this up," he said.

Then I heard the voice of Lestrade, accompanied by the pounding of his footsteps on the stairs.

Chapter 18: Watson

"You found it!" Lestrade fairly hugged himself with happiness as he saw the painting. Still breathless, he shouted down the stairs for a constable to come.

While waiting, he turned to Holmes. "I saw the two prisoners downstairs."

"The former Mrs. Stiles and her accomplice. Watson has her pistol here."

I handed over the weapon. "She shot the warder in The Three Pines Inn with this," I said. "Very likely she also stabbed the other warder at Hampton Court."

Lestrade nodded. "Her accomplice downstairs says the same. As does Mr. Stiles, in Holloway Prison. Both men say they'll tell all, if we'll just charge them for the robbery and not bring a charge of felony murder."

"What about what they did to me?" Flynn asked.

"It will be up to the Queen's Counselor," said Lestrade.

"We shall see that he is made aware of the facts," Holmes said.

"Meanwhile—" Lestrade crouched before the painting, gazing thoughtfully at the nails driven through the gilded frame. "I think we'd better take this priceless object of art back to Hampton Court, dresser and all."

For a moment, I thought Lestrade intended us all to go, and my pulse quickened at the thought. Then I realised that the time was now well after closing hour at the Palace and there would be no more tours until the following day.

"I don't expect The Lord Chamberlain's office will say much to the papers about how it was recovered," Lestrade said.

"You should take whatever credit can be allotted you," Holmes said.

"Thank you, Mr. Holmes."

"However, there is one thing you might do for me, if you can conveniently arrange it."

Lestrade's pinched features narrowed even further for a moment as Holmes came closer, but then he relaxed visibly, as Holmes said something too quietly for me to hear.

Chapter 19: Watson

It was nine o'clock Saturday morning. Save for the watery sun instead of grey fog outside of the window, the scene might have been identical to the one from three days before: Holmes sat slouched in his dressing gown before the fire, his violin lying carelessly discarded at his feet, his pipe clamped between his teeth, and his expression the particularly blank one that denoted either profound thought or profound boredom.

"Come Holmes." I seated myself in the chair opposite from his. "You cannot claim that this most recent case has provided no novelty or points of unusual interest."

"True." Holmes's expression lightened briefly. "It is indeed something of a novel experience to be hired by the criminal who committed the very crime which I am investigating."

"Speaking of the subject, how did you connect Mrs. Spenlow's story with the robbery at Hampton Court?"

"My dear Watson, you really ought to apply yourself more fully to the study of geography. If you recall, Mrs. Spenlow gave her place of residence as East Molesey. When a woman comes in and claims to hail from the town nearest Hampton Court Palace, it surely requires no very great deductive leap to surmise that she may be connected to a crime that took place at the palace mere days before. Particularly as it was plain from our first meeting that she had something to hide and was not who she claimed to be."

"I see."

Holmes drew once more at his pipe, relapsing again into moody silence.

"Very well, Holmes," I said, with a touch of exasperation. "Since you are apparently unwilling to communicate, I will ask you directly: what is it that is troubling you? Is it Zoe—"

I thought there might have been a quick flicker, as of pain or regret, in Holmes's gaze at the mention of her name. But he interrupted with a shake of his head. "You are mistaken, Watson. I am not troubled—not yet, that is."

I frowned, for the gravity of Holmes's expression belied his words. "Not yet? Wait a moment." I had caught sight of a sheaf of papers stuffed down into the chair beside him where they had plainly fallen from his hand. From the few words that I could make out at the top of the first page, it looked like a police report. "Officer killed on duty …" I read aloud, then looked up. "Is this the episode that Jack's Scotland Yard unit was called in to investigate? Lucy mentioned to me on the way back from Cable Street that a police sergeant whom he knew two years ago had been killed."

"No." Holmes picked up the stack of papers. "This is not the report on Sergeant O'Hara's death, but rather one from three years ago. The death of a police officer named Inspector Glen, who was killed in the line of duty while attempting to carry out the search of a house known to be a stronghold of one of the East End street gangs."

My eyebrows rose. "I see. And of what interest is the death of an Inspector from three years ago?"

"None. For the present moment. However, I have always found it prudent to prepare to face a threat when it is as yet nothing more than a distant cloud on the horizon."

"I see." I did not, of course, but what I did perceive plainly was that Holmes was unlikely to offer any more complete explanation than the one he had already given. "Perhaps my question should have been: who was this Inspector Glen?"

I thought at first that Holmes would evade giving me an answer to that question, as well. But then he said, his eyes on the fire, "An unlikable fellow, by all accounts. Rough-tempered, quick to anger … and there were whispers of corruption. In one or two of his cases, evidence that might have convicted a powerful or wealthy man was unaccountably lost. Interestingly, he also served as training officer for both the dead Sergeant O'Hara and for Jack."

"You think Jack will need our help?"

"He has been working the O'Hara investigation most strenuously and diligently since its inception." Holmes paused, glancing at his watch, then added, "Though I believe he has a paid leave day today."

From the street below, we heard the jangle of our bell-pull and the muffled voice of Mrs. Hudson.

"Now," Holmes said, getting to his feet and reaching for his scarf, "I hope you are prepared for activity, and perhaps a sporting wager as to whether or not Flynn will be joining us."

"Another case?" I asked.

"I hope not," he replied. He shouted, "Mrs. Hudson? Was that a delivery for me?" as he opened our door.

"There is no need to shout, Mr. Holmes," she said reprovingly. "I am right here. And here is your envelope. They did not ask for a reply."

I saw the Royal seal on heavy cream-coloured paper.

"From Hampton Court Palace," Holmes said. "Inside are six tickets for the noon tour, arranged by Lestrade. Lucy, Jack, and

Becky will meet us there, and I will give you odds that Flynn accepts their invitation to join them."

"I would not bet against you, Holmes."

"I thought not." He gave one of his quick little smiles. "Whatever storms may lie ahead," he said, "we may at least take full advantage of the calm before them."

THE END

Historical Notes

This is a work of fiction, and the authors make no claim that any of the historical locations or historical figures appearing in this story had even the remotest connection with the adventures recounted herein. However …

1. The portrait of Frances Stuart, Duchess of Richmond, is on display at Hampton Court Palace, along with nine other portraits of similar ladies of the court of Charles II, painted by Sir Peter Lely. Together, the portraits are known as the Windsor Beauties, because they were first displayed at Windsor Castle before being moved to Hampton Court in 1835. Since then, as far as the authors are aware, none of them has been stolen, even temporarily.

2. The authors both had the pleasure of visiting Hampton Court and are confident that Watson and the Baker Street team would have all appreciated a visit.

3. Frances Stuart was the model for the image of the legendary Britannica that appears on British coins such as this one:

POWDER ISLAND

Chapter 1: Watson

"Holmes," I said, putting aside my copy of the morning *Times*, "there was a massive explosion at Powder Island yesterday."

It was an April Monday, just after breakfast. The two of us were in our sitting-room, appreciating the warmth from the glowing coals in our fireplace. A cold rain lashed at our bow window.

"A man has died. Our old friend Gregson is involved. The report hints at murder."

Holmes leaned back in his armchair, fingers steepled and eyes closed. "Kindly be so good as to read the account."

This was the passage I read:

> **HORRIFIC EXPLOSION CLAIMS LIFE AT POWDER ISLAND**
> At a few minutes before 9 o'clock Sunday morning, an enormous explosion shocked thousands of British citizens. The blast came from the Rexford Gunpowder Factory on the banks of the Thames at Hounslow. In the factory rubble, police found the skull and several fragments of a human body, assumed to be the remains of Mr. Marcus Thiel, 60 years old. Mr. Thiel had been the company supervisor of operations. He leaves behind a widow and daughter. By all accounts, Mr. Thiel had been employed by the firm for many years and had been meticulous in the performance of his duties.

Authorities do not believe the explosion was due to carelessness. Inspector Tobias Gregson of the Metropolitan Police will lead an investigation into the cause of the tragedy.

Nearly four hundred workers at the factory have been suspended, including about 70 women. Until the investigation and rebuilding operations are complete, nearly all will remain unemployed.

I put down the newspaper. My heart felt heavy as I thought of the man's violent death, and of the four hundred employees without work, and their need for justice. I turned to Holmes. "'Not due to carelessness,'" I repeated. "That suggests a more sinister force behind the explosion, does it not?"

Holmes nodded. "I shall await a call from Inspector Gregson," he said. "It would be good to work with him again."

But springtime passed, and then summer, and then autumn, and finally winter began, and the call from Inspector Gregson did not come.

Chapter 2: Lucy

The shrill ring of the telephone yanked me out of sleep.

I opened my eyes and frowned, slowly coming alert. Snowflakes were falling outside our window. Jack's side of the bed was empty, and the telephone's ringing had stopped. Which meant that early as it was, Jack was already awake and had gone to answer it.

I got up, slipping on my dressing gown and heading for the stairs to follow him. I walked on tiptoe, on the chance that Becky was miraculously still asleep. I could hear Jack's voice coming from the front hall below.

"I want you to check every square inch of his rooms."

He had to be speaking to one of the police constables under his command. He was using what I thought of as his sergeant's voice: crisp and firm with authority. Although I thought this morning there was a more than usual grimness to his tone.

"Look behind the furniture, take up the carpets, send someone to sweep the chimney and unscrew the light fixtures if you have to. Understood, Hutchins?"

Constable Hutchins must have replied in the affirmative, because Jack hung up the telephone's speaking piece.

I would have sworn I hadn't made any noise, but he hadn't spent two years walking a beat in some of London's most dangerous neighbourhoods without developing a sixth sense as to whether or not he was alone.

He turned his head to look at me. "Good morning. Sorry if I woke you."

"It's all right." I tightened the belt of my robe and came the rest of the way down the stairs. "I was just waiting for you to add that if mathematicians can prove the existence of a fourth dimension, Constable Hutchins should search there, too."

Jack smiled, though briefly.

He was already dressed, his shirtsleeves rolled up and his dark hair rumpled as though he'd been running his hands through it.

I looked past him to our front room, where stacks of paper covered the table.

"Are those the reports on Sergeant O'Hara's murder?"

A little less than a week ago O'Hara had been killed. Jack had known him since the early days of their careers on the police force. Jack's unit at Scotland Yard had been assigned to the case.

Jack followed my glance. "That's right. Just going over witness reports."

"Witnesses?" O'Hara had been found in a dirty back alley in Whitechapel with a knife between his shoulder blades. I hadn't heard there were any witnesses.

"Witnesses might be too strong a word." Jack picked up one of the sheets of paper. "Just statements from people in the area. A couple of beggars who were parked in a doorway not far off at the time. A troupe of street performers—clowns." Jack raised an eyebrow. "I can't wait to hear what Hutchins has to say after interviewing them."

Unlike the cases Watson wrote about, which were generally solved with a single stroke of Holmes's brilliance, most police work was accomplished with hours upon hours of painful interviews and then combing through many possibly inaccurate, often contradictory reports, searching for the smallest details that might provide a fresh piece of the puzzle.

Jack picked up another paper, frowning. "Then there's a couple of sailors on shore leave who were going back to their ship after a night in the grog shops and heard shouts coming from the alley where O'Hara was found—or somewhere close by. They didn't think anything of it till they saw the story in the newspaper and came in to the Yard to make a report."

"Do you think they may actually have heard the murder?"

"I doubt it. Hearing shouts in Whitechapel is about as rare as a foggy day. And stabbing someone in the back implies stealth—you don't put your victim on his guard by shouting at him from behind."

Jack's voice was perfectly level, but the line of his mouth had tightened, and his eyes were dark with a cold, distant look that made a shiver slide through me.

He looked like a man who'd been fully expecting the worst and had just been proven right.

I opened my mouth, then closed it again.

None of this explained why Jack was so insistent that Sergeant O'Hara's room be searched. But—

Jack looked up at me. "You're about to ask why this case in particular bothers me."

"I didn't say a single thing!"

He smiled, if faintly. "Yeah, if you'd said nothing any louder, I'd be deaf right about now." He sighed. "It's not that I don't want to tell you—"

"It's all right. You don't have to, I understand."

There were always aspects of official police cases that Jack wasn't at liberty to share with me. It wouldn't be fair to try to make him tell me more than his duties allowed.

Jack shook his head. "No, I—"

Beside me, the telephone rang, making me startle. I reached for the receiver. "I'll answer. But it's probably Constable Hutchins again."

When I picked up, though, the voice I heard on the other end of the line belonged to my father, Sherlock Holmes.

"Ah, Lucy." As usual, Holmes forbore to waste time on anything as conventional as words of greeting. "I'm glad you are already awake. I have a question for Jack, if he is available?"

I felt my eyebrows edge upwards. It was seldom that Holmes needed to consult the police for answers, even his own son-in-law. "Yes, he's here."

Jack came to stand next to me, and I held the earpiece out so we both could listen.

"Good." Holmes's voice came crackling through the telephone line. "I need your recollections of the explosion at Powder Island."

Chapter 3: Lucy

Jack's expression registered surprise—as I was sure did mine.

"Powder Island?" he repeated with a grimace. "Not my favourite case."

"You worked it with Gregson, as I recall," Holmes said on the other end of the telephone line.

"I did. Nine months ago. Gregson was convinced it was arson and homicide, and so was I. He got into a good deal of trouble over it, poor bloke."

"How?"

"He trusted his superiors."

"Who, specifically?"

Jack looked uncomfortable. "I don't know, specifically. But someone high up didn't want him going on with that case. He persisted, and when he wouldn't back away, he lost his rank. Now he's been broken down to a beat copper, and he's walking the streets and alleys of Whitechapel."

"Can you get me the file?" Holmes asked.

Jack nodded, but his brows were furrowed. "How soon do you need it?"

"The factory owner wants to meet with me at eleven o'clock this morning."

"In that case, I'll go in to the Yard straight away."

"I'll come with you," I said. "You can give the files to me and I'll bring them on to Baker Street."

* * *

Snow was falling thickly as Jack and I made our way along the embankment towards Scotland Yard. Becky dashed ahead of us, the ends of her red scarf flapping as she tried to catch the flakes on her tongue.

She looked so joyful, even the surliest-looking passers-by didn't object when she narrowly missed bumping into them.

"That would be good news for Inspector Gregson," I said, "if his theory of foul play at the gunpowder factory could be proven correct."

"Hmm." Jack's eyes were on the Thames beside us, busy even in the wintry weather with steam launches and river barges, but I doubted he was seeing them. His voice and his gaze were both abstracted.

I looked up at him sharply. Jack was *never* abstracted—especially not when he was out on the streets with both me and Becky. He, like most police officers who'd seen far too much of the city's most violent side, constantly scanned his surroundings, noting details, evaluating potential threats. The habit was so ingrained in him as to be automatic by now.

"Maybe chimpanzees escaped from the Hyde Park zoo," I said. "They might have swum across the river, and let off fireworks to ignite an explosion."

"Could be."

"Jack!"

Jack started and looked down at me, then rubbed the space between his eyes. "Sorry. I was just thinking about—" he shook his head. "Never mind. What were you saying?"

"I was asking about the Powder Island case. Why couldn't Gregson prove it was actually arson?"

"We never really got that far. We collected the evidence, took witness statements—and then word came down from the assistant commissioner. The case was to be handed over to the Home Office. Gregson argued against it. Didn't want to give the investigation up. That's what lost him his rank. The Home Office men took offense—thought he should have given them better cooperation. Next thing I heard, he was broken down to constable."

"Was that the only reason? Just because he didn't cooperate with the Home Office?"

"How do you mean?"

"I don't know. But it feels as though there must be something wrong—or at the very least odd—about the case."

Particularly since Holmes was now involved. My father didn't undertake investigations unless either the stakes were especially high or the problem was an especially knotty one.

In the case of an explosion at a gunpowder factory, both of those conditions might well be proven true.

We had reached Scotland Yard. Becky came darting back to tug at my hand. "Lucy, can we go around to the stables and see the horses? Please?"

"All right." The Scotland Yard official horses were kept in a stable area in an inner courtyard of the building. "Jack can go and fetch the file and then meet us out there?" I glanced questioningly at Jack.

"That's fine." Jack paused, though, with his foot on the first step leading up to the Yard's entrance. He looked back at me with a puzzled frown. "Did you say something about chimpanzees?"

Jack looked grim enough, though, when he came outside and found us a quarter of an hour later.

Becky was delightedly feeding extra measures of oats to the horses and laughing when their velvet lips tickled the palm of her hand.

"What is it?" I asked.

"The files on Powder Island are missing."

"Missing?"

Jack took out a slip of paper and held it out. "This is all that's left."

The paper was a transfer slip, indicating the files had been signed over to the Home Office.

Jack nodded. "Everything else—all the notes and the statements taken from the witnesses—is gone."

I looked up at him, hesitating.

Jack sighed. "All right. I'll write a note to him."

"How do you know what I was about to ask?"

"Detective, remember?" Jack tapped his forehead. "Just be careful. Those aren't good neighborhoods to be walking around in."

"I will be."

Becky came back to join us, looking from me to Jack. "What's happened? Is something wrong?"

"Not yet. But after we visit Baker Street to tell Holmes about the missing file, we're going to make a visit to Whitechapel to track down Police Constable Gregson."

Chapter 4: Watson

A cab, an ordinary growler, cut across the snowy traffic lanes on Baker Street, heading straight for our home. I was close by on the pavement, returning from a morning errand, my boots growing steadily more soaked from the slush.

The cab was drawn by a single horse and driven by an ordinary cabman. The fellow wore a red wool scarf. He hunched over his reins. As soon as he reached the curb, he pulled his horse to a stop, directly in front of 221B and only a few feet ahead of where I stood.

The driver made no move to dismount. I saw no sign of activity within the enclosed carriage.

Perhaps, I thought, Holmes was about to dash off to some adventure without me. Using my own key, I quickly let myself in to our downstairs hallway and mounted the seventeen steps more briskly than usual.

But upon opening the door to our sitting room, it was plain that Holmes was very much at home and not at all about to depart. The papers from the past week lay in an untidy heap beside his desk, and Holmes himself lounged in his customary chair beside a blazing fire, pipe in hand, his sharp features enveloped in clouds of blue-grey tobacco smoke.

He glanced first at me and then at his watch.

"You ran up the steps," Holmes said. "Is he here?"

"You are expecting a client?"

"At eleven."

"There was a cab," I said. "I thought it was empty."

Holmes stood as I hung up my coat, and together we went to our bow window.

"Which cab?" Holmes asked.

For now, there were two cabs. The one I had noticed, with the forlorn-looking driver in his red scarf, had not moved. Behind it, however, another growler had stopped. Its driver had dismounted from his perch and was opening the door for a passenger.

"The first."

"The other has brought our client," Holmes said, "that tall, bearded fellow getting out now. Bradley Rexford is his name."

Rexford descended from the growler swathed in a black fur coat. Ignoring the cabby's proffered arm, he clapped a top hat onto his balding head, stuffed a folded note into the cabby's hand with a swift, final gesture, and then strode past, holding a black leather briefcase and mounting the steps to our front stoop. We heard the ring of our bell-pull.

Holmes grasped the window shade and pulled it down. Then he raised it once more, slowly.

I saw Flynn across the street, in the doorway of a coffee shop where he had been warming himself. Alerted by Holmes's signal with the window shade, he was looking at us.

"Why Flynn?" I asked.

"The first cab," Holmes said.

The cab driven by the man in the red scarf had not moved. But from here, I could see through the small viewing panel cut into the rear. A shadowy presence indicated a passenger was inside.

"Away from the window, if you please, old friend," Holmes said. "When our client arrives, I shall excuse myself. At that time, be so good as to entertain Mr. Rexford for a moment or two."

"You'll be giving instructions to Flynn," I was about to say, but the heavy footsteps on our stairs were nearly at our door and Holmes was pressing a finger to his lips for silence.

* * *

"Where is he going?" Rexford turned his square-cut face to me as the door closed behind Holmes. A greying beard fringed his jawline and chin, and it quivered with indignation.

"He won't be long," I replied. "Please. Do have a seat."

Rexford set down his briefcase and carefully draped his heavy, glossy coat over the back of our settee. Powerfully built, though somewhat stooped in age, he stood for a few moments to survey the room, his arms akimbo, reminding me of the great statue of King Henry VIII above the gateway at Saint Bart's hospital, in his characteristic pose of dominion and defiance.

I determined to be polite. "May I offer you a cigarette? A cigar?"

"I never smoke. Too great a hazard in my business."

"Which is?"

His lips pressed together for a moment. "I take it Mr. Holmes has not told you. I own the Rexford Works on Powder Island. Largest gunpowder manufacturer in Europe."

I recalled the newspaper article. "Where a significant explosion occurred last year," I said.

The pride in his expression turned to discomfort. "My appointment was for eleven. It is now—" he stopped, reaching into his waistcoat pocket. Then, abruptly, he withdrew his hand.

"I had forgotten. Misplaced my watch somehow." He quickly added, "It's a damn fine watch, but that's not what brings me here."

He sat down heavily on our settee. "And I won't want you writing about it," he said.

"You may rest assured," I said.

A moment later, to my relief, I heard Holmes's footsteps on our stairs.

"Just one more moment," Holmes said as he entered. He strode swiftly to our bow window and looked out. He watched intently, holding up his hand for silence.

Then he turned. "My apologies for the delay, Mr. Rexford. How can I be of assistance?"

In answer, Rexford withdrew a sheaf of papers from his briefcase and held them out to Holmes. "I want you to read this first."

Holmes took the papers without glancing at them. "Is that the Home Office report on the explosion at your factory?"

Rexford said, "I am impressed."

Now seated in his familiar chair by the fireside, Holmes crossed his legs, leaned back and steepled his fingertips. "Then please state your business."

"First, I wish you to clear up the uncertainty created by the report."

Holmes nodded. "Understandably." He nodded to me. "Watson, you may wish to refer to this—" he waved at the pages with a dismissive gesture. "Mycroft provided me a copy yesterday. It runs on for dozens of pages, close-set in type at the public's expense by Her Majesty's Inspector of Explosives, prepared for the Home Office. I shall summarise, in the interest of your time, Mr. Rexford, the thousands and thousands of words in the report and its exhibits. Pray correct me if I misstate."

Rexford nodded.

"There was an explosion some nine months ago in the glazing house of your gunpowder works. The blast was heard for miles and it demolished the building entirely. The scattered remains of only one man were found. The unfortunate victim was the supervisor of the works, known to be a reliable, conscientious and experienced man. At nine o'clock in the morning he was the only man scheduled to be on duty, for the day was a Sunday and work had halted for the Sabbath. The report lists ten possible causes of the explosion and dismisses eight of those ten, leaving as possibilities only the breakdown of a mechanical part of the mixing-equipment, which would have produced friction and thus a spark, or a flame from the heads of lucifer matches, which might have been scattered on the platform by a person or persons unknown for malicious purposes."

"Matches had been found on the floor in one of the other buildings," added Rexford. "A few days earlier."

"So now you come to me," said Holmes. "After nine months and a police inspection and a Home Office report, all with no results, you come to me. After the trail has gone cold, and after police have questioned all the witnesses. And you must know that I have no authority to require more answers."

"I had hoped the report—"

Homes held up his hand. "Pardon my interruption, Mr. Rexford. But you mistake my meaning. I did not ask why you waited to come, but why you come to me at all."

Rexford took a plain white envelope from his inside pocket and handed it to Holmes. "Because yesterday morning I received this."

The envelope contained a single sheet of cheap paper, on which had been pasted words clipped from a newspaper. The words of the message read:

Don't be too quick to celebrate. Another big bang is coming your way.

Chapter 5: Flynn

Flynn's icy fingers were slipping. It was awkward enough keeping his face away from the little window at the back of the slow-moving cab. Each time the wheels bumped over the ruts in the frozen slush, he lost just a little of his grip on the rooftop. He knew he would fall, unless he could somehow rebalance himself. Wiry, nearly twelve, Flynn was pretty sure he could do that.

Twisting his torso towards the back corner, he heaved himself upwards, scrabbling for the now-empty iron rail that would have kept suitcases from sliding off the roof, if there had been any suitcases. The fingertips of his right hand got around it. Numb though they were, they hooked the luggage rail like claws.

He was swinging his body back so as to get his other hand on the rail, when the cab stopped.

The side door clicked open.

Flynn bent to peer into the cab through the rear viewing pane. He saw a shadowy black-caped figure, and a gloved hand gripping the strap of a grey canvas holdall bag. Then the figure and the canvas bag were out the door. The cab lurched forwards just as Flynn dropped to the slush-crusted roadway. Off balance, Flynn fell into the slush, soaking the knees of his trousers. Thankfully, his boots kept the wet away from his feet and they gave him good traction as he stood. Mr. Mycroft had given him the boots, sturdy leather with strong leather laces, as a present for his work identifying some bombers just before Christmas. Flynn took no thought of that past success, though he was grateful for the boots. At the moment he knew he was on the verge of failing in the assignment Mr. Holmes had given him, first to watch the entrance to 221B Baker Street in anticipation of an important client this morning, and then to follow the cab driven by the man in the red scarf and not to lose sight of the passenger.

Out of the way, y' nickey dimwit!

A lorry driver was yelling that he was an idiot. The two big dray lorry horses were about to trample him. He'd be a dead idiot, he thought, if he didn't get a move on.

But across the street on the pavement, a black-caped figure in a white captain's cap was striding away from him, with a grey canvas holdall bag swinging alongside. The man was heading towards the round arches of the nearest building.

Flynn took that direction, scrambled after the caped figure, a hoof of the lead horse connecting with his retreating boot. The smack stung his ankle and knocked him off balance, but he kept on. He could read the sign above the arch. This was the entrance to the Baker Street Station of the Metropolitan Line.

He could buy a ticket, he told himself. He had a half-crown in his pocket. He would just see which train the caped figure boarded, wait to be sure the figure stayed on the train, and then climb onto the last car at the last minute.

A crowd was coming up the stairs, soot-covered and hurrying to reach the fresher outdoor air. As they surged round Flynn, he lost sight of the caped figure and the captain's cap.

Heart pounding, he pushed his way down the stairs. He waited a few steps above the platform, surveying the people waiting to board.

No white captain's cap.

No black cape.

No grey canvas holdall bag.

Flynn turned and scrambled back up the stairs. He hustled away from the entry doors, into the upper part of the station, where passengers could buy their tickets and get bread and coffee and meat pies and such. He made a quick circuit of the area.

No white captain's cap. No black cape. No grey bag.

Failure. He would have to go back to Baker Street at once and tell Mr. Holmes.

CHAPTER 6: WATSON

"What is the celebration to which this note refers?" Holmes said.

"Our factory is almost ready to resume full operation," Rexford said. "A dinner is being planned tomorrow at the local church." His expression softened, and his voice took on a note of appeal. "I am getting on in years, Mr. Holmes. The responsibility for the lives of others is a burden that grows heavier as one ages. I am only a man, after all. I beg you, do not mention this threat to anyone in the course of your investigation."

"You ought not to assume that I have accepted your case, Mr. Rexford."

"I shall pay five hundred pounds—"

"My fees are not in question."

"Five thousand—"

"Not unless I can determine that it would be worth your money and my time."

"There are many whose livelihoods depend on it. Four hundred employees and their families."

"And when the explosion occurred last April, all of them had been quite content with their positions and wages?"

Rexford stroked his chin. "I wouldn't say all. Not so rosy as that. We had our share of complaints. Some talk of forming a trade union. Not that our operation can sustain a pay raise—the government is our major customer, and they're not about to give us more generous terms. Not when they can get product from our competitors."

"Who is the current supervisor of the works on Powder Island?"

"My son Rex now manages the operation. He did not wish to do so, knowing what had happened to his predecessor. But he has taken up the task regardless of the risk and has done very well, by all accounts. Very thorough and conscientious—"

"Thank you. Are any others of your family employed at the works?"

"I have no other children. And my wife died fifteen years ago."

"Any other relations, more distant ones, perhaps?"

"There is my niece. My sister's daughter. She is my personal clerk."

"She telephoned me yesterday morning to make this appointment. And is your sister still alive?"

"She is. But her husband is not."

Holmes raised one eyebrow inquiringly.

"He was the previous supervisor of the works."

"Killed in the explosion."

Rexford nodded. "A sad day. I ought to have told you at first."

Holmes made a dismissive gesture. "And who is the beneficiary of your estate?"

"My son inherits all. Other than a small annuity for my sister and a few other bequests."

"And would that hold true if you were to float the business on the public exchange, as you are planning to do?"

Rexford's eyes widened. "How do you know that? The arrangements for incorporation have been a closely guarded secret."

"The government has its ways of learning when the largest supplier of a commodity essential to the security of the Empire is about to change ownership." Holmes paused. I immediately thought of Mycroft.

Rexford gave a great sigh. "Of course. And yes, my son's inheritance would be unchanged. But my son would inherit shares instead of direct ownership."

"He would attain wealth, without the burden of responsibility."

"I think it would be best for him. He is a fine, strong, adventurous lad—he reminds me of myself in my younger days. He has done well enough managing the operation these past nine months. However, he is still young."

"He does not know of your plans?"

Rexford's voice trembled. "No, Mr. Holmes, he does not! And I beg you, do not tell him."

"Why not?"

"Because he would think I had doubts as to his competence for the supervisory position. And concerns for his safety."

"But you do have such doubts and concerns, do you not?"

"Any father would. I shall be most relieved when an impartial new management selects a third-party supervisor. The death of my brother-in-law was a severe emotional blow."

"Where were you when the blast occurred?"

"In church, across the river from the factory. It was a Sunday morning. I was there with Rex. My sister and my niece were there too. It was a shocking moment, I can tell you, Mr. Holmes. The blast shook the ground and rattled the very benches we knelt upon. My son and I ran across the bridge, and we saw the smoking ruins from up close."

"You were able to keep up with your son?"

Rexford shook his head. "As I said, I am getting older far more rapidly than I would wish. I recall coming over the rise, and seeing his silhouette, bent over, slumped in dejection and shock. His hands were on his knees. Beyond him was utter desolation. The memory—well, it keeps me awake at night, Mr. Holmes."

"Understandable."

Rexford leaned forwards. "Now, Mr. Holmes, will you take the case?"

"One moment," Holmes said. He got to his feet, strode across to our bow window once again, adjusted the shade, and looked out.

CHAPTER 7: FLYNN

"You, boy!"

Flynn heard a woman's voice behind him. She sounded breathless.

About to mount the steps of 221B Baker Street, Flynn turned. He saw a young woman crossing the street towards him, her dirty face tarted up with rouge and lip colour, her dark hair bedraggled beneath a ragged linen scarf, her wool coat and skirt looking as if she'd slept in them, and in an alley at that. The hem of her long skirt dragged in the slush.

She stood just at the edge of the curb. "Saw you talkin' wi' Mr. Holmes, right there in 'is doorway."

"What of it?"

"I saw you hop on the back of that cab and stick to it like a bug."

She was trying to smile and talk at the same time, but she kept her lips together. Probably she was ashamed of her teeth, Flynn thought. She was all tight and tense, her hands clasped in front of her like she was praying, only she was holding something. Flynn couldn't see what it was.

"So?"

"I figured you'd fall off and come back to tell 'im wot 'appened, so I waited. And here you are."

"Tell 'im what?"

"Never mind." She shook her head, and the scarf slipped to one side. She quickly straightened it, awkwardly, because she was still holding the something in both hands. "I want you to do sommat for me. I want you to give this to Mr. Holmes."

And she held out a gold pocket watch. Flynn took it.

"Where'd you get this?"

"Nicked it, didn't I? I want Mr. Holmes to give it back."

"Wot you want to do that for? Looks a ream flash jerry."

For a moment she seemed confused. Then she recovered. "Oh. Right. But 'e'll kill me and my friend if 'e don't get it back. 'E knows she took it, you see. Or 'e will know, soon enough. And 'e's a right dangerous man to cross."

"Where'd you nick it?"

"My friend nicked it, really. At the Blue Bottle. 'E goes there to see 'er reg'lar, and she knows 'e'll figure out she's the one who nicked it, because 'e's a big powerful rich smart bloke, and now she's dreadful scared of wot 'e'll do to 'er."

"What's his name?"

"'E don't say it at the Blue Bottle, but there's writin' on the watch. Should be easy enough for Mr. Holmes to figure it out. That's why my friend is so dreadful scared. That's why she can't return the watch herself. Because now the rich bloke will think she knows 'is name."

Flynn looked up to Mr. Holmes's bow window. He saw Mr. Holmes, gesturing at him, indicating he should wait.

Chapter 8: Watson

After nearly two minutes at our bow window, Holmes turned back to us and addressed Rexford. "I crave your patience, Mr. Rexford. I must leave you once again, but it will not be for long, and upon my return I may be able to provide you the answer you are seeking."

Before Rexford could protest, Holmes was gone.

CHAPTER 9: FLYNN

Flynn saw Mr. Holmes leave the window.

Still holding the gold pocket watch, he turned back to ask more questions of the young woman. But she was running away, across Baker Street, one hand clapped on top of her scarf. Her boots splashed in the slush as she dodged a carriage. Then an omnibus blocked Flynn's view.

When it had passed, she had vanished.

What to do? No point in chasing her. Besides, he could not leave Mr. Holmes.

He turned back to the stoop.

Mr. Holmes was now standing in the doorway. He motioned Flynn to come up the steps and inside, shutting the outer door once Flynn was in the vestibule.

Flynn held out the watch to Mr. Holmes. "She gave me this—"

Mr. Holmes held up his finger for silence and looked at the watch, turning it over and inspecting the inscription.

He spoke quietly. "Tell me everything." he said.

Chapter 10: Watson

Waiting in the same room with Rexford became more and more uncomfortable. Plainly, the factory owner's patience had worn thin. He was standing before our settee, putting on his overcoat.

And then suddenly Holmes returned.

Rexford faced Holmes, his eyes blazing.

Holmes held out a gold watch.

Rexford's expression turned to one of astonishment.

Holmes said, "This is yours, I believe. The engraving proclaims as much."

Rexford gaped. "Where did you get this?"

"From someone who claims to know the thief. I may have more to say on that in the future, but for now I do not."

"You are indeed quite a marvel, Mr. Holmes."

"Nothing marvellous was involved. When do you last remember using the watch?"

"Only yesterday."

"In your office?"

"At the works, yes."

"Where, specifically, and for what purpose?"

A moment's reflection. "I was in the mixing house. I was observing the process of loading the mixed product into canvas sacks."

"What happens to the canvas sacks?"

"They are placed on a cart and sent to the green charge house."

"And how many men were working in the mixing house?"

"Only two. One to load the sack—"

"How?"

"Why, with a wooden shovel. To prevent sparks."

"And the other man?"

"He holds the sack open for the man with the shovel."

"Were you satisfied with their speed?"

"Actually, I was not. I told them we would need to produce at a faster rate if we were to meet our quota. You see, our orders have—"

Holmes held up a hand. "Where do you keep the watch when you retire for the night?"

"On my dressing table."

"And this morning?"

"It was not there."

"Can you clearly recall putting the watch on your dressing table last night?"

A long moment of hesitation. "I cannot."

"Please describe your movements yesterday evening."

"I had supper with my son. It was a late supper, because I had been occupied with work in the office. He kindly waited for me."

"What time did you begin dining?"

"Around eight-thirty."

"And how did you note the time?"

"Ah, I see, you are asking if I had my watch in my possession at that moment. But there is a tall clock in our entry hall, and I recall seeing the time there."

"And after your supper?"

"We each had a glass of cognac in the library."

"Only one glass?"

"I limit myself. Rex may have had two or three."

"What kind of cognac?"

"A French variety. Remy Martin."

"I know it. It comes in a very distinctive bottle. A blue bottle."

"No, you are mistaken there. The bottle is dark brown. Ordinary dark brown bottle glass."

"I will take your case."

Rexford gasped in surprise and happiness.

Holmes continued, ignoring the gasp and the proffered handshake of Mr. Rexford. "Watson and I will visit your facility this afternoon. My associate will also be there, if I can arrange for her to accompany us."

"Your associate?"

"Her name is Lucy James."

Chapter 11: Lucy

Tobias Gregson was a tall, gangling man with large, square hands and a long face that even at the best of times was rather melancholy-looking. Today, though, I thought he looked especially haggard. Since last I'd seen him, he had grown a drooping, scraggly moustache, and he had the gaunt, hollow look of a man who's recently lost more weight than he had to spare.

Jack was entirely correct; Whitechapel was one of the city's most desperately poor—and thus most dangerously criminal—neighborhoods. A decade earlier, the Ripper killings had terrorized the district's fallen women, the most vulnerable who walked these streets, and the area was very little improved in terms of security since then.

We were meeting Gregson at one of the few locations where I'd felt safe in allowing Becky to accompany me. The Mile End Section House was the police equivalent of an army barracks, offering accommodation to all unmarried constables and sergeants.

We had found Gregson in the canteen room. It was now past noon, but luncheon was still being served to the officers who either had just come in from walking their beats, or else were about to depart on morning rounds. Police officers sat in groups around tables, eating from the platters of beef, boiled potatoes, and tea that were today's menu.

Gregson hadn't touched his own food, except to poke moodily at it with his fork. Instead, he sat hunched on the chair opposite mine, his shoulders slumped and lines of worry or exhaustion bracketing his eyes and the edges of his mouth.

"The Powder Island case." He looked from me to the note he held in one hand—the one Jack had written for me to give to him. A scowl pulled his lips down. "Can't say I see the point of digging up the past."

He glanced at the sergeant who was keeping watch on the men from the head of the room.

The sergeant was watching a friendly wrestling match going on in one corner—probably to gauge the odds of it remaining friendly—and didn't have any attention to spare for our table.

Despite the fact that he wore his blue tunic and constable's helmet and was clearly about to go on duty, Gregson took a hip flask out of his pocket, poured a hefty measure of what smelled like brandy into his teacup, then returned the flask to his pocket and tossed back half the drink in barely more than a single gulp.

"The case is over—finished." His voice was rough. "The Home Office investigated and wrote up their report. What else is there to say?"

"I don't know. But there must be something more to it. The owner of the factory requested a meeting with Holmes. He met with him at Baker Street this morning, in fact."

Becky and I had stopped in at 221B on our way to Whitechapel to deliver the news of the missing police file, and Holmes had given me a brief account of his meeting with Bradley Rexford.

Gregson nearly choked on another swallow of tea. "*Rexford's* trying to hire Mr. Holmes to re-open the investigation?"

"That surprises you?"

Gregson snorted. "He was about as much use to our investigation as a sick headache. So yes, it surprises me."

"Do you think it was Mr. Rexford who campaigned to get the investigation handed over to the Home Office?" I asked.

But Gregson's momentary flash of interest was gone. "Maybe—how do I know?" He stabbed viciously at the potatoes on his plate with his fork, shoveling them into his mouth. "Look, I don't know what more help I can give you, and I'm due on duty in five minutes. So if you don't mind, I'd like to finish my—"

He hadn't given me any help at all so far, but I doubted if pointing that out would do anything towards winning his favour.

It was Becky, though, who interrupted Gregson in the middle of his dismissal. "In *A Study in Scarlet*, you told Mr. Holmes, *you should never neglect any chance, however small it may seem.*"

"A Study in—" Gregson frowned. "Oh, the Enoch Drebber case. Yes, well. That was a long time ago." His expression had softened slightly as he looked at Becky, but now he wiped his mouth on the back of his hand, his jaw hardening as he stared down at his congealing slice of beef. "I've learned things since then."

"Such as?"

Gregson transferred his glower from his plate of food to me. "Such as, this world will punch you in the face if you let it."

His gaze was so bitter, I almost flinched.

I could understand. Gregson was still a relatively young man. He must have devoted himself to the job fiercely and tenaciously to have risen to the rank of Inspector in so short a time. He plainly wasn't married, or he wouldn't be occupying quarters here at the section house.

His entire life had been wrapped up in his career at Scotland Yard—and because of his very unwillingness to drop an investigation without learning the truth, he had lost everything.

It was a monumental injustice.

"Maybe," I said. "Sometimes, though, you get the chance to punch back."

There was a long moment where Gregson simply sat and stared at me, his long, melancholy face unreadable. Then, so quickly I might have imagined it, his lips curved up in the ghost of a smile.

"Well, if anyone were to get to the truth of the matter, it would be Mr. Holmes. And I can't think of a man who deserves to be slapped in the face with the truth more than Bradley Rexford. So what can I do?"

"You can tell me more about Mr. Rexford, to begin with. Why didn't he want you investigating the factory explosion?"

Gregson picked up his empty teacup, but then set it down with a frown and without reaching for the flask again. "Because there weren't any good answers, from his point of view. He didn't want to hear of any criminal cause, since a criminal could strike again and the factory wouldn't be safe. A man who makes the British army's gunpowder doesn't want to admit he's let an enemy get the better of him. Mind you, he didn't want the explosion chalked up to negligence, either. But to him, it was the lesser of the two evils. He could pin the blame on some hapless factory worker who'd supposedly been careless and let safety measures slip. Make an example of him by firing him, and then offer a lot of talk about how safety and good repair processes had been improved to prevent a recurrence, and how he'd every confidence in the new protocols they'd now got in place."

His voice was heavy with irony.

"Is that what brought you into Mr. Rexford's bad graces? Your unwillingness to pin the blame on a hapless factory worker's lack of care?"

"Partly." Gregson pushed the food around his place. "That and he'd got the wrong idea about …" His voice trailed off as he thought. "Well, never mind. Suffice it to say, we didn't see eye to eye on a good many things."

"And you definitely thought the explosion was a work of deliberate malice," I said. I'd already had Jack's account of the investigation, but I wanted to hear what Gregson would tell me. "Did you have any suspects?"

Gregson opened his mouth, then closed it again, shifting position in his chair.

"Nothing definite. I'd barely started collecting statements from witnesses before I was ordered to turn the file over to the Home Office man and drop the case."

I had the impression he'd started to say something, then changed his mind. If he did have suspicions, he wasn't going to share them with me. And pressing him, I was fairly sure, would only bring about a rapid end to this conversation.

"Lucy?" Becky had been studying the wresting match over the corner and now turned to me. "May I go over and watch?"

Either she was bored with Gregson's conversation—or else, more likely, she thought he would speak more freely without her there.

"Yes, all right."

She skipped off. Gregson watched her go, a frown between his brows. "She's Kelly's younger sister?"

"That's right." I watched without surprise as several of the uniformed constables obediently moved aside to let Becky enter the circle of spectators; Becky had that effect on even seasoned policemen. "You don't have to worry. She'll probably be giving the contestants pointers on their wrestling holds before too long."

Gregson's eyes lingered on Becky a moment, and then he cleared his throat. "Can I ask a question? No, wait, hear me out first." He raised his hand when I opened my mouth to answer. "I realise I've no right to ask Mr. Holmes for details about his meeting with Rexford. That'd be breaking his client's request for confidentiality. And I've no official right to be kept informed, the lord knows, since I've been kicked off the case. So, I won't ask for details. But let me just ask: have you any reason to think Rexford may have an enemy or two behind this affair?"

I thought of the second cab that seemed to have been waiting for Mr. Rexford at Baker Street—and the odd behaviour of the woman who had begged Flynn to return Mr. Rexford's watch.

Holmes had told me—briefly—about both incidents when he'd summed up the morning's meetings. But we'd had no time to discuss the implications.

"What makes you ask?"

Gregson's expression lightened briefly in a smile that made him look both younger and less careworn. "Because I've told you Mr. Rexford did his best to shut down our investigation. The next logical inference would be to ask whether I'd ever thought Rexford himself was behind the explosion and the supervisor's death—maybe he'd had a quarrel with the dead man, maybe he did it for the insurance money. But you haven't asked it, or even hinted that it's what you and Mr. Holmes are thinking. Therefore, you must have reason to think Rexford himself is threatened."

Holmes had been entirely right in his estimation of Gregson's abilities: Tobias Gregson was by no means a stupid man.

It was the Metropolitan Police who were stupid—criminal, even—letting his abilities be wasted on the duties of a beat constable.

"Whether or not he's in danger, I don't know for certain," I said carefully. "But I think it's fair to say that some unknown person or persons are keeping an eye on Mr. Rexford."

Gregson nodded, but lapsed into silence, his thoughts clearly running along their own complicated inner track.

"What about Mr. Rexford's son?" I asked.

Gregson looked up. "What about him?"

"Did he share his father's unwillingness to help with the investigation?"

Gregson jerked one shoulder. "I wouldn't say that. He was willing enough—or what for him counts as willing. But if young Mr. Rexford ever had a thought in his head that didn't revolve around himself or his precious yacht club, I'd be surprised."

I'd brought the Home Office Report with me from Baker Street and scanned it in the cab on the way here. I opened to a page somewhere in the middle, where the author of the report finally got around to saying something definite after pages and pages of verbosity. I said, "According to the Home Office, a possible cause of the accident is 'matches maliciously placed on the platform by person or persons unknown.'"

"Matches." Gregson snorted again. "Right. I heard about that. A couple of witnesses said they'd seen matches on the platform of another building. Miss Thiel—Bradley Rexford's niece—was one of them. But that was days before the explosion, and the weather was damp—it was damp on the day the place blew up, for that matter. There'd been a spell of rain just the night before. If the thick-headed sods at the Home Office think a few scattered wet matches were the cause of it … well, they're even more lack-witted than I'd thought, or else—"

He stopped.

"Or else they've been either bribed or threatened into accepting the matches as a convenient explanation?" I suggested.

Gregson forked another bite of potato into his mouth and shrugged, one-sided, avoiding my gaze.

I waited a moment, then said, quietly, "So if I were to tell you that all of your files—notes, witness reports, everything else—are missing from Scotland Yard—"

I stopped. Gregson's expression had gone slack with shock, the colour slowly ebbing out of his face.

"I'd say—" he didn't speak for a long moment. He cleared his throat, but when he spoke his voice was husky. "Your husband Sergeant Kelly's a good man. First class copper. If he keeps on with the kind of work he's done so far at the Yard, he'll be made an Inspector one day. But not if he crosses the wrong people."

"The wrong people being …"

Gregson shook his head. He darted a look around as though seeking to make sure we weren't being overheard, then leaned in across the table. "I've said all I'm going to. Maybe I've been knocked down to a beat constable—but at least I'm still alive." He pushed away his plate and stood up, once again not meeting my gaze. "Take it from me, it's something to be thankful for. Now if you'll excuse me, I need to start on my afternoon rounds."

Chapter 12: Watson

"We spoke with Gregson about the case," Lucy said. "He believes there was a police conspiracy to quash the investigation."

Holmes grimaced. Then he said, "We have time to catch the next train to Hounslow Heath. Can you come with us?"

Becky asked, "Where is Flynn?"

"Downstairs, in Mrs. Hudson's kitchen," I said. "He's getting breakfast, and then he's going to a cab station to interview a cabbie in a red scarf. The passenger in the cab may be connected with the explosion case."

"I'll be right back," Becky said, and ran down the stairs.

"She'll want to go with Flynn," Lucy said.

"Is that wise?" I asked.

"After meeting Gregson," she replied, "I'd like to keep Becky as far away from Powder Island as we can manage."

* * *

So Becky stayed behind with Flynn. Letting Flynn and Becky loose in the city on their own was often an invitation to disaster. But they had sworn they were only going to the cab station, which I thought would limit their opportunities for getting into trouble.

During the hour-long train journey, Lucy told us more of her meeting with Gregson, and how wearied and worn down the demoted Inspector had become in his reduced circumstances.

"A pity he was treated so unfairly for taking an interest in the case." I said.

Holmes said, "Perhaps we can put things right."

Lucy asked, "What is our plan?"

"Watson and I will question the employees at the factory. I should like you to go to the church in the village, where a celebration of the factory re-opening is being prepared. Parishioners are more likely to speak freely with you than they would with Watson and me."

"I'll see what I can learn."

We arrived at the Hounslow Heath station shortly afterward. There we said goodbye to Lucy. Holmes whispered something to her as he closed the door to her cab.

Holmes then asked me to arrange for a cab while he placed a telephone call to London. I did not hear the conversation, but my curiosity overtook me when we were in our cab, on the way to the other side of the Thames and the Rexford works. "Who did you call?" I asked.

"My friends at Lloyd's," he replied.

"Why?"

"They run the Registry of Ships."

"I do not understand the connection."

"There is no need. It may come to nothing."

We could see most of the factory buildings as our cab approached. They were stone, each distanced from the next. The stones were blackened with layers of soot accumulated over the years. We dismounted from our cab and found ourselves at the base of a footbridge across the river from the mainland, facing a wrought iron entrance gate and a stone guard shed.

A grey-haired man with a military bearing emerged from the guard shed. "You'll be Mr. Holmes and Dr. Watson," he said, looking us up and down with an approving eye. "I've heard about you. And Mr. Rexford told us you'd be coming. Fairchild's the name. Naval Lieutenant till 1870, and here for the past thirty years. Do you have matches on your persons? If so, I would trouble you to empty them from your pockets and leave them with me."

"Company policy?" asked Holmes, as he handed over his box of safety matches.

"And strictly enforced, you may rest assured."

"The more so since the explosion, I'd expect," I said.

Fairchild shook his head, his brow furrowing between bushy white eyebrows. "I've been the enforcer, and I have not altered our procedures. No one passes through here carrying matches."

"But the Home Office report—"

"Pack of trumped-up nonsense. Said matches had been found days before the explosion. But they weren't dangerous."

"Why?" Holmes asked.

"Wet weather," Fairchild said. "But you gentlemen will make up your own minds. The office is the next building on your right. Miss Amy is expecting you."

"Miss Amy is Rexford's niece?" asked Holmes.

Fairchild nodded. "Amy Thiel." He looked at each of us in turn. "Stay on your guard. She has a sharp tongue, and I wouldn't be quick to rely on her."

"Did she tell the police that matches had been found?" I asked.

He shook his head. "I don't tell tales. Just a word to the wise. And you can pick up your own matches when you're ready to leave. I'll be here."

***

At my knock, Miss Amy Thiel looked up sharply from her desk. "Yes?"

Holmes spoke calmly. "Good afternoon, Miss Thiel. I am Sherlock Holmes, and this is Dr. Watson. Your uncle came to see me in London this morning."

She stood up quickly, walking briskly around her desk to stand before it, and then leaned back. Her blonde hair was neatly bound up into a bun atop her head in the fashion of the time. Dressed in black, she radiated a nervous tension, but she remained silent.

Holmes said, "We have come about the explosion, as I expect your uncle has told you."

She gave a curt nod. "My uncle telephoned that you would be coming. I do not understand why he wants to rake up the past, but there you are. He is the owner, after all."

She motioned us to the two wooden chairs facing her, and we sat. She remained standing, still leaning back against the desk. I had the impression that by standing she hoped to maintain a superior position. Or possibly there were papers on the desk she did not wish us to see.

Holmes asked, "Have you read the Home Office report?"

"Worthless," she said. "I hope we agree on that point. I believe the investigator thought he was being paid by the word. It is the quintessential blather of a government bureaucrat."

"You have some experience with bureaucrats?"

"Mr. Holmes, we are the largest gunpowder factory in Europe, and we sell most of our product to the British government. You can imagine the bureaucratic paperwork I must deal with every day."

"Indeed. Where were you at the time of the explosion?"

"I was in church. With my mother. In the second-row pew, behind Rex and his father. It was during the morning prayer when we heard the sound. We had just recited the words asking for salvation for the souls of others. I have tried to take some consolation in that, since it was the exact moment my father's soul had gone to meet his maker."

"What happened next?"

"Glass from the windows broke and fell. There was a general panic. My uncle and Rex ran for the entrance. I followed them, and saw them on the downstream bridge running towards the factory."

"You have had a great deal of work to do, since then."

"Yes, my uncle appointed Rex as my father's replacement, and I needed to teach him an enormous amount about our operations. Also, we had to build a new glazing-house, and other buildings had to be modified so we could continue production on a reduced basis. With less income, we had to lay off workers and reassign others. There was a significant amount of paperwork for those activities, which were in addition to all the usual operations."

"Difficult for you," I said.

"But important to the defense of England. So there really wasn't any choice."

"Do you get along with Rex?" Holmes asked.

"He is my cousin. We were childhood friends."

"How does he strike you—suited to the work?"

"He seems to have taken to it. A surprise to all. Before the explosion, he took little interest in the business. More interested in his friends at the yacht club and taking jaunts with his yacht."

"He fancies himself a sailor?"

"Well, he's given that up. At least he says he has. When he stops coming to work in his captain's hat, then we'll know it really is a new Rex." She gave an ironic smile, and then looked upwards, towards the doorway behind where Holmes and I were seated. "I see the postman coming," she said. "And my uncle is just behind him. Will you excuse me for a moment? I have some letters going out."

Holmes stood. I stood beside him. I noticed Holmes's gaze was directed to the desktop as Miss Thiel gathered up a stack of letters.

The topmost envelope was addressed to the Western Assurance Company office in London.

Chapter 13: Lucy

My cab drew to a halt outside the modest stone parish church of St. Andrews, in Twickenham.

"Miss James?" A woman came out from the shadow of the church's vestry to meet me, her hand extended in greeting. "Or perhaps you prefer Mrs. Kelly?"

I smiled. The palpable sense of fear that had rolled off Gregson during our meeting had all my nerves tight with uneasiness. His words felt like sharp-edged rocks, rattling inside my head. *I'm still alive. Take it from me, it's something to be thankful for.*

But there was nothing I could do for the moment save to put all of that aside and give my full attention to the investigation at hand.

"Either is fine."

The other woman looked me up and down. She was dressed in black, tall and stocky, with red hair going grey at the temples. "I am Janice Thiel. Brad Rexford's sister." She added, with another searching glance at me, "It's unusual to meet a woman investigator."

"Perhaps." I had learned a long time ago that, contrary to what the suffragettes' campaigns would have people believe, the harshest critics of my choice of employment were often other women rather than men—and that the only way to confront their disapproval was to meet it head-on. "But your daughter works at the gunpowder factory as Mr. Rexford's personal clerk, doesn't she? That's rather unusual."

Mrs. Thiel sighed, her shoulders slumping as any challenge seemed to die out of her. "Amy, yes. Although I wish to heaven I could persuade her to give up the work. She won't hear of it, though. She is too much her father's daughter. And Brad has been good to both Amy and me, of course. Kind enough to allow us to live in the Dower House at Rexford Hall—though that keeps her close to him when he wants to discuss business matters away from the factory. He's even set up a little office in the main Hall just for her."

Across the river, on Powder Island, Holmes and Watson were paying a visit to the actual gunpowder factory. My own assigned task, though, was to interview the local residents in an effort to find any other eyewitness accounts of the explosion.

Although the odds that those accounts would contain anything of value were depressingly slim. Nine months after the incident, any witnesses who appeared at this point were likely to be of the attention-seeking variety, happy to swear they'd seen a dozen sinister-looking strangers swimming across the river with sticks of dynamite clenched between their teeth, if they thought it likely to gain them a few minutes' fame.

Now, a grey-haired man emerged from the church door behind us, interrupting before Janice Thiel could go on. "Mrs. Thiel? Where do you want the banners and bunting hung?"

"Oh—yes, thank you, John." Mrs. Thiel turned, looking flustered. "There, on the outside of the church hall will be fine."

"Right you are."

The man vanished back inside the church, and Mrs. Thiel turned back to me. "Do you mind if we stay outside? We can be private, but there is to be a potluck supper here tomorrow night—in celebration of the new building opening over at the factory. I really ought to keep an eye on things."

"Of course."

I kept my voice level, but my pulse quickened as I recalled the words of the anonymous note Holmes had shown me on the train journey.

Don't be too quick to celebrate. Another big bang is coming your way.

Two men came out of the church—John, and one other—carrying a ladder between them, and started to hang large, brightly painted banners in the colours of the Union Jack flag along the side of the church hall.

Largest in Europe … We are Proud … Remain Largest … Safety is Our Guide.

"We used to hold these occasions monthly, but this is the first potluck supper we've held since the accident," Mrs. Thiel said. The worry etched on her face was more pronounced as she watched the men at work. "The livelihood of a good many of the parishioners depends on the factory's success. And since the explosion, management has laid off some of the workers, and cut back the hours of nearly all that remained."

"It must have been a very difficult time for everyone."

"Yes. Although my brother-in-law has done his best to help. Brad took out a loan and personally guaranteed it in order to rebuild and provide the workers some semblance of wages. Amy tells me keeping the workforce reasonably intact is good business, of course. But it was still a kind gesture, and one the people here appreciate."

Mrs. Thiel looked back at the church, where more workers were bustling back and forth, carrying chairs and tables.

"Did you know Mr. Rexford was planning to consult Mr. Holmes this morning?"

Holmes had suggested I ask, hoping to learn how the man in the conspicuous captain's cap and cape might have known of Rexford's visit.

"I?" Mrs. Thiel shook her head. "No. I suppose Bradley would have told my daughter—since it meant he would be absent this morning from the factory. But neither of them told me." A twist of pain or perhaps sadness crossed her expression. "I suppose they thought it would upset me, to hear the investigation was being re-opened."

I hesitated, wondering how to phrase the next question. "There is a witness who claims to have seen Mr. Rexford at a gin shop in the East End of London. A place called the Blue Bottle."

"Bradley?" Mrs. Thiel's eyes opened wide with astonishment.

"That surprises you?"

"So much so that I would say your witness must have been mistaken. It is not just a question of Bradley's morals—although I have never known him to be unfaithful to the memory of his wife. It is also his very character. Bradley is a man who appreciates his creature comforts. He likes the best of everything—the finest wines and cigars, the most well-tailored clothes. The thought of him voluntarily going to an unsavoury grog shop in the east end … well," she exhaled a half-laugh. "It's so absurd as to be almost impossible."

"What about Mr. Rexford's son?"

"Young Rex?" Mrs. Thiel gave me a sharp glance. "Are you asking whether Rex is more likely to attend a lower-class establishment than his father?"

"No offence meant." Mrs. Thiel's tone of voice gave me the answer, decidedly in the affirmative. "But I understand

Mr. Rexford's son is now the new factory supervisor? You called him Rex?"

"Yes. Of course, he is actually Bradley Rexford III, after his father and grandfather. But he has always gone by the nickname." The line of Mrs. Thiel's mouth had tightened perceptibly.

"You don't like him?"

"Not exactly. I—well." Mrs. Thiel exhaled a sharp breath and gave me a glance that held a brief flash of wry amusement. When she was not desperately worried, Janice Thiel was probably a very likable woman. "I'm not accustomed to speaking of private family matters to complete strangers. But it is pointless to hire an investigator and then refuse to give her the information she requires in order to investigate. A waste of expenditures, my daughter would probably call it. Or something of the sort. I usually get these accounting terms all wrong." She smiled briefly, then went on, "To be blunt, then, it is not that I dislike Rex. I doubt anyone could actively dislike him. I have known him from his earliest childhood, and he has always been a dreamer—no head for practical matters and very little taste for unpleasant tasks or responsibility. He was always playing at practical jokes. He had a wooden catapult, I remember—one of those toys boys love, the sort that fire small pebbles. He would hide in an upstairs window and use it to knock the feathers off the hats of fine ladies who came to visit his mother for tea—and yet it was difficult to be angry with him, he was such a happy, merry child. No, I like Rex well enough. I simply do not wish to have him for a son-in-law."

My eyebrows rose. As a part of bringing me up to date on the details of the case, Holmes had filled me in on the Rexford family background. But this was the first I had heard of a possible attachment between Amy Thiel and Bradley Rexford's son.

"And do you think it likely that your daughter will marry Rex?" I asked.

Our conversation was straying a fair distance away from the explosion at the factory. But it was one of Holmes's cardinal rules of investigation that one should always let a witness talk who was willing to do so. One never knew when an important detail might be revealed in the midst of seeming trivialities.

"I don't know." Mrs. Thiel looked troubled once again. "Girls today are so different from what we were in my young days—or perhaps it is only Amy who is different from what I was at her age. I cannot tell whether she cares for Rex at all. She is very … 'hard' isn't quite the word. Practical. Amy is all practicality and business and good sense. I'm afraid sometimes she might marry Rex simply because she believes it would make good business sense to do so—keeping the factory entirely within the family."

"And does Rex wish to marry her for the same reasons?"

"Rex?" Mrs. Thiel looked startled. "Oh no. No, I believe he cares for Amy quite genuinely. He has from the time they were young. And he was hardly business-like back then. His dream was to have the factory sponsor a big racing yacht, like Mr. Lipton's, which is just foolishness, if you know anything about the costs involved. Before he went away to school, he spent most of his time at the yacht club, or on his own little sailboat, out on the river. Then when he came back, he talked his father into buying a bigger boat that he docked at the club. He called it a yacht, though it was far smaller than most of the boats at the club, and nothing to compare with the big racing yachts. But he never took it out to sea. Then he sold it, just before the explosion. But he hasn't stopped wearing that captain's cap."

The back of my neck prickled. "Was he here this morning?"

Mrs. Thiel looked mildly startled. "Why, yes. Is it important?"

"Likely not."

Except that a captain's cap had been worn by the man whom Flynn had tailed this morning.

If it had been Rex, though, that begged the question of why he would have chosen to spy on his own father.

Mrs. Thiel went on, "Rex sold his 'yacht' last year, because he said the factory had some financial troubles and needed new capital to invest in new equipment." She gave another faint smile. "Then came the explosion. So the new equipment never was purchased. Whatever he received for the yacht was far less than what the factory needed. Though I suppose it is the thought that counts."

"But you still do not wish for Amy to marry him."

"No." Mrs. Thiel's voice hardened. "Rex may have genuinely changed and matured. I hope he has. He has proven a more capable supervisor than anyone would have supposed. Just this morning, he was here early—before going in to work at the factory—delivering pastries from the Rexford Hall kitchen to be served at the potluck supper. But still—" Mrs. Thiel gave a small, frustrated shake of her head. "I don't know, perhaps it is unreasonable of me not to trust him. Many young men sow their wild oats, as the saying goes, and then settle down to a life of sober respectability. But at a minimum, I cannot help feeling Amy and Rex's temperaments are utterly unsuited to one another as marriage partners."

"A short while ago, you spoke of the explosion as an accident. Is that what you believe?" I asked.

Mrs. Thiel pleated a fold of her skirt between two fingers, her lower lip caught between her teeth. "I don't know." She looked up at me. "I will tell you, though, that on that terrible morning, I had the most powerful feeling of dread." She looked around her with a kind of dazed pain in her eyes. "I was actually here, at church, when we heard the horrid sound."

I hesitated. Mrs. Thiel's husband had lost his life in that very same explosion.

I'd confronted murderers intent on adding me to their list of victims—many of them. But this was always the hardest part of an investigation.

"I'm sorry to make you speak of it," I began.

"It's all right." Mrs. Thiel's mouth twisted in a fractured smile that, this time, held no humour at all. "Heaven knows I have relived it often enough in my own mind. Speaking of it cannot make it hurt more than it already does—or alter the fact that Marcus is gone. What is it you wish to know?"

"Anything at all you can tell me. I know it is months ago—"

Mrs. Thiel interrupted. "I remember—I remember everything, every detail of that awful day. As I said, I had the most terrible sense of foreboding that morning. It was almost like an illness. I couldn't shake the feeling that something dreadful was to occur. I even begged Marcus to come here, to church with me, instead of going to the factory as he usually did. But he wouldn't hear of it, of course." Her voice wavered, and she stopped, wiping her eyes. "Marcus was so passionate about having risen to manage the operation of the factory. He worked his way up from a messenger boy. He felt obligated to set an example for the other workers. They had been wanting their wages increased, and Marcus kept saying that they couldn't expect any rise in pay if they weren't living up to their end of the bargain to help the business prosper. And now … now Amy is just like him. Just as hard-headed, just as driven. But you were asking about the explosion." She took a steadying breath and seemed to collect herself. "We were inside the church sanctuary when it happened. If you come with me, I can show you."

St. Andrews was a small church, the sanctuary designed in a simple style of white plastered walls pointing the focus towards an arched stained-glass window above the vestry. Mrs. Thiel led the way to the front two pews.

"My daughter and I were sitting just here." She gestured. "And Rex and Bradley were here, in the pew in front, when it happened. We heard the explosion—so loud, it was like nothing I'd ever known before. It broke some of the stained glass windows in the sanctuary. And then, just a few moments later, we heard the church clock chiming the hour." She shivered, her eyes darkening at the memory. "It was like a death knell."

"So Bradley—" I started to ask, but stopped as a sudden shout of alarm came from outside the church.

"Dear heaven, what now?" Turning, Mrs. Thiel ran back up the aisle and out the door, and I followed, my heartbeat quickening.

Several of the workmen who had been hanging up banners huddled around another man who lay on the ground, clutching his leg and moaning.

"Looks to me his leg's broken, missus," one of the others told Mrs. Thiel. "And he can thank his lucky stars it's not his neck. Upper rung of the ladder broke under him when he was working at hanging up the bunting."

Mrs. Thiel had gone very pale. "But that's Paul Jeffries! He's engaged to be married to my daughter's maid. Paul!"

She hurried forwards to kneel at the injured man's side.

The rest of the workmen grouped around them, discussing arrangements for who should be sent to fetch a doctor and whether a makeshift stretcher could be constructed from the chairs inside. Mrs. Thiel was insisting the man be brought to Rexford Hall, which apparently was not far away, and asking someone to use the village telephone to send word to that effect.

But I listened to the talk with only half an ear. No one was paying any attention either to me or to what I assumed was the faulty ladder, which now lay on its side near the church's outer wall.

I approached and crouched down so I could examine the broken uppermost rung, running the tip of my finger across the splintered wood.

"Miss James!" Mrs. Thiel had remembered me and now called out, turning from the injured young man. "I'm terribly sorry to cut our interview short, but I must go with Paul to Rexford Hall to wait for the doctor."

I straightened up quickly. "It's all right. I entirely understand," I told her. "I'll go with you, if I may."

"Oh—yes, of course." Mrs. Thiel gave a distracted nod, and I moved further away from the ladder—I hoped before anyone else had seen me examining it.

An upper rung had broken, true. But it had first been neatly cut, sawed nearly through so that only the very top of the wooden step remained intact.

It would have been primed to snap the moment any weight was placed on it.

Chapter 14: Watson

Holmes and I waited just inside the office building as the postman arrived. We saw him pick up the letters from Miss Thiel and give her more letters in return. She returned to her desk and began to sort out the day's mail deliveries.

Holmes and I waited outside as our client, Brad Rexford, approached. He was clad in the same heavy coat, hat and muffler he had worn for his visit in Baker Street, and he appeared ill at ease.

"Gentlemen," he said, "A private discussion, if you will. Could you step a bit farther away from the office?"

We did as he requested. He closed the door to the office without a word to Miss Thiel, who was still occupied with her letter sorting, and then stepped up to join us.

"I want to discuss financial matters," he said, looking around us as though worried our conversation would be overheard. "I should like to re-emphasize what people should know and what should remain private."

"We are at your service," Holmes said.

"First, my son Rex must not know of the proposed float of shares."

"Understood."

"Second, I have taken out a loan, in order to fund the rebuilding and remodelling required to operate in the interim. Proceeds from our insurance were not sufficient to cover those expenses. And our revenues were reduced, since we had to operate at reduced capacity after the destruction of our lower glazing house."

"Understandable," Holmes said.

"My son Rex knows about the loan. However, he does not know the loan is secured by a mortgage against the family estate not far from here. Rex lives there with me."

Holmes nodded. "So if the business fails, both of you lose your homes."

Rexford nodded. "I was not sure my boy could function properly, if he knew the risk involved in the decisions he had to make daily."

"He appears to have succeeded thus far," I said.

"Yes, he has. So I don't want him to know about the mortgage."

"We quite understand."

"The boy has given up a lot. It's more or less been all work and no play for him these days."

"And your niece says he has given up his yachting activities," I said.

"More than that. He sold his yacht. About a year ago we needed money to buy new equipment, and he gave up the yacht. Handled the sale himself. And then the explosion happened, so we had to use the proceeds to rebuild. But he hasn't complained, and he hasn't gone back to the yacht club. Why—"

Rexford broke off. Outside the gate, a very ornate and expensive carriage was rolling up to the guardhouse. A heavyset, florid-looking man got out.

Rexford's expression darkened. "Fairchild!" he shouted to the guard. "Keep the gate shut. Don't let that snake come a step further!"

He turned to us. "It's Jerrard. He owns a rival gunpowder works. Not as good as ours, but he's always hoping to cause trouble."

"I heard you, Rexford," said the florid-faced man, standing at the gate. He waved a document in one hand. "You owe me five hundred pounds, and it's due today. Give me my money!"

"Get off my property!"

Jerrard sneered, his face up against the bars. "Either you pay up or I'll foreclose. Then I'll come here any time I like, because I will be the owner."

"Over my dead body!"

"That would be a bonus!"

By now, the gatekeeper was behind Jerrard, about to place a hand on Jerrard's shoulder.

"Throw the man out!" screamed Rexford.

"No need for that," Jerrard said, moving away, and giving a final wave of the document. "I'll be off to court now, and the sheriff will be around to evict you, Rexford!"

He climbed back into his carriage and drove off.

"He's wasting his time," said Rexford, turning to Holmes. "I could pay the little swine today, but there is a grace period in the loan. I refuse to give him my money a minute sooner than absolutely necessary."

"Why are you both so emotional about a business matter?"

"He has blackened my reputation."

"How so?"

"Making false claims about defects in my products. The man has no principles."

"Though he did loan you five hundred pounds?"

"When I was in dire straits, just after the explosion, yes he did. But he did not make the loan out of kindness. He hopes to ruin my reputation so my company revenues will drop and I will fail to pay."

Then we heard a young man's voice. "Ahoy there!"

We saw a tall youth in a dark wool cape and white captain's cap approaching on one of the pathways within the factory campus.

"Ah," said Rexford. "There's my son. I've asked him to give you a tour of the property."

Chapter 15: Flynn

The cabstand was busy at this time of day, when rich people were either driving home from luncheons or going out to pay afternoon calls. Only two cabs were parked in the eleven available spaces, and the cab master was busy barking orders at a couple of men who were tending to a horse that had thrown one of its shoes.

Flynn had the number of the cab driven by the man in the red scarf, which meant he'd found out the fellow's name without too much trouble: John Todd. The harried-looking cab master had stopped barking orders long enough to wave at a man inside the small wooden shelter where the cabbies could rest from the cold or take a bite of food between searching for fares.

"He's actually here—that's lucky," Becky murmured, as they approached the shelter.

"I suppose." Flynn could see through the open doorway of the shelter that John Todd wore a red scarf, so he was pretty sure it was the same man.

But he couldn't shake an uneasy feeling that had been nagging at him since they'd left Baker Street.

It was the same feeling he'd had a week ago, when he'd been jumped and kidnapped while out on a job like this for Mr. Holmes. And the worst of it was, he couldn't be sure whether the uneasiness was real, and something he should pay attention to. Or just leftovers from being tied up and stuffed inside a steamer trunk for hours on end.

Flynn shoved the memories back, wishing he could stuff them inside the same kind of trunk.

But he couldn't stop himself from asking Becky, "Do you have a feeling something's wrong?"

"Wrong?" At least Becky didn't tell him he was crazy—or getting to be afraid of his own shadow. "How do you mean?"

"I don't know." Flynn exhaled a breath of frustration. He didn't like being scared—and he especially didn't like not being able to put his finger on why he should feel that way. "I just keep feeling like there's something ..." he glanced back at the street behind them, which was busy, too.

Omnibuses and wagons, shoppers, day labourers with picks and shovels over their shoulders—all were slogging through the dirty slush remaining from this morning's snowfall.

"You think someone is following us?" Becky asked.

"I don't know." Flynn frowned, trying to decide what about the street scene struck him as wrong. Or if there really was anything wrong.

A couple of vendors had set up shop near the cabstand: a knife sharpener, who was holding knives against his big spinning wheel, and a fruit vendor. The fruit vendor wasn't likely to have much luck; most of the apples he was selling looked half rotten.

Becky frowned, too, and looked like she might be starting to feel a bit jumpy, too. But then she shook her head. "Well, let's question the cab driver, and then we can work out whether anyone really is watching us."

Inside the shelter, cabman John Todd hunched over a plate

of boiled rabbit and pickled pork, and only grunted without looking up when Flynn asked if they could talk to him.

"It's a free country—or used to be."

"Do you remember taking a fare to Baker Street station earlier today?" Flynn asked.

The cabbie coughed, wiped his mouth, and looked up at them.

"Drive a lot o' fares all over the city." He coughed again and gave a gusty sigh. "Wind, rain, perishing cold, don't matter, still got ter be out there on top o' the cab. Don't pay any of 'em much mind—unless they don't pay."

His gloomy expression suggested this happened often. Although that could have just been his usual look. He was an older man, with a wrinkled, leathery face that made Flynn think of a walnut: just as hard, just as deeply furrowed. Deep frown lines ran down from the edges of his mouth almost to his bristly chin.

"You took this fare from 221B Baker Street to the station," Flynn said.

John Todd gave a grunt that could have meant anything from *yes* to *no idea* to *go away and let me eat in peace*.

"Can you remember anything about him?" Becky asked.

The cabbie looked up again, wheezing. For a second, Flynn was worried the man was having some kind of a fit, but then he realised the sound was what for John Todd passed as laughing.

"Oh, yeah." He blew his nose on the end of his scarf. "Make all of my fares sit for a portrait, I do, so I can be sure to remember what they look like."

Perfect, Flynn thought sourly. A down-in-the-mouth, sarcastic cab driver: exactly what they needed.

"This man was wearing a white captain's hat and a dark cape," Becky said. She dug into her pocket and brought out a sixpence—although she had sense enough not to hand it over yet. "And he may have been mixed up with something criminal. Do you remember him?"

Outside on the street, a blue uniformed police constable trudged past on his rounds. Maybe it was the sight of the police that made the cabbie more cooperative, or maybe it was the sixpence.

John Todd didn't ask what Becky meant by something criminal, but he scratched his chin, his eyes on the coin in her hand. "Maybe I do remember him now. Fat chap. Squeaky kind of voice."

"Squeaky?"

"High pitched—like maybe he'd got a touch of the croup. No surprise in this cold."

"Can you remember where you picked him up?" Flynn asked.

"Where was it, now?" The cabbie screwed up his face in an effort of remembrance. "I don't know as how I can recollect that."

Becky looked at Flynn, tilting her head to ask a silent question. Flynn nodded. He'd bet more than a sixpence they weren't going to get any more useful information by hanging about here—and the uneasy prickling feeling on his neck was back, making him want to keep moving.

Becky dropped the coin into the cabbie's hand.

"Piccadilly Station," John Todd said promptly. "Picked him up at Piccadilly."

Chapter 16: Watson

"I'd like to take you to our shot tower," said young Rexford when he had reached us at the factory office entrance. "You'll have a better view of the whole operation from there."

The young man's reddish-brown hair was barely visible beneath his white captain's cap. He had inherited his father's sturdy frame and commanding stature, but he was leaner, and his facial features were still clean-shaven and raw-boned. He moved forcefully, as though to demonstrate his position of leadership.

We followed.

After a brief trek through the snow, we reached the entry door to a tall tower, possibly one hundred feet tall. "Like a lighthouse, don't you think?" young Rexford said. "Come inside." He made a sweeping gesture, as though leading us into battle. "Onwards and upwards!"

We entered the tower and climbed up the massive stone circular staircase built against the thick stone interior walls. The centre of the great tower was an empty, hollow column. Daylight from a glass cupola above us illuminated the steps. When we reached the top, we stood on a stone platform with glassed-in windows all around.

As young Rex had foretold, the vantage point gave a good view of the snowy landscape and the factory buildings below.

"This tower was built by our family seventy years ago," Rex said. "Originally they used it for gunshot manufacture. Highly ingenious." He pointed to a basin hollowed-out from the stone platform. "They poured molten lead into that basin. Then they scooped it out and let the liquid drop from the basin. The lead fell nearly a hundred feet, down through the hollow core you see beneath you, and as it fell it separated into droplets, like rain. The droplets then landed in a water tank on the floor below. They cooled in the water into perfectly round little spheres, and formed gunshot pellets. So to this day, this building where we stand is called the Shot Tower."

Rex looked at us, obviously proud of his family business.

"Interesting," I said, out of politeness. Holmes remained silent.

"We don't make gunshot pellets here anymore," young Rex went on. "But we do use this building as a lookout tower. From these windows we can view any building in our operation, and if we see a fire hazard, we can give a prompt warning. I like to come up here and think about the future. My father and I have some great planning sessions right up here in this very spot."

Holmes asked, "Where were you when the explosion occurred?"

"Hasn't my father told you? I was with him in church. The explosion happened just during Morning Prayers." Rex pointed towards the window. "You can see the church right across the river."

We stood closer to the window. The river made a great black curving swath through the partially snow-covered countryside. A small stone church stood on the far riverbank.

"You can see the rooftops of all our buildings from up here. We keep the operations separate, for safety purposes, so one explosion doesn't destroy everything else on this side of the river, or harm the public on the other."

Holmes said, "Where did the explosion occur?"

"Right where the new building is now, the one where the stones and the roof slates haven't darkened with age. That's the part of the operation we're about to reopen. The glazing house."

"I see it is quite close to the river, with its own dock," said Holmes. "Do you think Mr. Jerrard could have set off the explosion?"

Rex looked shocked by the idea. He was silent. Then he asked, "How?"

"By boat, I would think. Jerrard or his associate might drift downstream in a small boat, with a dynamite charge of some kind. The dynamite could have a long fuse, giving the perpetrator time enough to get back in his boat and row out of harm's way."

Rex said, "You certainly are a clever one, Mr. Holmes. And you may have just solved the mystery! This will be a great relief to my father. Will you bring in the police now, and have Jerrard arrested?"

For a long moment, Holmes gazed down at the river waters far below. He seemed to be considering the idea. Then he shook his head. "I think not. Not just yet. We shall need more evidence."

Chapter 17: Flynn

"Where do we go now?" Becky asked when they were back on the street, outside the cabman's shelter. "Should we try asking at Piccadilly Station, do you think?"

Flynn shook his head. "Waste of time. Busy station like that, no one notices anything."

"Do we just go back to Baker Street, then?"

Part of Flynn wanted to—anything to get off this street. Which was exactly why he couldn't. If he lost his nerve, he'd be no good to Mr. Holmes or anyone else.

"There's still the Blue Bottle."

"The what?"

"The Blue Bottle. The place where the cockney woman said her friend had met Mr. Rexford and nicked his watch."

Becky was frowning, watching the fruit vendor who seemed to have given up and was now wheeling his cartload of rotten apples away up the street.

"Do you think she was telling the truth?" she finally asked.

"Don't know." There'd been something funny about the woman, although Flynn couldn't quite put his finger on what. But then he was getting good and sick of uneasy feelings he couldn't identify. Maybe the woman had been speaking the gospel truth. "Seems like it's worth looking into, though—see if anyone at the Blue Bottle knows if Mr. Rexford's a regular customer there."

Becky was still frowning, like she was thinking about something else. But she said. "All right. Do we walk or take a cab?"

Flynn took one last look up and down the street, which still looked just as ordinary as ever. "Cab," he said. He still wanted to get away from here as fast as possible. "Maybe we can get John Todd to take us, once he's finished eating."

John Todd hadn't been the first cabbie available, but another driver brought them to the East End, and Becky paid him before hopping out of the carriage. She eyed the gin shop doubtfully.

The Blue Bottle was a funny name for the place, she thought. East-enders sometimes called the police blue bottles. But from the look of the gin shop with the name in dirty gold letters over the door, it was the sort of place where people who wanted to stay far, far away from the coppers would go.

The outside walls were cracked and dirty, with piles of dirt and rubbish heaped against them. A pair of dead rats lay in the muddy gutter just next to the door, and half the windows were either broken or else boarded up.

"Mr. Rexford is a regular customer *here*?" Becky said.

Flynn shrugged, kicking a rusty tin can back towards the rubbish heap it had rolled from. "So the girl said."

Sometimes rich blokes did come down to drink and carouse down here in the poor neighborhoods. Slumming, they called it. Flynn had seen them. They thought it was all a big laugh or an adventure.

Mr. Rexford hadn't struck Flynn as that sort, just from the quick look Flynn had got of him, but you never knew.

"Were we followed here, do you think?" Becky asked.

"Can't tell." Flynn still felt jumpy, but then in a neighbourhood like this one, you'd be stupid *not* to keep your eyes open and your wits about you. "I didn't see anyone behind us in the cab, anyway," he said.

There weren't so many people about here, either. A pony-drawn rag and bone cart rumbled by. Across the street, a pair of flower vendors were quarrelling loudly over the rights to that particular street corner.

And closer by, there was a big, tough-looking boy a year or two older than Flynn selling cigars and cigarettes outside the gin shop. He had a tray looped around his neck with a bit of dirty rope and was scowling out at the world from under heavy brows.

"Where do we start?" Flynn asked.

Becky wasn't paying attention, though. She was frowning again, watching something up the road. Turning, Flynn saw a copper just turning the corner. It was getting to be late afternoon, with shadows closing in, and the police officer's helmet gleamed in the light from a gas lamp.

Flynn never would have thought he'd be glad to see a copper, but at the moment it was good to know that if they got into trouble, there'd be an officer of the law nearby.

"What did you say?" Becky asked.

"Do we go inside and ask about Rexford?"

Becky looked at the gin shop, considering. "I don't think we should bother, no one in there is likely to talk to us. They'll either laugh at us or try to rob us, but they won't be any help."

That was probably true, but it didn't get them any closer to finding out if Rexford had been here.

"We should ask him." Becky nodded to the boy selling cigars. "He looks like he probably sets up shop here often."

Flynn looked at the boy, who had shoulders like an ox and hands that looked like a couple of cricket mitts—and who was glowering as if he hated the entire world.

"Oh good," Flynn said. "How'd you know I was just hoping for the chance to get punched in the nose?"

"He'd have to catch you first. He's strong, but he doesn't look as though he'd be very fast," Becky said. "At worst, we can always run away."

That didn't make Flynn feel a whole lot better. He watched as a man who'd clearly had one too many came staggering out of the gin shop, waved a coin in the cigar boy's face, and then went back inside after he'd bought a bag of snuff.

Flynn sighed. He didn't have any better ideas, and he didn't want to go back to Mr. Holmes empty-handed.

"How do we want to go about asking him? Do we have any more money?"

"It wouldn't work. He'd just pocket the money and either refuse to say anything or tell us a packet of lies. He's already cheating all his paying customers. That snuff he just sold the drunk man? It was half sawdust—I could tell even from all the way over here."

"All right, then. Divide and conquer?"

And hope the boy was as slow as Becky guessed.

"All right." Becky didn't look worried, anyway. She slipped off up the street, where the growing darkness made it even harder to keep track of her movements.

Flynn put his hands in his pockets and strolled over to the dark-haired boy.

"Hello there. I'm looking for my sister."

The boy's upper lip curled in a sneer. "Good fer you. 'Ow about you look somewhere else?"

"No call to get nasty." Flynn held up his hands. "I was just wondering if you might have seen her in the Blue Bottle there. Dark hair, tan color wool coat, grey linen scarf? Think she's been here?"

The boy's scowl deepened. "I fink you'd better get outa my sight, 'adn't you."

Flynn stood his ground. If you had to go up against someone stronger than you, do it with confidence, he always said.

"You must not like your teeth much, mate."

"What?" The boy's expression creased in momentary confusion. "What're you talking about?"

"Her." Flynn nodded to Becky, who'd come up behind the boy, and now took hold of the rope holding his tray of cigars and jerked, yanking him off his feet.

Flynn had to admit it was a satisfying sight. The boy fell over with a crash, landed flat on his back on the muddy cobblestones, and lay gaping up and them, his mouth opening and closing like a fish as he tried to get back the breath that had been knocked out of him.

"Let's try this again," Flynn said. "Unless you want me to kick your two front teeth out, you'll answer my questions: have you seen a dark-haired girl hanging around the Blue Bottle? Wears a lot of face paint, looks like she got dragged backwards through a hedge in Hyde Park?"

The boy looked tougher than he really was, because he didn't try to get up or fight back. Still wide-eyed and puffing for air, he shook his head. "Don't fink so. Only woman who works in the Blue Bottle is old Maud what scrubs the glasses—and she's about a 'undred, with a face like a bulldog."

"What about a Mr. Bradley Rexford?" Becky asked. "Is he a regular customer here?"

The boy had recovered enough to give her the kind of look that said he couldn't believe how stupid she'd have to be to ask the question.

"And 'ow'd I know that? No one around here uses proper names."

Becky opened her mouth, but Flynn never got the chance to find out what she would have asked next, because someone screamed from further along the block.

Flynn's head jerked up and he stared through the grey dusk shadows, straining his eyes to see what had happened.

Becky gasped. "It's the police constable—look, he must have been hurt or taken ill."

Looking where she pointed, Flynn could see a man in a blue uniform lying on the ground. He'd have run as fast as he could in the opposite direction, but Becky had hopped up and was racing towards the crowd that had already gathered.

By the time Flynn had caught up to her, she had stopped short just a few feet away from the fallen copper, who was a tall, skinny fellow with a blond moustache and blond hair.

"What's wrong?" Flynn asked.

Becky looked like she'd just seen a ghost go swooping down the street. "That's Inspector—I mean Constable Gregson," she whispered. "I saw him just this morning with Lucy. And then I saw him walk past when we were at the cabstand—and again just now. He didn't come close enough for me to recognize him, but I thought he looked familiar. But then I thought maybe I was just imagining things!"

She bit her lip, looking over at Gregson.

He hadn't just been taken sick, that was certain. Flynn wasn't sure what had happened to him, but there was a dark, wet stain all down the front of his tunic. Blood.

"He was following *us*?" he asked.

"I don't know! Maybe. Is he still alive?"

Flynn couldn't tell that, either. Gregson wasn't moving, his eyes were closed—and he didn't look like he was aware of the crowd pressing in all around him.

A couple of the men who'd come running up—big, burly fellows who made the cigar boy they'd questioned look like a tame kitten—were crouching down and tugging Gregson's body, trying to roll him over.

"Think he's got anything valuable on him?" one asked.

The other one laughed harshly. "Never know. One thing, he can't arrest us for robbery, now can he? Not if he never wakes up."

"Stop!" Becky shouted.

Flynn wouldn't have gotten up and confronted the street toughs unless someone had held a gun to his head. He'd maybe have tried to rescue Gregson, but he would have tried a distraction first.

But Becky jumped right in between Gregson and the two men and faced them, her fists clenched and her eyes blazing fury.

"Get away from him! This man is a personal friend of Mr. Sherlock Holmes, and if you so much as touch him, Mr. Holmes will see to it that you spend the rest of your lives behind bars!"

Flynn didn't know if it was the mention of Mr. Holmes's name or if the men were just shocked at being told off by a girl. But they stopped, grunted, and then shuffled away. Pretty soon, the other onlookers did, too.

"He *is* still alive." Becky was feeling for the pulse in Gregson's neck. "But he needs help. Go and see if you can find another policeman, I'll stay with him here."

Flynn nodded. "All right." He stopped a second, though, looking down at the unconscious policeman. "What would he want to follow us for?"

"He worked the Rexford case. I heard him telling Lucy about it this morning. It's the reason he was demoted from Inspector to a beat constable. He must have thought there was a chance we could lead him to a clue."

"I guess it's good news if he was the one following us."

Flynn would rather have Gregson on his tail than whoever had planted a bomb and exploded a gunpowder factory.

"Maybe." Becky looked pale and scared as she tugged the folds of her coat more tightly around her. "I just realised something else, though. Remember that fruit vendor we saw outside the cabstand?"

It took Flynn a second to think back, but then he got it, too. His stomach dropped.

"His boots were new." He should have spotted it at the time.

"Exactly. Much too new. He'd never have been able to afford a pair like that with whatever he made selling half-rotten apples," Becky said.

"So, was he following us? Or Gregson?" Flynn nodded to the man still bleeding on the ground.

"I don't know." Becky shivered. "Just get help—and be careful."

Flynn's insides felt like they'd been scooped out and replaced with ice, but he nodded. "I'll get an ambulance. Then I'll send word to Jack so he can tell Mr. Holmes."

He took off up the street at a run.

Chapter 18: Lucy

I was alone in the Rexford family carriage. Mrs. Thiel had elected to ride to Rexford Hall with the injured man in a farm cart, so she could sit alongside and help support his broken leg.

We drove up the sweep of gravel drive at the front of the Hall, a handsome building of red brick, with two wings flanking a central, gabled entrance, making the footprint of the house resemble the shape of a letter *E*.

Legend had it that Queen Elizabeth had considered it a delicate compliment and been more likely to bestow her royal presence on manors built with her initial in mind. Although from the large scale of the construction, and from the fresh-looking exterior, I thought Rexford Hall was a newer imitation rather than an authentic Elizabethan manor home.

A slender, fair-haired young woman, dressed in black, came hurrying out to meet us. She went straight to the cart, and I heard her issuing brisk orders to the workers who had ridden along.

"Yes, bring him straight inside—carefully, now. I have the sofa in the downstairs parlour all ready. Yes, mother, I've already telephoned for the doctor, he should be here any moment."

This, then, must be Amy Thiel. She certainly seemed to be well in command of the emergency, her manner assured and entirely unruffled.

I got out of the carriage, watching as another girl hurried out of the house. The new arrival made for a striking contrast to Amy. Her dark-haired colouring was the exact opposite of Miss Thiel's fair complexion. She was small, and on the plump side, while Amy was willowy and fair. And her expression held all the worry and distress that Amy's lacked.

"Paul!" She reached to take the injured man's hand, and her voice, heavy with a broad Yorkshire accent, was also shaky with tears. "What's tha' done to thyself?"

"I'm all right." Paul Jeffries' face was white with pain, but he made an effort to smile. "Nothing wrong that can't be mended."

"Yes, Eliza, I'm sure he'll be all right," Amy said. She spoke more gently to the other girl than she had to the workmen. "Go along, you can sit with him and keep him company until the doctor arrives."

She stood back and watched as the workmen carried Paul's makeshift stretcher inside the house. Mrs. Thiel followed, with a murmur about asking Cook to prepare some tea and other refreshments for everyone.

Amy turned to me.

"You think this accident wasn't anything of the kind. Someone deliberately caused that ladder to break."

My eyebrows rose. Sabotage, of course, was precisely what the evidence seemed to prove. But it was unusual for an outsider to jump immediately to the same conclusion—especially since Amy hadn't seen the cuts made to the ladder's upper rungs.

"What makes you say that?"

Amy gestured impatiently. "I should have thought it obvious. You are an investigator, here with Mr. Holmes. Yet instead of going to join him on Powder Island, you came here with Paul. Therefore, you must have observed something about his fall to make you suspicious." She stopped, and now a line of worry did appear between her brows. "I'm afraid this will mean the opening of the new building at the factory will have to be delayed. As though people weren't already nervous enough! We'll be lucky if anyone is willing to come to a celebration dinner—much less come to work in the factory."

"The workers are uneasy, then?" I asked.

Amy shrugged her slim shoulders. "It's only to be expected, I suppose. After that sort of explosion—the entire building wasn't just damaged, it was obliterated. The workmen can't help thinking about what would have happened if they had been inside at the time—or if such a thing could happen again, despite all of my uncle's new safety measures." She sighed, then gave a slight shake of her head as though to throw off the moment's weariness, her eyes narrowing as she studied me. "I suppose you can't tell me what exactly about Paul's accident made you suspicious, since as far as you're concerned, I might be a suspect." She had a staccato, rapid-fire way of speaking, rather like the bullets fired from one of the machine guns her uncle's factory supplied with powder.

"I'm beginning to see why your mother described you as all practicality and business sense, Miss Thiel."

"Yes, poor mother." Amy's face turned wry. "She loves me, but she's also rather horrified by me. Just because I can't pretend to be a delicate, fainting, maidenly flower and never could. Please, come in," she added, leading the way through the still open front door.

Inside, Rexford Hall was decorated in the ornate style popular a half-century ago—and then only among the very wealthy: gilded furniture so ornate that it would have struck the Sun King himself as a trifle gaudy, walls papered in a rich blue brocade, and thick oriental rugs. Two large photographs hung on the heavy green wallpaper in the entry hall; one of them the Queen and Prince Albert, taken many years earlier, and one more recent, of the Prince of Wales at the helm of his yacht.

A tall mahogany coat rack stood to one side of the front door, with a white captain's cap and dark wool cape hanging from one of the hooks. The white cap was identical in style to the one worn by the Prince in the wall photograph.

I brushed by the cape as we passed. The hem was still a trifle damp.

"Those belong to Rex, my cousin," Amy said. "His room is upstairs, and of course, so is my uncle's."

"Is he here now?"

"I believe he's still at the factory. He was giving Mr. Holmes and Doctor Watson a tour. Probably stopped in here first for a dry cap and cape," Amy said. She led the way to the right of the front hall and into a small room that must, I thought, be the private office her mother had mentioned. It was far simpler in style than the rest of the house. The walls were painted a pale green. The furniture was well-crafted but plain: a wooden desk with papers tidily put away in individual dockets, a settee, a couple of chairs.

The window, looking out over the front drive, was covered only with a gauzy curtain that let in the winter's pale sunlight.

Amy seated herself behind the desk and motioned for me to sit.

"Now, what can I do to help your investigation? I've already spoken to Dr. Watson and Mr. Holmes."

"I'm sorry to make you go through it all again."

Amy waved that aside. "It's quite all right. The more times

one tells a story, the more likely it is for some forgotten or seemingly unimportant detail to come to light."

"That's quite true."

It was also unusual for an ordinary civilian to understand.

As though she'd heard my thought, Amy said, "Inspector Gregson told me so. When he was here to look into the explosion last spring."

"Yes, I spoke to him this morning about his investigation."

"You saw Tobias—I mean, Inspector Gregson?" Amy's voice altered, turning strained, somehow—as though she was trying to keep herself from sounding too eager. She toyed with a pen on the edge of her desk. "How is he?"

"He was demoted—he lost his rank of inspector and is now a constable in Whitechapel." I watched her as I spoke. "Apparently those in authority at Scotland Yard felt he had mishandled your case."

"But—" For the first time in our conversation, Amy looked as though she had been entirely shaken out of her briskly capable self-assurance. She stared at me, open-mouthed for what must have been a full five seconds before finally finding her voice. "But that is terrible! Worse than terrible—*criminal*!"

"You hadn't heard?"

It was difficult to believe that, as her uncle's secretary and assistant, Amy could have been unaware of Gregson's clash with Bradley Rexford. And yet her shock and outrage seemed genuine.

Amy shook her head. "No, I hadn't seen or spoken to him since … But how could anyone have faulted him? He only wanted to get to the truth!"

Twin bright spots of colour burned in her cheeks. One thing at least I was certain of: if Bradley Rexford had exerted his influence to get Inspector Gregson demoted, Amy hadn't been a willing party to the campaign.

"Did you share Inspector Gregson's opinion that the explosion was no accident?" I asked.

Amy gestured impatiently. "Of course I did."

"Do you suspect anyone in particular?"

A shutter seemed to come down across Amy's face, the outrage dying, leaving her expression hard and self-contained once more.

"No. I do not know what or whom to believe—but I know the explosion was deliberate." She drew a ragged breath, then went on, her calm almost fully recovered now, "If you'd like me to tell you about the day of the explosion … to start with, my father went to the factory to make his usual Sunday morning inspection. I said goodbye to him that morning at breakfast, just as usual—never dreaming that in just a few short hours, nothing about my life would ever be the same, or that I would never see him again."

Her voice was flat and almost toneless, but her face was etched with an echo of raw pain that hadn't yet been smoothed out by time.

Either she was an unbelievably good actress, or she genuinely grieved her father's death.

"Was it customary for him to go alone?" I asked.

"Oh yes. Father liked to go when no one else was about, to be certain he could perform his inspections alone and uninterrupted. He would go in at sunrise and then stay till he had walked through all the dozen or so buildings. He had slowed down a bit in this past year or two—he had arthritis in one knee that made it painful for him to walk. But he still never missed a day of work or a single inspection."

A carriage that I assumed to be the doctor's was rolling up the drive and would probably interrupt us in another moment or two.

"Would you mind if I asked you an impertinent question?"

Amy's brows rose slightly, and then a humourless smile quirked the corners of her mouth. "You've been talking to Mother, so let me guess: does it have to do with my marrying Rex?"

"Not for the moment."

Amy looked surprised. "No?"

"No."

It was a truism of the art of detection that assembling evidence was like putting together the pieces of a jigsaw puzzle. One didn't get to choose the individual pieces—or to throw a piece out simply because it didn't appear at first glance to fit in with the others.

I couldn't for the moment entirely see how the woman who had approached Flynn with Bradley Rexford's watch fit in with the factory explosion. But it did fit, somehow—and what was more, I was beginning to have a glimmer of an idea that it was important.

As important as the man in the captain's cap and cape whom Flynn had followed.

"What I wanted to ask you was this: do you think it believable that your uncle should have visited a grog shop in the East End of London, where he made the acquaintance of a—shall we say, lady of the evening?"

"Oh." Amy's expression was momentarily blank.

I watched her. "That doesn't appear to surprise you nearly as much as it did your mother. She thought it entirely out of character."

Amy gave a harsh laugh. "Mother also thinks it incredibly kind of Uncle Bradley that he allows us to live at the Dower House—and continues to employ me."

Her voice was bitter.

"And you don't agree?"

It wasn't the doctor's carriage after all. The carriage drew to a halt in front of the steps, and Holmes sprang out.

A cold weight landed in the pit of my stomach. Amy was still speaking, but I was already out of the door and halfway to the entrance hall when Holmes burst in through the front door.

"Lucy!" It was seldom that I saw Holmes jarred out of his usual imperturbable calm, but his expression now was urgent. "Jack telephoned to the Powder Island Factory. We must return to London at once."

My heart lurched and then skittered to a sickening halt. If Jack had telephoned, it meant Jack was still alive. But something could have happened to Becky, or to Flynn—

"Gregson was attacked," Holmes said.

Amy gasped. "What?"

I turned to find her standing behind me, swaying a little, her face gone ashen to the lips.

Holmes nodded. "He was stabbed in the chest—on the street outside the Blue Bottle in Whitechapel. He is currently in hospital, and it is uncertain whether he will survive the night."

Chapter 19: Watson

The white-painted corridor of Saint Bartholomew's Hospital smelled strongly of harsh soap and carbolic acid. We sat in a row on an uncomfortable wooden bench: Holmes, Lucy, myself, and then Becky and Flynn.

Gregson had been taken into surgery, and there was now nothing for us to do but await the surgeon's news of whether his life had been saved.

"This is my fault," Lucy said. I had seldom heard her sound more distressed. "I went to see him this morning, to ask him about the Powder Island case. I don't know what exactly I told him, but something I said must have made him decide to resume his own line of investigation—something that led him to alarm the wrong person when they heard what he was doing. And this is the result."

Holmes seldom wasted what he would consider valuable brainpower on expressions of reassurance or sympathy. But his manner as he addressed Lucy was more gentle than usual.

"Any investigation carries with it its own regrets. So I will merely ask what you imagine Gregson himself would say if he could hear you."

Lucy drew a breath and gave Holmes a shaky half-smile. "He would probably say I shouldn't waste time feeling guilty when I could be accomplishing something useful, such as catching whoever stabbed him."

"Precisely. And to that end—" Holmes paused, leaning back on the bench and half closing his eyes. "You say, Becky, you first noticed Inspector Gregson at the cabstand?"

"Yes. At least, I think it was him. I never saw his face."

"He might easily have seen you and Flynn, though. In fact, I think we may assume that he did see the two of you." Holmes put the tips of his fingers together. "I would reconstruct Gregson's actions thus: he learned from Lucy that we believed Mr. Rexford to be threatened. Inquiries on Baker Street would have produced a witness who could have told him of the man in the captain's cap and black cape who apparently followed Mr. Bradley Rexford to Baker Street in a cab. His mind operating along similar lines to ours, Gregson looked for the cabbie."

"Then when he saw us, he must have decided to follow us, instead," Becky said. She looked as downcast as Lucy. "Maybe he thought we might get into trouble going to the Blue Bottle and wanted to keep watch. If that's true, it's also our fault he got hurt!"

"You did well to summon help as quickly as you did," Holmes said. "If Gregson survives, he will have you as well as the surgeons to thank. Also, you are forgetting the fruit vendor you saw. The one with the suspiciously new boots."

Becky looked up quickly. "You think he was following Gregson?"

"You saw no such person in the neighbourhood of the Blue Bottle?"

Becky screwed up her eyes in an effort of remembrance, but finally shook her head. "I don't think so. Flynn?"

Flynn shook his head.

"No matter." Holmes looked regretful, but resigned. "We may take it this person changed clothing before continuing to

POWDER ISLAND 171

follow Gregson—and caught up with him when he was waiting for you up the road from the gin shop."

"But who was it?" Becky asked.

"Ah. That is the question, is it not?" Holmes leaned back a little on the bench.

"We know it can't have been any of the suspects in the Powder Island case," Lucy said. "Or at least, not Amy or her mother, and not Bradley Rexford or his son, either. They were all in Twickenham at the time Gregson was attacked."

"We must assume Gregson contacted an outside party before he set out to track down the caped man—someone outside of the immediate Rexford family circle," Holmes said.

Lucy said, her voice quiet, "I told him the police files on Powder Island had disappeared."

She and Holmes exchanged a long look. The implication was, of course, clear even to me: only someone within either Scotland Yard or perhaps the Home Office would have had access to those files.

Holmes cleared his throat. "However, speculating as to the identity of that person is less likely to bear fruit than solving the problem of the explosion on Powder Island. Questioning Scotland Yard or the Home Office will at best earn us a number of doors slammed in our faces."

"And at worst alert our man to our investigation," Lucy finished.

"Indeed."

"So we're going to let whoever stabbed Gregson get away with it?" Becky asked. She sounded outraged.

"By no means." Holmes's face had a granite-hard, focused look that I remembered well from past cases. No one seeing him now would think the malefactor who had sought to kill

Gregson would escape unscathed. "I am merely stating that an indirect approach is likely in this case to suit us best. Once we have identified the person who set off the explosion on Powder Island, the other pieces of the puzzle will fall into place."

"And we may hope Gregson will recover and will himself be able to identify his attacker," I said.

The words seemed to echo hollowly in the sterile, empty hospital corridor, where each passing moment made it less and less likely that our hope would be realised.

A nurse in starched white cuffs and collar approached, and we all stiffened in anticipation of what news she might bring—but she hurried past without speaking and entered a patient's ward further down the hall.

I stopped myself from looking at my watch in an attempt to calculate what progress the surgeon might have made by now in his valiant efforts to repair the damage done by the unknown assailant's knife. Instead I said, "We have another conundrum, in that all of our key players are also alibied for the time of the explosion. Both Rexfords, father and son, were in church when the blast went off, as were Amy and her mother. There is, of course, Rexford's enemy, Mr. Jerrard."

I paused, glancing at Holmes, but his face remained impassive. Unless I was much mistaken, Holmes did not seem to think Mr. Jerrard a likely suspect, whatever he had told Rex. The very fact he had spoken of the possibility so freely to Rex would have told me as much.

"But any of the family could have rigged a detonator and timer," Lucy pointed out.

"True." Holmes's tone was musing. "There is also the possibility that the dead man himself was in some way responsible—that his death was the result of some accident or clumsiness in handling the explosives."

I looked at Holmes in surprise. "Do you seriously suspect Marcus Thiel?"

Holmes made a dismissive gesture. "Neither more nor less than I suspect anyone else at this juncture. But he had a better opportunity than anyone else to both plant and detonate the explosives, therefore he must remain on our list of possible suspects. He could have been bribed or threatened to set off the explosion."

"I suppose that's possible," Lucy said. "But it seems out of character for him. His wife and daughter aren't exactly impartial witnesses, of course. But I gained the impression from both of them that Marcus was a highly conscientious man. Amy said he had been troubled by arthritis in his knee these past two years, but he still never missed a single Sunday morning's—what is it?" she asked Holmes.

Holmes hadn't spoken, but he had made a small, sudden movement, as though struck by something she had said.

Holmes waved a hand. "Nothing at all. Please, go on."

Lucy frowned, but said, "For that matter, it's difficult to see what motive *any* of them could have had for sabotaging the factory. Who has benefited by the explosion, or the death of Marcus Thiel? Not Amy or her mother. They certainly didn't benefit financially. Amy has exactly the same job she did before, but they've lost Marcus's income as supervisor. Her mother implied it was only Rex's generosity that allowed them to stay at the Rexford Hall Dower House. And both are genuinely grieving for Marcus, I'm certain of that."

"Quite." Holmes's long fingers beat a restless tattoo on his trouser leg. "Bradley Rexford has been thrown into financial difficulties by the explosion. He is attempting to solve that with the incorporation. Meanwhile, his son Rex has been forced to go to work and give up his carefree life of yachting. According to his father, he has not been sailing since the explosion."

"He apparently hasn't retired his yachting apparel, though," Lucy said. "His cape and captain's cap were on the hall stand at Rexford Hall—and the hem of the cape was still damp."

"Ah." I caught a familiar gleam in Holmes's half-lidded gaze. "That is interesting. He was wearing a cape and captain's cap when he gave Watson and me a tour of the Rexford Works." He thought for a moment, and then said, "Flynn."

Flynn had been sliding further down on the bench, looking as though he were halfway to falling asleep, but he jerked upright at Holmes's mention of his name.

"Yes, sir?"

"Can you recall anything else about the girl who approached you with Mr. Rexford's watch?"

"I don't think so." Flynn rubbed the bridge of his nose. "Except for what I've already told you. She looked scared. She was out of breath when she first came up to me, and she said she didn't dare mention the name of the man who owned the watch ..."

Holmes interrupted. "Her appearance, though. Was there any detail that struck you? Anything odd about her?"

"Well." Flynn considered. "I dunno if it's odd, but her clothes were all rumpled, just like I said before. And she'd got her face painted—but it was just smeared on anyhow, smudged all over her face, not just on her lips and cheeks."

"But that *is* something odd!" Becky sat up straighter. "A girl wouldn't bother to put on rouge and lip colour if she was going to do that bad a job of it. She would use a mirror—and even if she was too poor to afford one, she'd borrow one from a friend, or else use a shop window to see her reflection."

"Wait!" Flynn held up a hand. "I'd forgotten before, but something else was strange. I said the watch looked like a flash jerry, and she didn't know what I meant."

"Flash jerry being Cockney slang for an expensive pocket watch," Holmes said. He leaned forwards, definitely alert, now. "Can you repeat everything she said to you—her precise words—in as exact detail as you can?"

"I'll try." Flynn's brows knitted together. "She said she'd seen me talking to Mr. Holmes. And then she said, *I want you to do sommat for me.*"

Holmes held up a hand. "That will do."

Flynn looked at him, startled. "That's all?"

"Yes, that is quite enough confirmation."

"Confirmation," I repeated. "You know, then, who the guilty party is?"

"I would not go so far as to say that." Holmes looked at Lucy. "But we have narrowed the field down to two possibilities, each with roughly equal likelihood of being proved correct, would you say?"

Lucy pursed her lips, considering. "I might put the split around sixty-forty."

Holmes gestured to Flynn and Becky. "I have an assignment for the two of you," he said. "Tomorrow I want you to go to Rexford Hall."

Flynn and Becky listened thoughtfully as he spoke further, quietly, out of my hearing, and then nodded.

I sighed. "I assume when all of this is over, I will discover what all of you are talking about. But for the moment—"

I broke off as a white-coated doctor approached our bench, his expression tired and grave.

"Mr. Holmes?"

"Yes?" Holmes's tone was sharp.

The doctor cleared his throat. "I'm happy to tell you it looks as though Constable Gregson will pull through. It was touch and go—and of course we must hope that he avoids infection—but I believe I may say he is for the moment out of danger."

"Ah." Holmes released a long breath. "Thank you, doctor." He remained motionless a moment, then stood up with renewed energy and made to stride off.

"Where are you going?" I asked.

"This news accords quite well with our plans." Holmes spoke over his shoulder. "I intend to find a telephone and tell those at Rexford Hall that Gregson is still unconscious, but expected to make a full recovery."

Chapter 20: Lucy

I positioned myself near the massive stone gate of St. Bartholomew's Hospital, looking out upon the stone-paved, noisy neighbourhood of the London Central Meat Market. A statue of Henry VIII crowned the stone archway—an unlikely figure, I would have said, to offer hope or reassurance to the sick. But the street outside the gate was crowded, even at night, with a steady stream of the ill and injured seeking relief. The uniformed porter was busy with mothers holding sick and crying babies, men with their arms done up in makeshift bandages or slings, and one old woman begging to have a rotten tooth extracted.

I waited in the deepest part of the shadows, pinching myself to keep awake as the clock of a nearby church tower chimed first one o'clock in the morning, then half past the hour, and then two. I ought to have been too on-edge to be tired, given that it was an attempted murder we were expecting—*another* attempted murder, meant to remedy the first effort's having failed.

But it had been a long day, and the cold and the darkness—and the constant parade of human suffering and frailty before me—were making it hard to stay focused.

Becky and Flynn had long since gone back to Baker Street to sleep out the remainder of the night, so as to be fresh for the next day's assignment Holmes had given them. Holmes and Watson were still here. But the Western Gate was far from the only entrance to the huge hospital building, and we needed to take every precaution that none of our suspects slipped in and caught us unaware.

The porter escorted an old man in, directing him to the out-patients' ward to the left of the gate.

I watched him totter off, clutching his own brown glass bottle in which to carry home any medicines he was prescribed. Then I stiffened.

The porter's back was still turned to the outside gate as he, too, watched the old man make his unsteady way across the cobblestones. And while the gate was momentarily unattended, a tall, slim figure slipped inside, briefly joined a group of mothers who were sitting on the steps of another ward, waiting for the matron of the infants' department to arrive—and then stood up and made for a door leading into the hospital's main floor.

As the figure moved, a beam of light from a gas lantern in the courtyard fell on it, showing fair hair and a young woman's pale, nervous face.

My heart dropped. I had agreed with Holmes that there was a forty percent likelihood of this outcome. But I was still sorry.

I hadn't wanted it to be Amy Thiel for whom I was waiting.

I straightened, stepping quickly out from the shadows and following Amy into the hospital. I stopped at the end of the corridor, where the hallway opened out into a reception lobby, with a matron on duty behind a central desk.

There were more people about here—patients and doctors and nurses hurrying to and fro. But I heard the heavyset and stern-looking matron telling Amy in a clipped tone that visiting hours were over for the day and would not commence again until nine o'clock tomorrow morning.

"I understand." Amy's voice, higher than usual, and sounding frightened, reached me. "But if you could just tell me what room Constable Gregson is in? Please? Then I could come back and see him tomorrow. He is—that is, he is a very close friend of my family."

My eyebrows edged upwards. It was one of Holmes's maxims that a murderer always made at least one mistake—but it was seldom so great a blunder as openly inquiring as to the location of their proposed victim.

I missed hearing the matron's reply, but she must have been more soft-hearted than she first appeared, because Amy stepped back from the desk with a look of quick relief and a heartfelt, "Thank you! Oh—thank you!"

She turned away, walking slowly towards an outer door, but then, as soon as the matron began to attend to another patient, she reversed direction, heading quickly towards a door marked *Recovery Wards*.

I slipped my hand into my pocket, making sure I had ready access to the revolver I carried there, and followed.

Chapter 21: Watson

The door to Gregson's hospital room opened and I heard stealthy footsteps approach the bed.

I was there at Holmes's direction. Gregson lay quiet, still unconscious from his surgery. I had stationed myself behind a fabric hospital screen, hidden from view.

Now, looking around the edge of the screen, I saw someone in a captain's cap and a long cape, standing beside the bed, and a pair of hands holding a pillow. The attacker was reaching towards Gregson, about to smother him.

I sprang from my chair. A moment more, and I had clapped my hand onto the attacker's wrist.

I saw my adversary, his face twisted in surprise and rage.

Young Rex Rexford.

My own fury surged. I thought nothing of tactics or how I might be disadvantaged by my greater age. My thoughts were focused solely on protecting Gregson from this would-be murderer. I tackled him, but he stayed erect. He tried to twist out of my grip, but I clung to him. I saw a pistol in his belt, beneath his cape. Locked in our struggle, we stumbled into the hospital hallway. I bore down on him, throwing him to the tiles of the hallway floor, and I heard a woman's voice.

"Rex!" It was the voice of Amy Thiel. "What are you doing here?"

"He was about to kill Gregson," I said.

Rex said nothing. His hand scrabbled for his pistol.

"Drop it," came Lucy's voice, hard and cold. She had her Ladysmith drawn, and she pressed the muzzle into Rex's cheek, just below his eye. "Now, do I have your attention? You can simply nod. I don't want any more noise to disturb Inspector Gregson."

I peeled back Rex's cape and took away his pistol. Lucy kept her Ladysmith aimed at Rex as I removed his belt and used it to bind his wrists behind his back.

"Now," said Lucy, "I suggest we all go peacefully to the visitors' waiting room. It is empty, and we can speak there without creating more disturbance."

We sat on the wooden benches in the waiting room. Rex kept his eyes down, unable to meet the questioning gaze of Amy. He said nothing.

A few moments later, Sherlock Holmes arrived, along with two constables.

"We have the papers from the sale of your yacht, Mr. Rexford," Holmes said. "Courtesy of the Registry of Ships."

"What of it?"

"The papers reveal your true purpose for selling."

"I was raising capital for our family company. Everyone knows that."

Holmes cut him off. "You were acquiring a murder weapon, in a way you thought would not be traced to you. But in your usual careless fashion, you failed to read the paperwork for the conveyance of the yacht, and by so failing, you have betrayed yourself. Do you care to explain how you engineered the explosion?"

Rex sat mute, lips compressed, eyes staring blankly.

"Very well. The evidence we have is enough to arrest you. The constables will soon take you to the Old Bailey for your arraignment. Do not hope for bail, for it will not be granted, considering you were just now caught in the act of attempting the murder of a Metropolitan Police officer."

Rex remained mute.

Amy Thiel said, "I truly don't understand, Mr. Holmes. Can you please explain what the papers connected to the sale of Rex's yacht have to do with the explosion?"

"The papers called for the vessel to be sold in 'voyage-ready' condition. It was not. One important piece of equipment, required by government and insurance safety regulations, was missing. The papers record that the seller of the yacht gave a credit to the buyer in the purchase price in order to compensate, and that the buyer assumed all liability resulting from the lack of the missing component."

Young Rex's lip curled in a sneer. "Just what component was missing?"

"The papers make it quite plain. The missing component was the safety flare gun, otherwise known as a Very pistol, required for emergencies to call for help."

"Trivial," Rex said. "I can't be bothered with those details. I just signed the papers that they put in front of me. If there was something missing from my yacht, this is the first I've heard of it."

"You set off the explosion with that flare gun. You used a tripwire."

"I deny it," Rex said. "Nothing of the kind was found at the site."

"But you and your father were the first on the scene after the explosion, and your father recalls you running ahead. You hid the wire and flare gun and then returned to dispose of them later."

"You cannot prove it, Mr. Holmes."

"When we spoke at the top of the shot tower, I noticed how pleased you were when I suggested that Jerrard had rowed to the building and lit the fuse to a bomb. In fact it was you, Rex, not Jerrard, who rowed there. You came to the building at night, when no one could see you. You connected a tripwire to the cocked trigger of the flare gun from your yacht. Then you rowed back to the Rexford Hall dock and crept to bed. The next morning, you went to church with your father. Then when the parties were all in church, each with an alibi, the explosion occurred."

"I don't understand," said Amy.

"Rex's goal was not merely to destroy the glazing works building. He wanted to kill your father."

"No!" Rex cried.

Amy turned to Rex, her eyes brimming with tears. "Why would you do such a thing?"

For the first time, Rex's air of confidence seemed to desert him. He lowered his gaze and sat silent.

Holmes said, "Miss Thiel, Rex had a financial motive, and perhaps another. Your father had begun to support the other workers in their demands for better wages. With him out of the way, factory wages could be kept low and profits maximized. Isn't that correct, Rex? Or did you have a second reason? Did you somehow imagine that the loss of her father would make Miss Thiel more vulnerable, and thus more susceptible to an offer of marriage from you?"

Rex stared at the floor.

Amy's face was horror-stricken.

"The only way to be certain that Marcus Thiel was present when the building exploded was to have him *cause* the explosion.

And, knowing that Marcus dragged his feet when he walked, due to his arthritic knee, Rex used a tripwire. When Marcus shuffled into the glazing building, hitting the tripwire, the flare gun fired, and the burning flare ignited the gunpowder."

Amy's voice was raw and ragged. "Rex. Tell me it's not true. Tell me Mr. Holmes is wrong."

Rex took a deep breath, and somehow his air of confidence seemed to return. "Not to worry. No one's going to prove it. My father will get me a top-shelf barrister."

Amy stared at Rex for a long moment. Then she turned her back on him.

After a nod to the two constables from Holmes, Rex was taken away.

"Will he get away with it, Mr. Holmes?" asked Amy. "Will he really walk free after killing my father?"

Holmes's face was grim. "We have Dr. Watson's testimony to support a charge of assault on Constable Gregson here at the hospital, and perhaps attempted murder. That will be enough to hold him temporarily. But if Rex is to be convicted for your father's murder, my deductive reasoning, accurate though it may be, will not be enough. We will need hard, convincing evidence, and in sufficient quantity to convince a jury."

Chapter 22: Watson

Outside Gregson's hospital room the street was dark, barely illuminated by a few gas lamps. I stood by his window for a moment, my thoughts swirling. What would Holmes do to find the evidence we needed? And how would we protect Gregson from those who were trying to silence him? Young Rex had been caught, but who else was out there in the darkness? I thought of the flare-gun young Rex had used. I thought of the murderous air-gun used by Colonel Moran.

I closed the curtain.

In his bed, the unconscious Gregson continued to breathe peacefully, still under the influence of the sedative he had received.

Holmes turned to Amy. "I still have two questions, Miss Thiel. First, why did you follow Bradley Rexford in the guise of his son? And second, why did you pretend to be a cockney woman from the Blue Bottle who wished to return your uncle's purloined watch?"

Amy opened and closed her mouth, but no sound emerged.

"You were the passenger in the cab, Miss Thiel, wearing the cape and the captain's hat." Holmes said. "Only someone who knew your uncle had made an appointment to see me in my Baker Street rooms could have arrived there first. And only someone connected with your family would have chosen the conspicuous captain's cap and cape. You knew, because you had arranged the appointment. And you had access to Rex's wardrobe, since you had your own office in Rexford Hall, where he lived. From your choice of disguise, you expected to be seen by your uncle, and to be incorrectly identified as his son. Am I correct thus far?"

"I—" Amy still seemed unable to speak.

It was Lucy who appeared to take pity on her. "You knew, didn't you," she said quietly. "You knew it was Rex who had caused the factory explosion."

"I didn't *know*." Amy flung out her hands in a gesture of appeal. "I suspected. But I hadn't a shred of proof to confirm my suspicions. My uncle would never have believed me—his own son? Guilty of sabotage and murder? I could scarcely believe it—I didn't *want* to believe it. I had known Rex ever since we were children! And yet I also knew how little obstacles mattered to him, when it was a matter of getting his own way." She stopped, biting her lip. "I thought if I disguised myself as Rex and followed my uncle to Baker Street, he might see him, lose confidence in Rex, at least a little, and make him more likely to believe anything Mr. Holmes uncovered to discredit him."

"And the purloined watch?" Holmes asked.

Amy lowered her head. "That is the action of which I am least proud," she said. "But I wanted to stop the incorporation my uncle was planning! I knew a board of directors would never permit me to keep my position—a young woman in a position of authority at a gunpowder factory? They would die of horror at the very notion. So, I thought that if I could cast a shadow on my uncle's character, perhaps it would be enough to make the underwriters not want to go through with the incorporation."

"Was that the only reason you wanted to prevent it—so you could keep your job?"

Amy sat up straighter. "Not just that. Part of my job was to correspond with the insurance company. We had insurance coverage that included more than enough to rebuild. We had a 'lost profits' clause that should have provided enough money to pay wages to keep the factory running. So, most employees should have been able to continue work."

"So you think funds from incorporation weren't needed?"

Amy sighed. "Yes, I'm sure there was something wrong. At any rate, I thought that my uncle having his watch supposedly stolen by a lady of the night from the Blue Bottle, a notorious late-night haunt for disreputable men and women … well, it would surely be enough to besmirch his reputation."

"You were not very convincing as a cockney barmaid," Holmes said.

She nodded. "I was afraid you would see through me. When I saw you talking to that street boy on your doorstep, I panicked. I told the cabman to drive off. But then I saw the street boy following and thought he might be taken in more easily. So I stopped the cab at the railway station and made sure the street boy had seen me. In the station I stuffed the captain's cap and cape into my canvas holdall, put on my lip rouge, and hurried back to 221B."

"Where you waited for Flynn and told your tale of the stolen watch," Holmes said.

"Which wasn't a crime," Lucy said.

"I am sorry for it, though. I believe—" Amy gave a shake of her head and exhaled a shaky breath. "I believe I have been almost unbalanced with grief for my father these past months.

Perhaps the more so because I could not admit my suspicions of Rex to myself. How could I have been foolish enough to work for a man like him all these months?"

"You didn't know," Lucy said.

Amy's eyes moved to Gregson's pale, still figure on the bed. "You will—" she swallowed. "Will you please let me know how he fares?"

Again, it was Lucy who answered her. "Yes, of course we will."

Amy bowed her head. "Then I must return to my mother and my uncle. The news of Rex's arrest will devastate them."

We watched her depart, her face pale but her posture brave, square-shouldered and erect.

Holmes was the first to break the silence. "Watson, I propose we should take the rest of the night by Gregson's bedside in shifts. Would you prefer to remain on guard first, or shall I?"

"Guard?" I repeated in blank surprise.

Holmes's expression was grimly set, his voice determined. "I think this matter is very far from being over and done. And we have a great deal of work to do."

CHAPTER 23: LUCY

St. Andrews Church was filled with celebrants for the opening of the new building. The mood of the gathering felt cautiously optimistic. I hadn't spoken to Mr. Rexford personally, but according to Holmes, he had taken the news of his son's guilt more calmly than might have been expected, being more concerned with proving his innocence and keeping the case out of the newspapers. Perhaps as a parent he had fewer illusions than anyone about the strength of Rex's character.

Nor, it would appear, had the factory workers and their families been overly fond of Bradley Rexford, Junior, or overly grieved that he would no longer be their supervisor. There was, it seemed to me, *a good-riddance-to-bad-rubbish* attitude towards Rex's arrest, and a feeling that perhaps now the celebration tonight could truly mark a fresh start.

Jack and I, though, were standing outside the church in the freezing cold—and I was beginning to wonder why.

"I don't suppose Holmes told you what we're supposed to be looking for?" I asked.

"Anything suspicious or out of the ordinary was as much as he'd tell me," Jack said.

"We're looking for a needle in a sea of other needles, in other words."

"Your father's obviously expecting trouble," Jack said.

So was I, if I was honest. My skin was crawling with a nameless, uneasy sensation that had nothing to do with the chill weather.

"The man who walked in a few minutes ago—tall, heavyset, with a green checked waistcoat and a red handkerchief in his pocket," I said. "What colour boots was he wearing?"

"Brown," Jack said without even a pause for thought. "The lace on the left foot was fraying. Why? You think that's important?"

"Not really. I just wanted to see whether I could trip you up as to any of the details."

"Is that a challenge?"

A few latecomers from the village were still trickling in, and his eyes tracked them, taking in, I was certain, every detail of their appearances, from the tarnished belt buckle on one man to the colour of the feather in a stout woman's hat.

"Maybe."

Jack grinned. "What stakes are we playing for?"

If I were Becky, I'd ask for the privilege of picking desserts for a week. "If I win, you tell me as much as you can about Sergeant O'Hara?"

A shadow crossed Jack's gaze. "I'd do that anyway. Lucy—"

"It's all right," I interrupted him. "What we really ought to do for now is split up and make a circuit of the church. This is the main entrance, but there are others. All were locked on Holmes's orders, but we should make certain of that—and that everything else is as it should be—before the speech-making starts."

Jack nodded. "All right. North or south?"

"I'll take north." That would make my route include a circuit around the banquet hall. "We can meet in the middle."

Jack turned and started around the southern side of Saint Andrews. I watched him go, trying to identify where the cold, crawling sense of some looming disaster was coming from. It wasn't just Holmes's warning—

I stopped as I caught sight of a familiar figure in a blue police uniform approaching the church, then disappearing around the side of the banquet hall.

Gregson.

His presence here wasn't suspicious, per se, but it was unexpected. Holmes had arranged for an official police guard to be placed in Gregson's hospital room after he and Watson had completed their night vigil. Jack had been getting updates from the doctors about Gregson's condition, so I knew he was recovering well and ready to be discharged.

What had brought him here, though?

Frowning, I started after him.

Then I saw the answer.

Gregson and Amy were standing close together in the small, sheltered alcove of the church's south porch. Gregson was speaking, his voice rough and husky. I caught only the final words.

"—insane. You deserve so much better. What would your mother—or your uncle—say about you marrying a common police constable?"

Gregson broke off. He had just caught sight of Jack, coming around the church from the other side.

"Sergeant Kelly."

To judge by his expression, Jack had heard as much of Gregson's words as I had done, but he said only, "Good to see you up and about again, sir."

Gregson's face jerked, as with a quick flash of pain. "No need to call me *sir* anymore. You outrank me these days."

"Maybe not. Sir," Jack said. His eyes met mine in silent

question over the top of Gregson's head, and I nodded. "But I'd still be glad of your thoughts on the security measures in place for the event this afternoon," Jack finished. "We haven't got enough manpower to vet all the late arrivals."

"I—yes, of course." Gregson went to join him, and they moved off together, towards a handsome black carriage just rolling up to the front of the church.

Amy lifted her head and saw me. Her expression quivered, and for a moment, it seemed likely she would simply bolt past me without a word. But then she lifted her head.

"I suppose you heard that." She didn't phrase it as a question, nor did she give me time to answer. Her cheeks were flushed, her eyes over-bright and glittering with unshed tears. "Are you going to tell me I'm insane, as well?"

"For wanting to marry a policeman? Hardly. That was my husband who just went off with Constable Gregson. You didn't know?"

"Your—" Amy stared. "Oh. No, I didn't know." She looked past me towards Jack and Gregson, her expression softening a little. "It was good of him, not to make Tobias feel inferior because he's lost his rank of inspector."

"Jack *is* good." I paused, then added, "And not that your choice of a husband is any of my business, but he also tried to give me much the same speech Gregson was giving you just now—about how I deserved better than to be married to a low-ranking police constable. He was only a constable when we got engaged."

"And what did you say?"

"That I'd somehow missed the vote where he was put in charge of deciding what was best for me."

Amy gave me a small, fractured twist of a smile. "I wish I could hope that would work as well on Tobias. He—" She stopped, frowning as she apparently caught sight of something behind me. "Why, that's Mr. Jerrard's carriage pulling up. What on earth is he doing here?" Her frown deepened. "He and my uncle loathe one another. If my uncle catches sight of him—"

Jerrard, a heavy, florid-looking man in a black top hat and fur-trimmed overcoat, was just descending from the newly arrived black carriage. His lips were pursed, his nostrils pinched as though all the world had a faintly rancid smell. Or maybe he was just indignant because his carriage driver hadn't come round to put down the set of steps so he could climb down from the carriage with ease.

The coachman was muffled in several layers of scarves that covered the lower half of his face, and had a hat pulled down low over his eyes. His brown boots appeared new. Instead of attending to his passenger, he seemed to be fumbling with something placed in the box under his seat.

I saw what he'd picked up. Just a fraction of a second later he stood tall, pistol in hand.

"Jack!"

My scream caught Jack's attention, and he looked in a flash from me to the carriage. Gregson, too, caught sight of the gun, and he and Jack both broke into a run towards the coachman.

But Mr. Rexford had come out of the church—and he, too, was armed.

"For God's sakes, what do you think you're doing?" he shouted at the coachman. "Drop your weapon or I'll fire!"

The rest seemed to happen in a blur that left me unable to tell who had fired first, the coachman or Mr. Rexford. But the sharp crack of a gunshot rent the air—

And then, a bare split-second later, the carriage exploded in a deafening roar and a flash of yellow-orange flames.

CHAPTER 24: WATSON

We were at the rear of the St. Andrews church sanctuary, just within the sheltered area beneath the south alcove. I was treating Gregson and Jack for the minor burns and cuts they had sustained from the blast. All I had available was cold water and a towel from the church kitchen.

I had every confidence that both men would make a full recovery from their surface wounds. However, I was keeping a close eye on Gregson. Already weakened from being stabbed yesterday, he had now been knocked unconscious and had possibly sustained a concussion.

We had carried him away from the explosion site. Getting him into a seated position, I thought, would accelerate his return to consciousness and also give me a better opportunity to assess his condition.

Now both he and Jack were side by side, in the rear pew. Jack, fully alert, was with me watching Gregson. Both of us were waiting impatiently for signs of wakefulness.

After several minutes had elapsed, Gregson's eyes flickered. His head came upright. "What happened?" he asked.

"Mr. Jerrard and his coachman were both killed," I said.

Gregson closed his eyes for a moment. Then he asked, "Amy?"

"She's gone with Lucy to fetch some proper dressings for your injuries: burn ointment and gauze," I said. "Don't make any sudden movements. Just stay calm and rest for a bit. Jack is here beside you."

"Where is Holmes?"

"He's outside, examining the site of the explosion. Mr. Rexford is with him."

A few moments later, Lucy and Amy arrived. Each insisted on ministering the burn ointment directly to her respective man. I encouraged this, knowing the medical risk in their misapplying the ointment was far outweighed by the strong emotional reward. For a patient to have a loved one care for him is often the best aid to healing.

Holmes returned, with Mr. Rexford close behind him. He took in the scene at once, and I thought I saw a momentary smile of satisfaction as he nodded towards Lucy and Jack.

Rexford's eyes were on Holmes. It was apparent that Holmes had not yet shared his conclusions.

Then Holmes spoke. "The carriage was packed with sticks of dynamite. One of the bullets fired must have struck the dynamite, causing the shock that set off the explosion."

Mr. Rexford shook his head wonderingly. "I suppose Jerrard must have planned to drive his carriage up to the church and detonate it as an act of sabotage."

"Someone certainly planned for tonight's explosion," Holmes said.

The odd note in Holmes's tone must have struck Mr. Rexford, as well, because his brows lowered. "What do you mean, Mr. Holmes?"

"I mean, Mr. Rexford, that I have seldom met a man with his hand in so many tills at the same time."

Mr. Rexford drew himself up. "I find your tone offensive."

"Then you will find the facts I am about to state still less to your liking. You and Mr. Jerrard have maintained the appearance of being rivals and enemies in public. But in private, the two of you were working closely together."

"Ridiculous!"

"So closely, in fact, you were even willing to make your own son into a murderer in order to uphold your end of the bargain."

Mr. Rexford's jaw dropped open, and a dull, brick-red colour began to suffuse his cheeks.

"Are you suggesting—"

"I am more than suggesting, Mr. Rexford." Holmes's voice had the crisp, cold snap of a whip. "I am telling you. I do not imagine for a single moment that the idea of blowing up the factory and incidentally murdering Marcus Thiel came into your son's mind without assistance. His admiration for you made him easy to manipulate. You must have worked on him gradually—hinting to him that if something were to happen to Marcus, he would be eligible to step into the position of factory supervisor, and how you had every confidence he would do well in that regard. You likely spoke approvingly of a marriage with Amy, and of the dynasty such a marriage would create. We saw the photograph of the Queen and her cousin, Prince Albert, in your front hallway, as well as another photograph of the Prince of Wales, at the helm of the Royal Yacht. The marriage with Amy would emulate the Royal intrafamily connection."

"Those photographs are evidence of my son's patriotism and family loyalty. As far removed from evidence of a crime as they could possibly be."

"Your son is indeed loyal. Even though not denying his guilt, he refused to incriminate you. Did you suggest how easily an explosion might be touched off by a flare gun, and how the explosion would put many of the employees out of work and make them appreciate the wages they had once been paid? No more attempts to organise a trade union to demand better working conditions. The workers would be grateful to return to their jobs and would no longer ask for higher pay. The business would grow and prosper and might one day sustain the full-size racing yacht your son yearned for. And you told him the insurance proceeds would cover the costs of rebuilding."

Mr. Rexford seemed to make an effort to speak, but no sound emerged.

"Then, in keeping with your policy for never treating honestly with anyone, you also pocketed the insurance payment after the explosion," Holmes went on. "And all the while you pretended that the factory was in dire financial straits and needed you to take out a loan, and to bring in capital through incorporation."

Rexford finally found his voice. "Completely untrue!"

"The 'loan' was really a bribe from Jerrard to sabotage your own business and temporarily close down most of the factory. When the new building was complete, and your employees were eager to get back to work, you and Mr. Jerrard could have played out another pretty little comedy like the one you enacted for Watson's and my benefit, pretending once more to be mortal enemies. Mr. Jerrard expected to further that performance when he arrived here today. Then the two of you come to a business settlement, the corporate underwriters would take over, and you both would split the proceeds of the incorporation."

"Mr. Holmes, you are completely deranged."

"But you needed the support of the underwriters. So you brought me in to investigate the first investigation to impress them with your zeal to uncover the truth. To induce me to take the case, you sent yourself the anonymous letter made with newspaper clippings. Of course, you thought your crimes were too well concealed for me to uncover."

"You haven't uncovered anything. You are only speculating."

"We shall see about that," Holmes replied calmly. "You had also paid or bribed one of your own employees, first, to follow Gregson and kill him, and when that did not succeed, to take the place of Mr. Jerrard's coachman. He bought new boots with some of your money. You also gave him a gun—an empty one, no doubt—and instructed him to wave it around and make a show of frightening Mr. Jerrard. He, unfortunate soul, thought along with everyone else that Mr. Jerrard was an enemy trying to destroy his livelihood. He did not know you had arranged for dynamite to be loaded into Mr. Jerrard's carriage. Nor did he know that you, using the coachman's weapon as an excuse, would fire your own revolver into the carriage, detonating the explosion. You planned to keep both Mr. Jerrard's bribe money, what remained of the insurance payout after the building had been replaced, and, later, the proceeds of the incorporation, without anyone being the wiser." Holmes stopped and regarded Mr. Rexford with a cold, steel-hard gaze. "But now you will need to spend much of your money to organise legal defence teams for both yourself and your son."

"I admit nothing," said Rexford. "And you have no evidence."

Amy, her face aghast, stood up and strode forwards to come face to face with her uncle. "You are as evil as your son," she said. "I am ashamed to have wasted so many years working for you."

To my surprise, Rexford pushed her away with a violent shove.

She staggered back and collided with me.

Then he whirled and ran for his carriage.

I started to run after him, but Holmes put a restraining hand on my arm.

"Give him a minute," he said, "and then he may lead us to evidence."

"I'm with you," Jack said.

Chapter 25: Flynn

While everyone was away at the celebration, Flynn and Becky had broken into Rexford Hall, acting on Mr. Holmes's instructions. They were ransacking the place for clues.

But they hadn't found anything so far, and now they heard a carriage rattling up the driveway.

On the ground floor, they'd found a white canvas holdall in the closet of a small office. On the upper floor, they'd found some business papers in Mr. Rexford's desk. Flynn stuffed those in the holdall. The dustbin was empty, which was a disappointment, for Mr. Holmes had asked particularly that they check the dustbins and retrieve everything, especially old newspapers.

They'd moved into the bedroom and office suite at the other end of the hall, where young Mr. Rexford had lived until he'd been taken off to jail. They were searching Rex's room when they heard the clatter of wheels and hoofbeats and saw a big, bearded man in the coach-box, lashing furiously at the horses, coming closer to the house.

"We've got to get out!" Becky said, looking down from the window. "He's almost here!"

Flynn said. "In a minute." The dustbin in this room was also empty. But there was a neat stack of newspaper-looking magazines on the bookshelf. Neat, that is, except one in the middle, the spine of which bulged out oddly from the edge of the stack.

Flynn examined it, and found that the entire contents had been removed. Only the magazine cover remained. It showed a picture of an enormous sailing vessel, and the name on the cover was *Yachting World*.

They could hear Mr. Rexford stomping up the front porch stairs and opening the door.

Flynn had an idea.

"Take the back stairs to the kitchen. Hurry!"

"Why?"

"Because up here the maid emptied the dustbins. But maybe she hasn't finished burning the trash downstairs."

Mr. Rexford's boots clumped up the carpeted front steps. Flynn and Becky eased themselves down the back stairs, practically sliding, leaning onto the railing and taking as much weight off their feet as they could.

They crept into the kitchen. There were two dustbins, one large, by the fireplace and the other, the smaller one, by the back door.

The large dustbin was full of papers.

"Quiet," said Flynn. They'd forgotten to close the door to the back stairs, and they could hear Mr. Rexford going from room to room, slamming one door after the other.

Which meant Mr. Rexford could hear them.

Becky held the canvas holdall open while Flynn stuffed in the papers. Some food wrappers. Some envelopes and catalogues. The day's newspaper. Yesterday's newspaper.

And a group of smaller pages, magazine-size newsprint, with *Yachting World* printed across the top of each.

Flynn riffed through the pages. He held up one.

There were two rectangular holes in that page, where two words had been cut out.

Becky's eyes lit up. Flynn stuffed the magazine pages on top of everything else in the holdall. But as he turned to go, the holdall swung out and knocked a metal pitcher off the big centre kitchen table. Becky and Flynn froze at the racket as the pitcher clanged and clattered on the hard tile floor.

A roar came from upstairs, and then came the sound of heavy footfalls pounding down the steps.

Flynn grabbed the holdall and mimed the word, "Run!"

On the way out, he carefully knocked over the other dustbin, the one with the food waste, spilling the foul-smelling contents onto the porch steps.

Then he and Becky ran, trying not to slip on the snowy path, until they reached the garden.

Hiding for a moment behind a tall hedge, they saw Mr. Rexford stumble out of the kitchen and fall onto the back porch. He hauled himself up, his face florid, trying to wipe the putrid garbage from his hands, his head turning right and left as he scanned the property.

Flynn gave a smile of satisfaction as he saw the big man's trouser legs were soaked through at the knees.

Then he saw Rexford pull a pistol from his pocket.

Flynn picked up a rock and hurled it as far as he could, to the woodpile at the right side of the building. It landed with a clatter.

Mr. Rexford took a few cautious steps in the direction of the sound.

Flynn and Becky took off running in the opposite direction. From behind them they heard Mr. Rexford, bellowing, "I see you! Come back or I'll shoot!"

They ran to the front of the Hall.

And saw a police carriage racing up the drive, the driver lashing at the horses.

The driver was Mr. Holmes. Beside him on the driver's box was Jack, holding a shotgun.

From behind them a shot rang out.

"He's got a pistol!" Flynn yelled, pulling Becky down with him alongside the road.

Jack raised the shotgun to his shoulder. "Drop it, Rexford!" he shouted. "Hands up!"

They heard the pistol hit the gravel driveway.

Flynn and Becky stood aside as the police carriage drove past. A moment later, both Mr. Holmes and Jack had leaped from the carriage. Jack hauled Mr. Rexford around and was locking handcuffs onto his wrists.

Becky waited while Flynn gave Mr. Holmes the canvas holdall.

"We've got it, Mr. Holmes," she said.

Mr. Holmes said, "Well done."

He gave each of them a pat on the shoulder.

Chapter 26: Lucy

I approached the door of flat 221A Baker Street, then stopped at the sound of voices from inside.

"Stabbed and blown up in the self-same week." Gregson's voice was weak, raspy with fatigue.

"Ought to set some kind of record with the Force," Jack agreed.

On Holmes's insistence, we had brought Gregson—still drifting in and out of consciousness—back to Baker Street to recover from the effects of the bombing. We had been taking it in turns to sit with him, and I had been about to spell Jack so he could return to Scotland Yard.

"I need to get up—get out of here," Gregson's voice came from behind the door panel.

"Oh? Why's that?"

I seemed to be making a habit today of eavesdropping on Gregson's private conversations, but his next words kept me rooted in place outside the door.

"The same reason I can't have anything to do with Amy. Because I'm a danger to anyone who gets too close to me." Gregson drew a ragged breath, then said, his voice so low I could just barely make it out. "The Syndicate's behind this. And if you don't know what that means—" he broke off, and I pictured him searching Jack's expression. "You do know. Don't you?"

"I know."

I almost shivered at the tone of Jack's voice. I had never heard him sound quite so grim.

"Then you'll have heard what happens to anyone who sets himself against them."

"Yeah. I know that, too. But I also know there's no place safer in London for you than this room right here—and that the shape you're in, you might as well sign your own death certificate if you try to walk out now."

"But—"

"Get some rest," Jack said. "We'll talk more about this later."

Gregson must have felt even worse and weaker than I imagined, because he didn't argue, only fell silent. A moment later, Jack appeared in the doorway.

He didn't look at all surprised to see me. He'd probably heard my footsteps on the stairs.

"The Syndicate?" I asked.

Jack ran a hand across his face. "Crime. Highly organised crime. Not just your run-of-the-mill street gang kind. They've got members everywhere—a whole network of bribery and corruption that runs straight up to the highest levels."

"Including the police force and the Home Office, obviously." I was oddly surprised at how calm and quiet my voice sounded. Cold was burrowing into me, but my words came out flat. "If someone either at Scotland Yard or the Home Office was being paid to squash the investigation into Powder Island … can we take it that either Mr. Rexford or his late associate Mr. Jerrard—or both—were Syndicate men?"

Jack gave me a wary look. He was probably surprised at how calm I sounded, too.

"Jerrard's the more likely candidate, I'd say, from the look of those papers Becky and Flynn found. Rexford's trying to move up in the world, but he's not rich enough or influential enough for the Syndicate to bother with him."

I nodded. "How long have you known about them? Wait—no. It would have to be since your training days, wouldn't it? Since you knew Sergeant O'Hara when you were going through police training together."

"Yes."

"And Sergeant O'Hara somehow tried to fight back against the Syndicate, and they killed him for it? That's what's been troubling you about his murder?"

Jack shook his head. "Years ago, O'Hara and I had the same training officer. Inspector Glen. He was … well, let's just say he was as dirty as they come. Accepted bribes to look the other way when a murder or robbery was committed—or to misplace evidence, or maybe send the name of a key witness to someone who could put that witness out of the way before they could testify. He wasn't above beating a confession out of an innocent man, too, so he'd have someone to pin the blame on. It didn't take O'Hara and me long to discover what he was up to, but what could we do about it? We weren't even official police constables yet, just recruits in training. Who'd take our word above Glen's?"

I studied Jack's face. "I'm guessing you still tried, though?"

Jack released a breath. "Yeah. We tried. We went to the Superintendent and told him what was happening."

"And?"

"And the Superintendent was found dead the next day. Stabbed through the heart. A botched street robbery was the official conclusion."

I swallowed against the cold lump wedged in my throat.

"How did you and O'Hara escape being victims of the same type of unfortunate robberies gone wrong?"

"I'd guess only because the Superintendent didn't name his sources of information. He may not have realised the full extent of what Glen was a part of—just thought he was corrupt but working on his own. That's what O'Hara and I thought, until the Superintendent died. We might have still been in danger—it wouldn't have taken Glen long to work out who'd gone to the Superintendent about him. But then a day or two later, Glen himself was shot in a raid on a criminal's hideout."

"So whatever he knew or suspected died with him." I searched Jack's expression again. "You wouldn't have left it there, though." I didn't have to ask myself what I would have done in Jack's position; I already knew. There were some battles that couldn't be won by a direct assault. But that didn't mean you walked away or stopped fighting. "You and Sergeant O'Hara. You've been investigating quietly ever since, haven't you? Secretly gathering information, assembling evidence."

Under ordinary circumstances, Jack might have grinned and said something about the drawbacks to being married to Sherlock Holmes's daughter. Now he just nodded, his expression equal parts grim and tired. "We never met in person, even off-duty. We didn't want to risk our names being put together. But we'd worked out a system for sending information back and forth. Always in code. We had a couple of places around London where we could leave messages when we had something new to report."

"And it's something to do with those reports of Sergeant O'Hara's that have gone missing now? That's why you wanted his lodgings searched so thoroughly?"

Jack was looking out the hallway window into the street beyond, where carriages were rolling past through the inch or two of wintry slush and mud on the ground. "Yes. I was at O'Hara's lodgings myself just after he died, and I didn't find anything. All the notes he'd kept, the evidence he'd gathered … it was all missing. That doesn't mean the other side's got them. O'Hara could have had another hiding spot—even rented a safe deposit box in a bank somewhere."

"But it also doesn't mean the Syndicate *doesn't* have access to whatever O'Hara knew." And Jack's name was bound to be all over whatever records Sergeant O'Hara had kept.

"You're right."

I said nothing; just looked at him.

Jack turned, meeting my gaze. "You think I should have told you."

There was no point in lying. I knew Jack couldn't always disclose the confidential details of his police work to me, but this was different entirely. To have kept a secret so huge … it felt as though he'd slid a knife between my ribs.

"Yes."

"I wanted to." Jack caught hold of my hand. "I swear I wanted to. But I was afraid. More than afraid. Terrified." He drew a shallow breath. "It's been years. Four years O'Hara and I spent, trying to dig up any kind of evidence to let us fight back. And you know what we've got? Lists of dead witnesses. Lines of investigation that snap as soon as you try to run them down. And now O'Hara's dead."

Jack reached to touch my cheek, and his voice when he went on was both ragged and yet controlled, his eyes dark. "Not much scares me, Lucy. But the thought of what could happen to you if the Syndicate thinks you're any kind of a threat … I'd die if I lost you, Lucy. I'd never leave Becky on her own, but if anything happened to you, everything alive inside me would be gone—killed, too."

He meant it. He meant every word.

I shut my eyes for a second. Tears pricked behind my lids.

I had grown up alone, just as Jack had, wondering what it would be like to have a family of my own. Back then, I would have given anything in the world to know that someday someone would love me this much.

I opened my eyes, drew back, and punched Jack in the shoulder—a solid right hook that made him stagger back a half-step.

"That's what I get for trying to keep all this from you?" he asked, when he'd recovered his balance.

"No. That's what you get for making it very hard to stay angry with you, even though I've every right to."

Finally, Jack gave me a crooked half smile, though it faded almost at once. "I suppose it's no good asking you to stay safely out of this?"

"No." I took his hand and laced my fingers with his. "If you haven't got anywhere on your own in four years, then it's time to see what we both can do."

Chapter 27: Watson

Two weeks had elapsed since the explosion of Jerrard's coach and the arrest of the Rexfords. Father and son were still in custody, awaiting trial.

Bail had been denied, given the nature of the purported crimes. The list was impressive indeed: evading arrest, attempted murder of a police officer, attempt to defraud an investment company, actual defrauding of an insurance company, endangerment of the public safety, and the murders of Marcus Thiel, Mr. Jerrard, and his coachman. Those latter three offenses would likely earn father and son the gallows.

Flynn and Becky had been basking in well-deserved praise. The papers and newspaper clippings they had taken from Rexford Hall provided ample hard evidence needed to hold the Rexfords. A search of Jerrard's rooms had also yielded fruit for the prosecution: records of payments to Rexford, and also payments made to a bank in Switzerland. The Queen's Counsel was confident of achieving a guilty verdict, after which both Rexfords would be hanged.

Now, on a snowy Wednesday afternoon, our doorbell rang, and Amy Thiel arrived at our rooms at 221B Baker Street. I took her coat and hung it up. She declined tea. I invited her to take a seat on our sofa. She shook her head.

"Miss Thiel," said Holmes, who had been standing by the mantel. "Please." He gestured towards our sofa.

After a long moment she nodded and sat across from our fireplace, stiffly upright, her blonde hair neatly coiffed, her hands clasped together in her lap.

She drew a breath. "I have come to speak to you about two matters."

Holmes had his attention apparently on refilling his pipe from the Persian slipper, but at that he turned, brows slightly elevated, and took his customary chair to face her. "Please proceed."

She leaned forwards. "First, I have come about the incorporation of the Rexford Works. I have spoken to a group of legitimate underwriters, and they believe the business itself is strong enough to be sustained with Rexford and his son no longer involved. They are willing to proceed with the incorporation, but they would appreciate a short interview with you, simply to assure themselves that your investigation did not uncover any other fatal flaws about the operation."

"They knew of my involvement?" Holmes asked.

"My uncle had told them he would hire you. You were right—he was confident any investor would look favourably on a company investigated by Sherlock Holmes."

"And incorporation would yield far more than the bribe money and the remains of the insurance payments that he had already received," Holmes said. "For such a reward, he was willing to take what he thought was a very small risk."

"He thought his crimes were so clever that even you could not uncover his guilt," I said.

Holmes said, "I shall make myself available for an interview with the underwriters."

Amy relaxed a bit. "That is a relief. Thanks to you, the business will go on," she said, "and four hundred workers will be able to support their families."

Holmes gave one of his fleeting, momentary smiles. "Now, what is the second matter?"

She sat fully upright once more. "Whatever criminal investigation Tobias is involved in—whatever led to his being stabbed. I wish to take part. To help."

"Miss Thiel—" Holmes began.

But Amy interrupted once again. "At least neither you nor Tobias can claim I would be bringing embarrassment to either myself or my family by taking part in a criminal investigation." Her lips twisted. "With both my uncle and my cousin in prison for murder, I should think any damage I do to our family's reputation ought scarcely to register."

"I was not thinking of scandal, Miss Thiel," Holmes said, "But rather the possibility of danger. These are highly unscrupulous people with whom we are dealing. They have already attempted Gregson's murder, and succeeded in many more."

"Please. Give me credit for at least a rudimentary degree of intelligence, Mr. Holmes." Amy's voice was crisp. "I understand there are risks involved. I still wish to offer my services to you in whatever capacity may be most helpful. I cannot bring back my father, but I can help fight against those who tried to kill Tobias."

Holmes considered her a long moment, during which the only sound was the hiss of sleet against the windowpane and the crackle of the coal fire at his back.

"In that case, Miss Thiel," he said at last, "I believe I may have an assignment for you."

THE END

Historical Notes

This is a work of fiction, and the authors make no claim whatsoever that any historical locations or historical figures who appear in this story were even remotely connected with the adventures recounted herein. However …

1. The explosion at the fictional Rexford Factory at Powder Island was inspired by an incident at the gunpowder factory of Messrs. Curtis and Harvey, in Hounslow. In 1887 an explosion obliterated one of the Hounslow factory buildings while killing the single man who was present at the time. Many of the details of the explosion in this story were taken from the 1887 newspaper account, and from the lengthy Home Office report on the explosion.

2. The Home Office report concluded that, of the many possible causes of the explosion only two, in the judgment of the preparer of the report, were reasonable. "1. The fracture of a portion of the machinery; and 2. Matches maliciously placed upon the platform by some person unknown." As far as the authors are aware, the unknown person was never found, and no arrests were made.

3. The cover image for this adventure is taken from a photograph of the Hounslow Shot Tower, which is the only building from the factory that survives today.

4. The land once occupied by the Hounslow gunpowder factory is now Crane Park Island, a nature preserve managed by the London Wildlife Trust.

5. The massive stone statue of King Henry VIII, erected in 1702, still stands atop the entrance gate of St. Bart's Hospital in London, a brief walk from the Smithfield Market.

6. Corruption in the London Metropolitan Police was a very real problem in the past century. It was vigorously opposed and somewhat eradicated under the watch of Commissioner Edward Bradford, who held many official positions during his distinguished career. Commissioner Bradford appears as a character in many of the Sherlock and Lucy adventures.

Lucy James will return.

MURDER
AT THE ROYAL
OBSERVATORY

Chapter 1: Lucy

"Hello, Missus." The man standing at our back door leered ingratiatingly. "Yer good man at 'ome, by any chance?"

Most people being confronted with Harold Bailey—who for some unknown reason went by the name of Nibbs to all who knew him—would have slammed the door in his face.

Tall, gangly, and thin as a scarecrow, Nibbs looked as though he had been dunked in a vat of glue and then rolled through someone's trash bin. His clothes, tattered and filthy even by the standards of the London streets, were held together by odd bits of string or knotted rags. His shoes were wrapped in twine to keep the flapping soles joined to their tops a little longer. A rough length of tar-stained rope that he'd probably picked up at the docks was wrapped double around his waist for a belt. His black stove-pipe hat was stuffed with sheets of old newspapers to fill in the holes that could have been chewed by a thousand moths. His pockets were filled with empty bottles, tin cans, broken match sticks, pen wipers, torn playing cards, and whatever other odd assortment of trash he'd picked up and thought he might either be able to sell or put to use one day.

And because his visits had become something of a regular occurrence, I didn't slam the door on him, but instead stepped back, allowing him into the kitchen.

"Yes, Jack's right here."

Jack was just putting on his coat. Broad-shouldered and athletic, with a clean-shaven, handsome face, he was at twenty-six young for a Scotland Yard police sergeant. But he also had the kind of quiet, hard-edged authority that came from years of first-hand experience with London's most dangerous elements.

Nibbs winced at the sight of him—or rather, at sight of the blue police uniform he was putting on.

Old habits were hard to break, and the past year or two of working as a police informant hadn't yet counteracted his instinctive aversion to any police officer, borne out of a lifetime of petty crime.

"Ah." He transferred the ingratiating smile to Jack. "I came early, on account of I was 'oping to catch you before you'd left for work."

Jack reached for his wide leather belt and buckled it on. "By which you mean that you were hoping to come at breakfast time so that you could get a free meal."

One thing I had learned about Nibbs from former visits was that it was quite literally impossible to offend him.

"Very kind o' you to offer." He beamed, folding his long frame to slide onto a chair at the kitchen table. "Whatever you're 'aving, it smells a treat."

Without comment, I slid a plate of eggs and bacon onto the table in front of him. I'd also learned that it was far easier to accept the inevitable when it came to Nibbs' visits.

"Ah, thank you kindly." Nibbs smiled at me, displaying a row of broken and stained teeth that would give a dentist a lifetime's worth of nightmares. "Wouldn't say no to some mustard, too, if you've got it."

I passed the mustard pot across, watching in fascination as Nibbs spooned mustard into a towering heap on top of his eggs.

"I assume you're here because you have something to tell me?" Jack asked.

"Wha'?" Nibbs paused with a strip of bacon halfway to his mouth, then nodded. "Oh—yar. A china o' mine says the street is that there's bottles offerin' bees to anyone as can offer a chirp about the inspector wot turned up brown bread a coupla years ago."

I had spent my entire childhood in America, but by now I had lived in London long enough to consider it my home—and even to occasionally feel as though the great city accepted me as one of her own, too.

Then I spent three minutes listening to Nibbs or one of his fellows, and felt as though I might just as well have stepped off the boat from New York yesterday.

I was still laboriously working out that *china* was short for *china plate*, which rhymed with *mate*, which meant that Nibbs' source of information had been a friend of his, when Jack sat down in the chair opposite from Nibbs.

Having grown up on the same streets that Nibbs frequented, he didn't miss a beat.

"You mean Inspector Glenn?"

"'S'right." Nibbs finished crunching bacon and started shovelling mustard and eggs into his mouth, then gave a derisive snort. "As if they'll get anyfink but a lot of porkies from them's as noses fer a livin'."

Porkies was short for *pork pies*, which was rhyming slang for lies. And a nose was a paid police informant.

Jack could have said something about pots and kettles, considering Nibbs' own happy acceptance of payment for any information he could give. But he knew Nibbs as well—better, in fact—than I did, and didn't bother. His lean, angular face was perfectly calm, his voice neutral. Only if you knew him very, very well would you catch the undercurrent of tension in his manner as he said, "You've heard something more useful, though?"

"Dunno. That's the question, in't it?" Nibbs swallowed the last of the eggs, using the edge of his fork to scrape every last molecule off the plate. "This mate o' mine, like I was tellin' you, 'e said as how the bottles was splashin' bees about, lookin' for information, like. And 'e said to me, wot about it, on account of 'e'd run into a china o' his, wot claimed 'e'd been paid fer doin' some jolly work on the day this 'ere Inspector Glenn met 'is maker, and did I fink the police would want t' know about it? So I says to meself, Nibbs, I says, why don't you go along and have a chin-wag wi' yer good friend Sergeant Kelly, and see what 'e makes of it all?"

Jack hadn't moved, but I could tell from the controlled, still-muscled calm of his whole body that something Nibbs had said was important.

"This friend of a friend of yours. Did he say who'd paid him to act the jolly?"

"Nah." Nibbs shook his head. "Mind you, 'e might recollect more, wif some proper motivation, if you understand me."

He winked broadly, laying one grime-encrusted hand palm-up on the table.

"Right." Jack dug in his pocket, produced a half-crown, and dropped it into Nibbs' hand. "Give him this. See if he remembers anything else."

"Will do, sir, will do. That is, so long as I can find him again," he added, crinkling his brow in a conscientious frown. "He's a hard man to track down sometimes, this mate o'mine."

"Here's for your trouble." Jack dropped another half-crown

into Nibbs' hand. "See if you can spend it on something other than drink or tobacco."

"Why, thank you, sir!" Nibbs gave an exaggerated start of surprise. "Thank you kindly! The soul o' generosity, that's what you are."

Jack acknowledged the thanks with a nod, then said, frowning, "And Nibbs? This stays between us. No trying to cash in twice by taking this somewhere else."

Nibbs' eyes widened in a look of angelic innocence. "I wouldn't dream of it! Even if I did, I couldn't tell who to trust." He got up and sloped towards the door, bowing deeply to me on his way. "Thank you for the breakfast, missus. Yer a pearl among women, and yer eyes are like … like two pools of water wot's got a bit of algae growin' in them. Green, like."

With which odd but no doubt well-intentioned saying, he slid, crab-like, through the kitchen door. A moment later, to judge by the rattles and clanks, he was rummaging through the trash bin that stood against the wall outside.

I waited until the sounds had stopped and Nibbs could be judged safely away before turning to Jack.

"Act the jolly?"

Jack's brows were drawn together, and the darkness in his eyes indicated his thoughts were following some inner and unpleasant track. He said, almost absently, "A jolly's someone who's paid to start a riot. Usually it's so that one of their gang can commit a robbery while everyone's attention—including the constabulary's—is on the mob pounding each other in the street."

I frowned, thinking back over the conversation with Nibbs.

"So what Nibbs came to tell you is that on the day Inspector Glenn died, a friend of a friend of his was paid to start a riot? Was there a riot that day?"

"There was." Jack's eyes were still focused on the middle distance, seeing something else entirely from the familiar kitchen table and breakfast dishes. "That was when things went wrong. We were making a raid on a fencing ken on Earl Street in St. Giles." He glanced at me. "That's—"

"A house where stolen goods are distributed," I finished for him. "I may have grown up in Connecticut, but I do know that one. Although if you intend to start speaking like Nibbs does, I may resort to talking about being boondoggled and dusted and any other Americanisms I can think of."

Jack smiled. Though the shadow crossed his dark brown gaze again as he went on.

"A riot did start, just as we were about to break in the door. It was chaos—just bloody chaos. That neighbourhood's a powder-keg anyway; all it takes is one lighted match to make it all blow sky-high. That day, it was men pounding each other, women and kids in danger of getting trampled. And somehow in the middle of it all … Glenn was shot."

I watched Jack's face. "And no one ever knew who shot him?"

There was a fraction of a pause before Jack answered. "No. We never found out if it was someone from inside the fencing ken who'd shot him or just someone in the riot who'd got a grudge against the police."

"Which in St. Giles describes practically everyone," I said. "What was Nibbs saying about bees, though?" I tried to remember. "Bottles passing out bees?"

"Bees and honey—money," Jack said. "And bottles are—"

"Police," I finished. "Bottle and Stopper. Copper." A chill had wrapped around me, sliding inch by inch down from the nape of my neck. "The police are suddenly offering reward money to anyone who can give them any information about Inspector Glenn's death? Why would they be doing that, more than two years after he died?"

Whatever the answer turned out to be, it was unlikely to be good. Inspector Glenn had been part of a web of bribery and corruption known as the Syndicate. Information about their organisation was in short supply. But we did know that they had—still had—members in the police force, officers more highly ranked than Inspector Glenn.

"Is that why you told Nibbs not to try to take advantage of the offer of money?" I asked. "You think whoever is behind this sudden quest for information on Inspector Glenn's murder is a part of the corruption?"

I already knew the answer, even before Jack tipped his head in confirmation. "If an official investigation's been opened, it's being kept quiet—otherwise I'd have heard about it at the Yard."

"But if it's unofficial, run by the Syndicate, using the policemen they already have under their control …" I liked nothing about this. I especially didn't like the possibility that had just wormed its way into my thoughts. "Nibbs said that all they were likely to get was a lot of lies—witnesses willing to say anything for the reward money. Do you think that's all they're after? Informants willing to swear to anything, just so that they can pin the blame for Glenn's murder on someone of their choosing?"

The other police officer who'd been with Jack at the time of Inspector Glenn's murder was dead himself. Sergeant O'Hara had been stabbed in the back a few weeks ago by an unknown attacker. Although, considering that he and Jack had been privately investigating and gathering evidence again the Syndicate together, we both knew exactly the force—if not the actual hand—that had driven the knife in between Sergeant O'Hara's shoulder blades.

"All the evidence that you and Sergeant O'Hara assembled," I said. "It's still missing. Your name would be all over it. You were present that day when Inspector Glenn got shot. And now suddenly someone wants very much to find witnesses to his death—or people willing to pretend they were witnesses."

It was like a twisted version of the printed games for children, where drawing lines to connect the dots on a page turned those seemingly random dots into a picture.

Questions might be asked in inconvenient circles if Jack turned up stabbed in the same way Sergeant O'Hara had been. But there were other methods of getting someone out of the way. Including accusing him of murdering his police training officer, for example.

The grimness that etched Jack's expression told me he'd already followed the same line of reasoning, but before he could say anything, the telephone rang outside in the hall.

I started to get up, but I heard Becky's footsteps clattering down the stairs, and then her voice saying hello.

A few moments later, her blonde head appeared around the door to the kitchen, her eyes bright with excitement.

"Lucy? It's Mr. Holmes. He wants us to come to Greenwich this morning to meet him and Dr. Watson. There's been a murder at the Royal Observatory. And it looks like the killer might be someone from the planet Mars!"

Chapter 2: Watson

Two uniformed constables stood at the gated entry to the Royal Observatory, eyeing us up and down and squinting into the morning sun. They stood with arms folded across their chests, probably trying to warm themselves, for here at the top of the hill the wind from the river came in hard and sharp. The air was unusually clear for February, when our London air was normally loaded with coal smoke from more than a million chimneys, and the blue sky promised a cold day.

Then the constables saw Lestrade, who was behind Holmes and me. Quickly they came to attention as Lestrade, impatient, stamped his feet.

"Constable, kindly open the gate at once. We are expected by Mr. Harewell."

One constable opened the gate, the other waved us through with a salute, and we proceeded along the uphill path that led to the Observatory.

The young man whose body we had come to see lay on the paved path, a few yards in front of the gateway to the great domed Royal Observatory tower.

Holmes crouched over the prostrate, hatless form. The face lay in a small pool of drying blood that had issued from a massive wound at the right temple. But more disturbing than the bloodied wound were the awkward angles at which his arms and legs were flung out.

I suppressed the urge to shudder. The victim resembled a child's rag-doll, carelessly thrown aside by some giant's hand.

Lestrade appeared worried, and more haggard than usual, possibly due to the early hour, for it had been six AM when he had telephoned us at Baker Street.

"The victim is Emmett Frazier, one of the computers at the Observatory," Lestrade said. He turned to a tall, pleasant-featured man who had come down the path. Lestrade said, "Introductions are in order. Mr. Harewell, I'd like you to meet Sherlock Holmes and Dr. Watson. Gentlemen, this is Christopher Harewell, Astronomer Royal to Her Majesty."

"For my sins," said the other man, with a diffident smile. "My apologies for calling you here so early, but I am terrified of the consequences and implications of this horrible act."

Holmes nodded acknowledgement of the Astronomer Royal, but continued his examination, now crouching at the right side of the body.

Alongside it lay a polished brass telescope, perhaps two feet long.

"An expensive telescope," Holmes said. "Was it the property of the dead man?"

"I have no idea. I can tell you that it does not belong to the Observatory. Is it important?"

"I cannot say for the moment. I thought at first that it might be the murder weapon," Holmes said. "But it bears no trace of blood. Also, the damage to the victim's head is consistent with a fall rather than a blow from a weapon."

As he spoke, Holmes continued to study the victim, standing up and walking carefully around the dead body, his face bearing the singularly keen, remote expression that meant his attention was fully absorbed in noting even the minutest detail.

At last he raised his head. "Well, gentlemen. It is clear that something of an unusual nature occurred here last night. You will of course have noted that this man has fallen from a great height. Note the angles of his arms and legs, the bones of which were broken by the fall. Although fortunately for him, he was at that juncture already dead. He was obviously dropped here—but from where?"

Holmes tilted his head back to survey the sunny blue sky overhead.

He knelt again, examining the pavement beneath the dead man.

"It appears that he fell straight down. Moreover, there are no footmarks whatsoever. Neither the dead man nor his presumed attacker appears to have left so much as a trace of how he arrived."

I startled. I had been so taken up with the sight of the dead man that I had neglected to notice the points which Holmes mentioned. But now that I looked more closely at the crime scene before us, I could see that Holmes was entirely right.

There were no footprints, no scuff marks, no signs of a struggle or of anything having been dragged to the entrance site. The body of Emmett Frazier might have been flung down from some passing cloud—or from the stars above—for all the signs that had been left on the ground.

"However," Holmes went on, "the peculiarity of those circumstances alone does not explain the agitated—some might even say hysterical—telephone call that I received this morning. I presume that the answer lies in the odd greyish black powder that is visible around the victim's nose and mouth? I shall want samples of that collected and analysed, by the way," he added to Lestrade.

In answer, Lestrade's narrow features grew even more pinched and sour looking than usual.

"Also, Lestrade, I should like a copy of the beat patrolman's report from last night through the present. Perhaps the man noticed something that may be helpful."

"I shall look into that," Lestrade said.

Mr. Harewell took out a handkerchief and mopped his brow. He seemed to be having difficulty in deciding how to begin, but at last said, "You are familiar with the popular novel written by Mr. H. G. Wells called *The War of the Worlds*?"

"I have heard of the story. A fictional account of an attack by creatures from Mars."

I, too, had heard of the popular tale, which had been published a year or two before. In Mr. Wells' work of fiction, giant, spider-like alien creatures, having depleted the resources of their Martian home world, had looked to Earth for a new home and come to conquer mankind.

"The alien beings arrived in steel ships that emitted a flash of green light, and they killed their victims with a poisonous black smoke," Mr. Harewell went on.

Holmes's brows edged upwards. "I see. And you believe the traces of black powder around the nostrils and mouth of Mr. Frazier—and the lack of footmarks—point to Martian involvement?"

Mr. Harewell's cheeks flushed at the irony in Holmes's tone. "Put like that, I realise that it sounds farcical—too wild a tale to appear outside the pages of fiction."

He broke off, applying the handkerchief to his forehead once again.

Holmes's keen grey gaze swept across the Astronomer Royal's face, but he said only, "I take it you were the one to find Mr. Frazier's body?"

"I was. I was in early, for this day is a very important one for us at the observatory. I arrived at 5am."

"Did you see anything unusual at the gate?"

"I did not see anything at the gate. I came to my office from my residence, which is inside the gate, within the observatory campus."

"Pray, continue."

"I heard a commotion."

"Can you describe it?"

"Raised voices. Only for a moment or two."

"Were the usual astronomers on duty making their observations last night?"

"No. They had been given the night off, to compensate for being required to come in early today."

"Why?"

"We must all make preparations for a fundraising dinner tonight."

Holmes continued to regard Harewell with a steady look. "There is some further detail which you have yet to disclose." His tone made it a statement rather than a question. "Something more, which you yourself either heard or witnessed."

Harewell hesitated, then seemed to come to a decision. He spread his palms. "I have to be truthful, much as it pains me." He took a deep breath. "I saw a flash of green light."

"Not your imagination?" Holmes asked.

Harewell shook his head.

"Where were you when you saw the green light?"

"I was in my office, standing at that window." He indicated a tall window on the side of the Observatory building, without curtains, and framed with an arch at the top.

Holmes lifted his gaze to the window, as well. "How long was the light visible?"

"Perhaps one second, maybe two. No more."

"Did you see any smoke?"

"No, but I would not expect to. This was before dawn, and the area was dark, as I said. I was simply musing on the upcoming events of the day, getting my thoughts in order for the pressing matters that would be forthcoming. Then there was the light."

"And then you heard something?"

"No, I heard the raised voices a few moments before. That was why I was at the window."

"But understandably you do not wish that level of detail to be made public."

Mr. Harewell's throat muscles contracted as he swallowed. "We do serious work here, Mr. Holmes. Thousands of mariners and indeed the British Navy rely on our almanacks to support navigation across the seven seas. I cannot afford to become the subject of ridicule, as I certainly would be if word of this got out."

Lestrade mused, "'Employee murdered by Martian green rays and black poison smoke, says Astronomer Royal.' Yes, that would sell quite a few newspapers."

"And discredit us in the opinion of the important people whose donations are essential to continuing our work."

Holmes nodded, returning his attention to the body. "Dr. Watson, would your estimate of the time of death be consistent with its having occurred shortly after 5am?"

I considered, having already taken note of the temperature and rigidity of the victim's limbs. "Unfortunately, I cannot be so exact as that. The cold weather makes it difficult to give a precise time. I can only say that a death somewhere between 2am and 5am seems most likely."

Holmes tipped his head in acknowledgement. "And the cause of death?"

"That would require a postmortem. The victim's muscles are particularly rigid, however, and the black powder about the mouth would seem to suggest poison. Although it is more likely to be of earthly origin than Martian." I smiled briefly.

I expected Holmes to make a remark about the mistake of theorising in advance of data, but instead he turned to survey the surrounding area. "I take it this is the entry path the employees will follow as they arrive for work today?"

"Yes. In about one hour."

"Inspector Lestrade, could you please have the constables remain on watch?" Holmes waited for Lestrade's acknowledgement, and then addressed the two constables directly. "Gentlemen, would you please take note of those who come through, and report to me any that take more than an ordinary notice of this location."

"Sir?" One of the constables looked bewildered.

"Anyone who appears not to be simply arriving for an ordinary workday. Please get their name. Use whatever pretext you please."

The man nodded.

Holmes turned to Mr. Harewell. "Do you have any idea about what this unfortunate man hoped to see with the telescope? Was he familiar with Mr. Wells' story?"

Harewell's expression became, if possible, still more pained. "He was fascinated by it. I believe that is why he had come here last night with his telescope."

"Why here?"

"We have the best vantage point in London for observing the night sky. Which is why the observatory is located here, of course. Frazier knew he would not be permitted to use the Observatory equipment for his own purposes, so he quite correctly remained outside the gate and brought his own telescope."

"Assuming that the telescope does indeed belong to him," Holmes said. "We will learn more by looking into Frazier's background."

"You can be sure of that," added Lestrade.

"Lucy will be here soon. I shall ask her to interview Mrs. Frazier," Holmes said. "I understand he lived with his mother."

Holmes appeared about to turn away, but then looked back at the unfortunate victim's body and moved to crouch beside it once more. He drew back the dead man's sleeve an inch or two. "Dr. Watson, will you kindly give me your opinion as to these marks on the forearm?"

I bent, peering more closely at the raised red marks that blotched the skin just above the wrist.

"It looks to me like a rash—a touch of eczema would be my diagnosis."

"Nothing serious, then?" Holmes asked. "Nothing to do with the cause of death?"

"I would not say so, no." I spoke carefully, for long experience with Holmes had taught me that even such minor and seemingly innocuous details could not be entirely dismissed.

Holmes nodded, springing easily to his feet once more. "And now, Mr. Harewell, perhaps this conversation would be better continued in your office. Extraterrestrial intervention aside, there is another point of potential significance about the attack on Mr. Frazier."

I was at a loss as to Holmes's meaning, but Mr. Harewell sucked in a sharp breath.

"I refer, of course, to today's date," Holmes said.

Holmes did not elaborate, because at that moment Lucy arrived, along with Becky. Holmes took them both aside to give them background details and instructions.

Chapter 3: Lucy

Mrs. Geraldine Frazier was a small, sweet-faced woman whose greying hair was parted in the middle and drawn smoothly back into a bun at the nape of her neck.

She and her son lived in a small villa on Blackheath, near enough to the Observatory that Becky and I had been able to leave Holmes and Watson to their investigations and walk here in only about twenty minutes' time.

The landscape here was almost park-like, with tall evergreens shading winding pathways—almost as far from the constant noise and dirt and bustle of the London streets as could be imagined.

When she'd opened the door to us, Mrs. Frazier's eyes had been red with weeping, and her expression had the dazed, bewildered look of the recently bereaved, when the loss is so raw, so fresh that the full reality of it has barely sunk in. But she had immediately agreed to answer our questions.

"I will do anything"—her voice shook, but her expression was fierce—"to help you find whoever has done this terrible thing to my son."

"Thank you, Mrs. Frazier," I told her. "I'm sorry to have to ask, but do you know of any enemies your son may have had? Anyone who might have wished him harm?"

We were sitting in the front parlour, a small, cheery little room with chintz-covered chairs and arrangements of dried flowers on the bookshelves and mantle.

"Enemies?" Mrs. Frazier pressed an already crumpled handkerchief to her eyes, and gave me a small, heartbroken smile. "If you had known my son, you would know what a laughable suggestion that is. No, Emmett had no enemies. He had few friends, mind you. He always said that he found numbers far easier to understand than people. And people often found him overly serious, solemn. But I cannot believe that anyone would have hated him enough to … to kill him." Her voice cracked. "He ate, slept, lived, and breathed for his work as a computer at the Observatory. And what is there to murder anyone in that?"

Mrs. Frazier might be surprised. I had observed that one of humanity's more depressing characteristics was our seemingly boundless capacity for finding petty reasons to hate one another. But I could hardly say that to the dead man's grieving mother.

"Had your son been worried in any way lately? Anxious or upset?"

"No, just the opposite." Mrs. Frazier shook her head, shutting her eyes, although a tear still leaked out beneath her lashes. "Emmett had been working very hard of late—staying longer hours at the Observatory, coming and going in the middle of the night. I told him that he would make himself ill if he did not stop to rest and take proper care of himself. But he said that I was not to worry, that he was especially busy just now working on a project of his own—a discovery he had made, that he was in the process of cataloguing and writing down. But he said that it would be finished before much longer, and then he would be ready to amaze the world."

"Amaze the world?"

"Those were his very words." Mrs. Frazier's voice caught, and she shut her eyes again. "Poor Emmett, he sounded so happy—he was always at his happiest when he was immersed in his calculations, and when whatever he was seeking to prove was going well. I suppose I must take some comfort in that."

"And do you know what the amazing discovery he had made was?" I asked.

"I'm afraid not." Mrs. Frazier's smile was brief and sad. "I'm sorry to say that I have no head for mathematics myself or anything along the scientific lines. Emmett tried once or twice to explain his work to me, but the truth is that I did not understand more than the barest fraction of what my son did for a living. He had probably discovered something quite esoteric, like a new way to calculate the light emissions of a star or the distance between Saturn's rings. Not but what those are important discoveries, to those who care about such things," she added quickly. "And my son was beginning to gain attention in scientific circles. He had a publisher—a Mr. Pike, I think Emmett said. A very important businessman who expressed interest in printing his—"

She broke off with a sudden gasp as from the rear of the house came the distinct sound of a crash, as of glass breaking.

I stood up instantly. "Is there anyone else in the house?" I asked in an undertone.

Mrs. Frazier shook her head. "No. Our servants don't live in, they only come to oblige in the mornings, and I sent them home today. I couldn't bear ... that noise came from Emmett's room," she whispered. Her eyes were wide, and her face had gone very white. "He had a room downstairs here, at the back of the house, so as not to wake me when he came in late—"

I was already moving towards the parlour door, though I took the time to look over my shoulder at Becky and say, "Stay here with Mrs. Frazier. Promise me."

Becky's expression was testament to how little she liked the idea, but she gave an unwilling nod.

As silently as I could, I eased the door open and listened. After the first crash, all had gone quiet, and I could hear nothing now. I tiptoed towards the end of the hall, paused to draw the Ladysmith pistol I carried, then flung open the door, taking care to step aside out of the doorway, in case our intruder was also armed.

Nothing happened. No shots fired, no sounds of movement from within. Although when I looked cautiously into what must have been Emmett Frazier's bedroom, I drew in a quick breath.

The place was in shambles—books taken off the shelves, papers scattered on the floor, even the sheets and blankets pulled off the bed. A lamp with a broken chimney had no doubt been the source of the crash we'd all heard.

An open window with mud on the sill showed the path the intruder had taken to escape. I crossed to look out, but there was no sign of anyone—and little hope of catching whoever it had been, although I still debated making the attempt.

"Lucy?" Becky's voice, high and frightened-sounding, came from back in the parlour. If I had to guess, she was standing at the very edge of the doorway, obeying the strict letter of the law, if not the entire spirit.

"It's all right." I couldn't leave Becky here, not when the intruder might circle back while I was out trying to track him or her down. I raised my voice to call back to her. "Whoever broke in has gone, now. Mrs. Frazier, perhaps you could ring the police? Then come here and try to tell us whether anything from your son's room is missing."

Chapter 4: Lucy

"I don't understand." Mrs. Frazier looked with tearful bewilderment at the wreckage in her son's room. "I don't understand at all. Why should anyone break in here? What could they have hoped to find?"

"That is what we must try to uncover," I told her gently. "Can you tell whether the intruder took anything?"

The police had already been summoned, using the telephone which Emmett Frazier had used to communicate with the Observatory. Lestrade or one of his officers would be here shortly. And I had examined the dirty smears on the windowsill, though the marks told me little except that the intruder had recently walked through mud—which accounted for roughly ninety-eight per cent of the population when the winter was beginning to thaw.

There were no distinct foot marks, and since the Fraziers' house was surrounded by neat beds of gravel, no footprints leading away from the window, either.

"I don't know," Mrs. Frazier said. "I don't think anything is missing. But those papers were to do with his work." She gestured to the sheets that were scattered all over the floor. "I wouldn't have the faintest idea whether any of them had been taken or tampered with."

I nodded, picking up one of the papers from the floor. It

was covered with line upon line of mathematical calculations, worked in a slightly cramped but very neat hand.

I wasn't anything close to an expert, but the formulas on the page I was holding seemed to have to do with orbital mechanics.

I turned to survey the rest of the room. There was nothing in particular that caught my eye. Charts marking the movement of the stars and planets on the walls. Shaving brushes and a razor on the wash stand, together with a jar of patent skin cream.

One book with a well-worn cloth cover had escaped being flung on the floor like the others from the bookshelf. It had been left lying open on the night stand.

Becky moved over and picked it up, so that I saw the title on the spine: *The War of the Worlds*.

Another detail with which the press would have a proverbial field day if they were to get hold of it.

"The police will want to see all of this," I told Mrs. Frazier. "But we needn't wait here ourselves, if you'd rather go back to the parlour."

Mrs. Frazier's eyes lingered on the open window.

"Do you think whoever did this will be back?"

"I'm not sure. Someone was clearly looking for something. But they'll have to assume that the police will be on guard against another break-in. Have you anywhere you can go tonight, so that you don't have to stay here alone?"

Mrs. Frazier swallowed and nodded. "Yes, there's my sister. She lives in Chelsea."

"Good. Then after the police have finished, why don't you pack a bag and go to her?"

Meanwhile, I was fairly certain that Lestrade would leave at least one constable on guard here—just in case our intruder did return.

"I will." Mrs. Frazier took one last look at the wreckage, then squared her shoulders. "But you wanted to ask me some more questions about Emmett, didn't you?"

"Only if you feel up to it."

"Yes. I would rather help—I would rather do something—than simply sit idle."

She led the way back to the parlour, and when we were settled once more on the chintz easy chairs, asked simply, "What more can I tell you?"

"What about beginning with Emmett's colleagues at the Observatory?" I asked. "Did he get on well with them?"

If Emmett had made some important discovery, then jealousy—professional, rather than personal—might constitute a motive for wishing him out of the way.

"Yes." The word was slightly drawn out, though, in a way that gave doubt to the assertion.

"Please, Mrs. Frazier, I know how difficult this is, but if you can think of anything, however seemingly trivial, that might explain why someone would wish Emmett harm—"

"I understand." Mrs. Frazier bit her lip. "It's only that it seems so … well, so silly, really. And it happened … oh, it must be four or five years ago, besides. But Emmett and a colleague of his—Clyde Brooks was the young man's name—both admired the same girl. Veronica Cowell." Mrs. Frazier's expression hardened as she said it. "She worked at the Observatory, just as Emmett did, doing calculations. And Emmett and Mr. Brooks used to compete with one another—who would be first to open a door for her, who would be allowed to walk her home from work, that sort of thing."

"You didn't like Veronica?" I asked.

"No. She always seemed to me a hard young woman—all brains, very little heart. But then, perhaps I am being unfair to her, simply because she did not happen to return my son's affections." Mrs. Frazier's eyes filled once again as she shook her head. "Poor Emmett, he wasn't very adept at courting. Although as it happened, Mr. Brooks didn't seem to fare any better. In the end, Veronica threw both of them over and left the Observatory to open a dress shop."

"A dress shop?" It seemed an unexpectedly frivolous choice for a young woman who had worked as a mathematician for the Royal Observatory.

"Yes, one of those fashionable couture places on the Brompton Road, not far from Harrods." Mrs. Frazier sighed. "She came into an inheritance, I believe, and used it as capital to start her business."

As far as motives for Emmett's murder went, I had to agree with Emmett's mother that this one seemed thin. A rather lukewarm romantic rivalry, and four or five years in the past, besides. And yet—

"Mrs. Frazier, I know you said that this business with Veronica ended years ago. But something must have brought it into your mind now?"

"Well, yes." Mrs. Frazier seemed to hesitate, then said, "The fact of the matter is that I hate to tell you, because I'm afraid it may reflect badly on me—that perhaps I may have done Veronica an injustice." She gave another small, sad smile. "But of course, that hardly matters now, does it? Emmett would certainly say that it does not. He had a passion for the truth—the exact truth. It was one of the reasons he liked numbers so much. He used to say that they never lied." She wiped her eyes, then straightened her shoulders. "The truth, then, is that three days ago, Veronica Cowell came here."

"Here to this house?" I was surprised.

"Yes. It was quite early in the morning. Emmett had not even left for work yet; he was still asleep. She came knocking on the door, and when I answered it, she seemed dreadfully upset. Agitated. It was most unlike her. She said that she must speak to Emmett—that it was of the utmost urgency that she talk to him."

"Did she say what it was that she wanted to talk to him about?" I asked.

"Not a word." Mrs. Frazier shook her head. "She was almost … well, incoherent is really the only word for it. I'm afraid I thought that she might have been"—she lowered her voice—"inebriated. You know. Drinking. Really, her manner was so very unlike anything I'd seen from her before."

"And did she speak to Emmett?"

"Not that morning." Mrs. Frazier rubbed at a slight smudge of furniture polish on the arm of her chair. She looked troubled. "I'm afraid that this is the part of the story that does not reflect very well on me. But I … well, I told her a falsehood. I said that Emmett wasn't home, that he had already gone to work at the observatory, and that if she wanted to find him, she would have to go there. It was petty, I know. But I wanted to protect my son." She raised hand in a gesture of appeal. "Emmett seemed to have gotten over his feelings for her. He hadn't so much as mentioned Veronica's name in years. I didn't wish to give her the chance to entrap him again. But now I wish … if something was truly wrong, if something had happened to seriously upset her—I did mention it to Emmett, when we were sitting at dinner together that night, that Veronica had called to see him. My conscience demanded at least that much. But even the mention of her name must have upset him terribly."

"Was he angry?"

"No, no, it was nothing like that—nothing that he said, even. But that very night, I heard him in the hall outside my room. I thought perhaps he had been taken ill, so I got up and went out to see what had brought him upstairs. He was standing at the hallway window. I was frightened, because the window was wide open, and he was leaning so far out that I was afraid he would overbalance and fall. I thought at first he had got out of bed to look at the stars—he did that often, ever since he was a little boy. So I called to him to be careful. And he turned to me and said quite seriously that it was all right, because he had learned how to fly. That was when I knew that he was asleep—dreaming. Fortunately, he allowed me to take him by the hand and lead him back to bed. He remembered nothing at all about it in the morning, though he said that he had been troubled by very strange dreams. But you see, if only hearing Veronica Cowell's name was enough to give him nightmares, I thought that seeing her in person would be bound to be worse still."

"And do you know whether Veronica ever did find Emmett at the Observatory?" I asked.

If her visit here had been three days ago, there ought to have been plenty of time for her to have tracked him down before he died.

"If she did, he never mentioned it to me." Mrs. Frazier pressed the crumpled handkerchief to her cheek. "But then, he mightn't have told me. He knew I didn't approve of her. Oh!" Her eyes widened as though in sudden realisation.

"You've thought of something?"

"Last night. The last time I saw him." Mrs. Frazier's lips trembled. "He said as he left the house that he would be meeting someone. I've just realised that perhaps it was Veronica."

"Did he say where he was going?"

"No. I just assumed that he would return to the Observatory. He seldom went anywhere else. But he didn't actually say that was where he was going."

"Mrs. Frazier, did your son own a telescope?" I asked.

"A telescope? No. He always wanted one of his own—he was saving for it—but he could never afford one, not on the wages that the Observatory paid."

A fresh rush of tears spilled from Mrs. Frazier's eyes, as though she had just realised that her son would never get his telescope.

I was about to end our interview. Later, something else of importance might occur to Emmett's mother, but it seemed cruel to keep pressing her now.

Becky, though, spoke up. "Mrs. Frazier? Did this book belong to your son?"

She held up the copy of *The War of the Worlds*, which I saw she had carried with her from the bedroom.

Mrs. Frazier looked at her blankly a moment, then her face crumpled. "Yes, that was Emmett's. He was almost ... almost obsessed with it, really. Not the black smoke and the Martian beings and their heat guns—he found all of that rather silly. But the idea that there might be other planets with life on them besides ours ... it was part of what drove him onward in his work at the Observatory." She drew a shaky breath and wiped her eyes again. "The thought of what a discovery for humanity it would be if he could find—or even establish contact with a world beyond our own."

Chapter 5: Watson

Morning sunlight filled Harewell's office, streaming through high-arched windows and rebounding off the white-painted walls and high white ceiling. The floor was bare. Six well-varnished work tables with matching high-backed chairs were spread around the large and airy space. Harewell's desk, also varnished wood, was positioned out of the glare at the far side of the room. It faced the wall, as if to indicate his intention to do desk work here rather than to welcome his subordinates.

He turned his chair around to face us, beckoning Holmes, Lestrade, and me to sit. Each of us took one of the high-backed chairs. I found mine uncomfortable enough, and it occurred to me that the design and furnishing of the room, where people likely worked during the night, had been arranged to discourage any employee from falling asleep at his post.

"Now, gentlemen," Harewell said, after ordering a coffee cart to be sent in, "Mr. Holmes has already touched on my added source of anxiety."

Holmes nodded. "Indeed. Exactly six years ago today, an anarchist bomber fatally wounded himself outside the gate to the observatory campus. The anarchist was carrying a bomb, which apparently went off by accident. He was unable to provide any explanation before he died, but police did uncover evidence of his association with an anarchist group in London."

"Had the bomb not detonated outside, the anarchist might have carried it into the observatory and killed many of our employees," Harewell said. "As it was, most were too distraught to continue working."

"Understandably," I said. "And now, you think they will react in the same way?"

"I hope people will not make the connection, since there was no bomb involved today. Indeed, it is crucial that they not do so." Harewell drew a breath. "We are about to dedicate our new observation building with a fund-raising dinner tonight."

"You scheduled the date deliberately?"

"Indeed we did. Every year, we celebrate all the accomplishments that have come after that most disturbing incident. A show of confidence—or bravado, some might say. And I supervise the preparations. Also, today the printer will be delivering the bound copies of our latest almanac. There are a dozen crates coming this afternoon, and I must inspect them."

"Crates of books?" asked Lestrade. There was a note of skepticism in his voice. "You're unloading crates of books?"

"That may sound like a mundane task, but the books are our life blood. Our very reason for existence is to assist navigation, according to our charter."

"Who is the printer?" Holmes asked.

"Lovejoy & Son, in Great St. Thomas Apostle. They have always printed our almanacks. Very regular and reliable. In fact, the books have been crated and ready for nearly a week, but the delivery had to wait until today."

"How many books?"

"Twelve hundred."

"Does Lovejoy & Son manage the delivery?"

"That is done by Pike's Transport. We use them for all our major deliveries. Scientific instruments, telescopes, large items."

"Their rates are particularly attractive?"

Harewell smiled. "They are owned by one of the principal benefactors of the Observatory. As is Lovejoy's. And yes, the relationship is mutually beneficial. They provide most attractive rates for their services."

Holmes gave one of his tight little smiles. "And when the almanacks are delivered by Pike's, you store them here?"

"Yes, in our basement. We ship them from here to the various customers who need to keep their navigational information up to date. I will need to be ready with personally autographed copies for tonight's thirty dinner guests. I need to prepare personalised inscriptions of thanks and hopes for continuing support, if you take my meaning. I hope the volumes will be well received."

Holmes inclined his head. "Lestrade, will you see that this telegram gets delivered immediately?"

He drew a sheet of paper and pencil from his pocket and scribbled down a few words. I saw the name of the public house to which he often directed messages for Flynn, the head boy of his team of Irregulars. He must have some assignment that he wished Flynn to carry out back in London.

Holmes turned back to the Astronomer Royal. "We pass then, from the realm of the practical into the speculative. Can you, Mr. Harewell, think of anyone with a motive for disrupting tonight's fundraiser?"

"No one." Harewell's answer came readily.

"Or anyone with a motive for killing Mr. Frazier?"

Distress puckered the Astronomer Royal's brow. "Again, no one. He had no enemies that I know of, and yet ... I did not know him well, of course. It may be that inquiry into his private life will yield some unknown person with a reason for wishing him ill."

The somewhat cynical thought passed through my mind that it would certainly be the best possible outcome for the observatory if the motive for Frazier's murder were to be found in the young man's private life, rather than in his professional one here.

"Mr. Frazier's work here—it was satisfactory?" Holmes asked.

"Yes. For the most part."

Holmes looked inquiring. "For the most part?"

Harewell shifted in his seat, looking uncomfortable—perhaps at the idea of speaking ill of the dead. "Well, he was a diligent fellow, capable in his work here. Intelligent. But the truth is that of late he had been … distracted is the only word for it. Three of his most recent sets of calculations were found to have errors in them and had to be done again."

"I see. And have you any idea of the source of Mr. Frazier's distraction?"

"None."

"Did he appear unhappy?"

"Not unhappy—excited, more like. I thought perhaps it was a lady—you know what these young fellows are. I told Frazier last week that he had better apply his attention more fully to his work, he promised that he would, and as far as I knew that was the end of it."

"Until today."

Harewell looked regretful. "As you say, until today. I wish of course now that I had questioned him more fully—urged him to confide. But I had no notion that anything was seriously the matter with Frazier, and I have a full load of responsibilities—"

If he was hoping for either sympathy or reassurance from Holmes, he was doomed to disappointment. Holmes stood. "Then we shall trespass no further on your time and leave you to get on with said responsibilities. Thank you for your candour about the flash of green light that you saw. It may provide a valuable clue. We shall not mention it unless it becomes absolutely necessary."

Harewell also stood, his hands clasped to his chest as though in prayer. "Thank you, Mr. Holmes."

Holmes turned to Lestrade. "I would hope you and your men can establish the whereabouts of each person on the staff between the hours of midnight—" he began.

The door to Harewell's office burst open and a young police constable stumbled in, breathless.

Lestrade fixed him with a censorious eye. "What is the meaning of this, Rogers?"

Constable Rogers removed his helmet and stood at attention. "Beg pardon, sir. But we've found something outside when we were making a search."

Holmes was instantly alert. "What have you found?"

The constable's gaze swivelled in Holmes's direction, and he swallowed, visibly shaken. "Well, sir, it's hard to … the fact is, sir, I think you'd best come and see for yourself."

Chapter 6: Lucy

"Are we going to talk to Veronica Cowell next?" Becky asked.

We had waited with Mrs. Frazier until a pair of Lestrade's constables arrived to take charge, and had Mrs. Frazier's assurance that as soon as the police gave her permission to go, she would leave for her sister's home. We were walking away from the Fraziers' house, beneath the tall canopy of evergreens that lined the road on either side. It had felt quiet and pastoral before our visit with Emmett's mother. Now the back of my neck was buzzing with the unpleasant awareness that we were out of sight of the Fraziers' villa, and, save for a pony cart I could see in the far distance, there didn't appear to be another soul about besides ourselves.

I pushed the uneasiness aside before it could infect Becky, though.

"I think we must definitely pay a visit to Veronica. Both to her and the Clyde Brooks whom Mrs. Frazier mentioned. So far, they're the only people we've learned of who might have even a shadow of a motive for wishing Emmett harm."

"It doesn't sound as though Veronica was angry with him, though," Becky said. "Not if she came to see him when she was upset."

"Unless it was something Emmett himself had done that had upset her."

Although at the moment, it was hard to know what that something might have been.

The impression I'd gleaned both from Mrs. Frazier and the dead man's room had been of a quiet young man, deeply private, solemn and shy.

I tried to imagine him ... what? Forcing his unwanted attentions on Veronica after a break of several years?

I shook my head. As Holmes would say, speculating in advance of data was always a waste of time.

"What do you think, Lucy?" Becky asked. "Do you think that there might be alien creatures living on Mars?"

"I don't know." I cast an involuntary look upwards, although what little I could see of the sky was patched with the thick evergreen branches above. "Our own galaxy is vast—so huge that it's difficult to even comprehend. And beyond that, there are more galaxies, and more ... it seems self-important somehow, to think that ours is the only planet that supports life, in all that immense space. But if you're asking whether I think that Emmett Frazier was killed by a race of murderous aliens intent on overthrowing earth, then no. I should say that was unlikely in the extreme."

"I suppose. It is odd, though—the way there were no foot marks around the body or signs that he'd been dragged to where he was found. And you know what Mr. Holmes says about eliminating the impossible, and whatever remains—however improbable—must be the solution."

"Yes. But I don't think we've yet proved that it's exactly impossible for Frazier to have been dropped outside the observatory by something other than an alien spacecraft."

"Well, yes, there is that," Becky admitted. "But it would have been fun to track down an alien creature." She sighed, with clear regret at having to dismiss Martians from our list of possible murder suspects. "It is a splendid story," she added.

Mrs. Frazier had spontaneously offered to gift Becky with Emmett's copy of *The War of the Worlds*, and now she hugged it a little more closely to her chest.

"I read the first few chapters while you were talking to Emmett's mother," she said. "It's very exciting. The Martians arrive in a big cylinder and they have heat-ray guns that can blow up entire towns, and then they assemble their fighting machines—tripods that walk on three legs and that can wipe out an entire army—" She paused for breath. "I do think it was a bit rubbish that as soon as the Martians invade, the narrator takes his wife and just dumps her off someplace where he thinks she'll be safe, though. He ought to have let her stay and fight!" She frowned, looking down at the cover of the book. "Perhaps I'll write to Mr. Wells in care of his publisher sometime and tell him so."

I smiled. I, for one, would pay good money to witness Mr. H. G. Wells' expression on receiving such a letter from Becky.

"Did Emmett Frazier write down any notes in the book?" I asked. "Anything that might give us a clue as to the important project he was working on?"

"I don't think so. Although I only had time to read the beginning part." Becky rifled the pages of the rest of the book. "No, there's nothing—oh, what's this?"

A small sheet of paper had fluttered out and fallen to the ground. Becky picked it up, and I was about to ask to see it when a twig snapped on the path up ahead of us.

I looked up sharply and Becky gasped as two men stepped out from behind a screen of bushes.

They were so identical in appearance that I might almost have been seeing in double. Both were tall, heavily muscled, and both were dressed in suits of plain, unrelieved black, with black bowler hats that shaded their eyes.

Both also held snub-nosed revolvers which were currently aimed directly at us.

Becky gasped and clutched at my hand. I squeezed her fingers once, trying to signal her to stay calm—and quiet.

I looked from one man to the other. "To what do we owe this honour, gentlemen?"

I was mentally rifling through our options as I spoke, and I had to admit that I didn't like any of them. Even if I'd stood a chance against the pair in close hand to hand combat—which I doubted I would—they would never let me get close enough to catch them off guard. I had a gun of my own, true. But my Ladysmith revolver was currently tucked away inside my bag, where it might as well have been on the moon for all the good it would do me.

Both of the men in black looked competent enough with their weapons to shoot me before I could even get the clasp on the handbag open.

The man on the right—who upon further study was distinguishable from his companion by the squareness of his jaw and a few more pounds on his heavyset frame—cleared his throat.

"We don't want any trouble."

I raised an eyebrow. "Do you know, that statement would be far more believable if you would put your weapons away."

The two men ignored that suggestion—not that I had really expected them to take it—and continued to regard me with flat, expressionless gazes.

"We're agents of Her Royal Majesty's government," the heavier man went on.

"You're what?" Becky asked. Either she had misunderstood my request to stay quiet, or more likely was simply ignoring it.

The man gave her a swift, dismissive glance before refocusing on me.

"Acting on Her Majesty's orders, we have some questions for you in regards to the death of Emmett Frazier," he said stolidly. "My name is Agent Wilson, and this is Agent Thompson. If you'd be so good as to come along with us?"

It was actually something of a relief to hear him bring up Emmett Frazier's name. My first thought when the men appeared on the path was that they had something to do with Jack, Scotland Yard, and the investigation into Inspector Glenn's death.

"I'm assuming that is more of an order than a request?" I said.

I was still silently running through possible escape plans—and still not coming up with anything that I could credit with more than about a thirty-five per cent chance of success. Alone, I might have chanced it. With Becky, I needed better odds before I would take the risk.

The two men continued to stare at me with all the expression of twin Easter Island statues.

"Just come along with us," the heavier one—Agent Wilson—repeated.

I fixed a bright smile on my face. "Of course. Well, if you're under orders from Her Majesty's government—"

Then I'm the Queen of England.

"Then that makes all the difference," I finished out loud, still beaming.

The two men exchanged a brief, but telling, glance. I had just thrown off whatever plan they were working from.

They were expecting to need threats and intimidation to get their way. Ready compliance confused them.

They also weren't the ones in charge of this attempted abduction—if that's what it was. If they were independent, they'd be able to pivot more smoothly when the unexpected did occur. Right now, their identical expressions of guarded puzzlement telegraphed an urgent wish that they could speak to whoever had given them their orders.

Not much, maybe, in the way of information, but at the moment I would take any small crumb of intelligence I could get.

"Have you a carriage somewhere nearby, then? But of course, I suppose you must, you wouldn't have come all this way from London on foot." I kept my smile fixed firmly in place and kept speaking quickly and brightly, in the chattering tone of someone whose tongue has been loosened by relief. "That is, I suppose your offices must be in London, in order to be closer to Her Majesty's government? Does the Prime Minister know about your work, or is it too secret even for him to be kept informed?"

The men were still about ten yards away, their weapons not lowered, but not held quite at the ready, either, as they continued to give me looks of confusion.

I spoke under my breath to Becky, too low for the men to hear. "When I give you the signal, I want you to run. Keep off the paths, stay hidden in the trees as much as possible. But run back to the Observatory and find Dr. Watson or Holmes. They should still be there, they were going to wait to return with us to Baker Street."

I felt the ripple of shock run through Becky's small frame. "I can't leave you—"

"Yes, you can. You have to. One of us needs to get help, and there's a better chance that you'll be able to get away."

Becky was better dressed for an escape attempt in a sailor dress and sturdy black boots. My own pale-yellow linen dress and low-heeled white leather shoes were appropriate for making a call on a grieving mother; less so for dashing through a forest and across uneven ground.

And the men were less likely to chase after Becky than me. Especially since I planned to strongly discourage them from trying.

"But they might hurt you—they could even try to kill you!" Becky whispered. She was still clinging tightly to my hand.

I squeezed Becky's hand again and added, under my breath, "If they do, they'll find out quickly that I'm very difficult to kill."

Becky finally gave me the ghost of a smile.

"What's that you're saying?" Agent Wilson asked, his eyes narrowing with suspicion.

I raised my voice. "Nothing, it's just that you're scaring her with the guns. Could you please put them away, there's really no need."

The two men exchanged another look, then Agent Wilson shrugged and lowered his weapon. Agent Thompson followed suit.

"All right," Becky whispered. "Tell me when."

We started forwards. My heart was pounding as I tried to calculate the optimal distance. Not yet … not quite yet …

When we were about ten feet away from the pair of men, I let go of Becky's hand.

"Now!"

Instantly, Becky spun and dashed away, crashing through a patch of green shrubbery at the side of the path.

Stunned, the men gaped at her a moment, then Agent Wilson shouted at his companion, "Don't just stand there, get after the brat!"

Agent Thompson obeyed, breaking into a run. I stepped into his path, tripped him, kicked his leg out from under him while he was off balance, and then aimed another swift kick to the underside of his jaw while he was on the ground.

He managed to roll out of the way, and the blow that should have knocked him unconscious or at least stunned only glanced off his nose and chin.

But with another kick, I at least succeeded in knocking the gun from his hand and sending it flying off into the underbrush.

"Why you—" Agent Wilson seized hold of me from behind.

I pulled my feet up, hitting him with my full weight, and he stumbled. I elbowed him hard in the abdomen, and was rewarded with the sound of a pained grunt. Although his grip on me didn't slacken, and the next moment I felt the barrel of his gun jab my back in between my ribs.

"If you want to live, don't move," he ground out.

"You want me to go after the kid, St—Wilson?" Agent Thompson asked. He hauled himself to his feet and stood, looking significantly less anonymous and intimidating, with his hat knocked off and blood dripping from the end of his nose onto the pristine front of his black suit.

Agent Wilson kept the gun pressed into my rib cage. I didn't bother to fight anymore. There was no chance I could break free, not against two of them, and anyway, that had never been the plan. I'd only meant to delay them enough that Becky could get away.

Heart pounding, I stood straining my ears to listen for any sound that would signal Becky's location.

The forest was silent, though, the only sound the soft rustle of the pine branches in the breeze and the sharp call of a bird from somewhere nearby.

After what seemed an eternity, Agent Wilson said, "Don't bother, she's just a kid. We've got the woman, that's the main thing."

He jerked me round to face him. His heavy-boned features were flushed with anger, and I braced myself for at best a smack across the face with the butt of his gun—at worst, a shot.

He drew in a breath, though, hardening his jaw, and said, "Now, come along quietly, and no one has to get hurt."

Chapter 7: Flynn

Something bad was about to happen, Flynn thought. His run of good luck on this assignment couldn't last.

This was a tailing job, but he wasn't slogging through the crowds on the pavement or dodging cabs and lorries on the street. He was riding *inside* a cab, just like a proper gent. He had a warm coat too, a blue navy pea jacket that fit him, almost, being just a bit too tight under the arms.

Ahead on the right he could see the target, the loading dock at Lovejoy & Son, framed by a grey, weather-worn doorway. The doorway was open. Backing up to the doorway was a big lorry with a painted sign that read "PIKE TRANSPORT."

Twelve crates, Mr. Holmes had said. See all twelve delivered to the observatory safely and with no tampering. Then report.

A bit more than an hour's ride, he reckoned. In a cab.

Entirely too easy a job.

Flynn watched two men from the Pike lorry get down and walk to the loading dock. They walked bent over, as if their backs were sore. Neither of them noticed Flynn in the cab.

Flynn craned his neck through the cab window to see inside the loading dock, but the angle was wrong. So he told the cabby to wait while he hopped out. Now he could see perfectly. The two Pike men were at the edge of the dock, waving some papers and shouting. With the noise of traffic Flynn couldn't make out all the words but he did catch "'op to it, will yer!" and "don't 'ave all day."

Soon two men from inside the Lovejoy loading dock came shuffling out, took a look at the papers, and walked slowly back inside. They, too, walked bent over. Flynn didn't know what he'd be doing for a living when he reached their age, but he hoped he wouldn't be walking like they were.

The Pike men backed up their lorry a few feet from the loading dock. A few minutes later a wheeled cart emerged from the warehouse, piled up with a stack of crates. The two warehouse men pushed it right up to the edge while the Pike men opened the back doors of their lorry. Flynn could see inside the lorry. It looked full, but he guessed there was room at the back for the crates.

The warehouse men helped the Pike men hoist the crates into the lorry, one by one. The crates looked heavy. All four men needed breathing time after manoeuvering each crate onto the back of the lorry. Finally, the twelfth crate had been settled into place. The Pike driver pulled his team forward so his helper could shut the two back doors.

Flynn told the cabbie to follow the Pike lorry and climbed up into his seat, keeping his window open so he could look out. Next stop, he thought, was the Royal Observatory in Greenwich.

CHAPTER 8: WATSON

We quickly went down the steps from Harewell's office to the Observatory exit. Outside, the frightened constable ran ahead of us into the park. "It's just over there, Mr. Holmes," he called, "and it's not like any footprint I've ever seen!"

Holmes followed. His confident, easy stride bespoke an assurance that I did not feel.

I hesitated. Looking across the wide green lawn of the park to the faint line of the buildings of London far away at the edge of the river, I thought how small and insignificant they seemed beneath the vast expanse of cold blue sky overhead.

Unbidden, my memory produced recollections that I had locked away and never wanted to recall again.

Twenty years earlier, I had stared at that same blue sky as I lay wounded and helpless on the dust-ridden Afghan battlefield at Maiwand. I had uttered a cry for help, though it was a silent one. The enemy soldiers were not far, and they were looking for survivors to eliminate. Then my thoughts turned to all my fallen comrades. Were they, too, calling out silently, hoping for divine aid?

Yet the blue sky, far above the soaring, craggy mountains—seemed cold and immobile and silent.

And then aid had come, in the form of Murray, my brave and loyal orderly, without whose assistance I would never have survived.

"Watson!"

Holmes's call shook me from my reverie. He was with the constable a few dozen yards away, in the park, pointing downward at something in the grass. Moments later I was at his side, my memories and musings vanished as though blown away by the cold wind. I had work to do.

"What do you make of it, Watson?"

Holmes gestured at a depression in the turf, perhaps six inches wide and two feet in length, and perhaps two inches deep.

For some reason, an image flashed into my mind. "Road construction," I said. "Workmen tamp down the soil or the gravel. A heavy metal plate and a wooden pole."

"Bravo, my friend. And what if I told you that there are two other similar depressions, each within fifty feet of this one, forming the points of a triangle?"

I recalled the Martian battle vessels imagined by Mr. Wells. "Someone wished to create the illusion that a large object supported by a tripod had landed here and then taken off again."

"The illusion?" Holmes had an amused expression on his hawk-like features. "You do not think these impressions are the remaining traces of a Martian landing?"

I felt my spirits and confidence rising. "I do not. These impressions are too clear. The grass and soil around the edges would have been disturbed, pushed sideways one way or the other had there been a landing and subsequent takeoff. But the edges are straight. And at any rate, the idea that creatures advanced enough to travel the great distance between here and Mars would make such a journey merely to kill a hapless mathematical worker, create a few footprints, and then fly away—well it hardly bears consideration."

"You are in good form today, Watson," Holmes said. "Now, walk with me a few paces."

We walked with the constable until we had come within a few feet of a hedge-row that marked the boundary between the grassy park and a wooded area beyond. Holmes pointed to a circular patch where the grass had been badly scorched. The blades were withered or gone altogether, the soil was black, and there were flecks of grey ash around the rim.

"Intended to create the illusion of a blast from a Martian heat-gun," I said.

"Again, why only an illusion?"

I considered. "It is circular," I said.

"What of that?"

"If it were caused by a gun pointed from high above and a substantial distance away, as it would be if it had been shot from the top of a huge tripod, its shape would have been elliptical."

"Bravo again, Watson!" He crouched down and picked up some of the blackened grass and soil. "Hold out your hand."

I did so, and he dropped a pinch of the black mixture onto my outstretched palm.

"Now, what does your nose tell you?"

I sniffed. "Holmes, the odour of turpentine is unmistakable. More evidence that this was done by human beings."

The constable said, "It's been a relief to hear all this, sir."

"But we must remain vigilant, constable," Holmes said. "Whoever did all this may not be an adept or completely convincing illusionist, but that someone is still a murderer. And more murders may be planned."

"Yes, sir."

"Now, have you anything to report from your observations

earlier today? Any employees taking an unusual interest in the site as they arrived for work?"

"No, sir."

"Anyone suspicious try to come into the Observatory grounds?"

"No, sir."

"Any strangers in the neighbourhood?"

"No, sir."

"Nothing unusual at all?"

"No, sir." The constable folded his arms across his chest. "Unless you call a farmer's cart something unusual?"

Holmes's voice sharpened. "What of the farmer's cart?"

"Oh, nothing in particular. Just that I saw it this morning. When I first came on duty. Just before you and Dr. Watson arrived."

"How did you know it was a farmer's cart?"

"Why, because it had a load of hay piled up in it. I saw that hay, and I said to myself, where's he takin' that, now? Who around here has horses?"

"And did you see where the cart went?"

"I didn't watch long, because you gentlemen came. But it was driving along the road leading into the park. Do you think it's important, sir?"

Holmes did not reply.

At the next moment, Becky emerged breathless from the woods.

"Lucy's been kidnapped!" she cried.

Chapter 9: Flynn

The lorry was turning off the street.

Watching through the window of his cab, Flynn saw the lorry drive into a large warehouse. The name "Pike" was painted on the side wall, in big red letters.

Flynn could see through the open warehouse doors. A smaller lorry was waiting inside. The horse was facing away from them.

The large lorry pulled up alongside the smaller one and stopped.

Beyond, more light filled the space as two doors on the other side came open.

A cold feeling slithered across the back of Flynn's neck. The warehouse doors on Flynn's side were closing.

"Can you drive around the back?" he asked the cabbie.

"There's traffic," came the reply.

Flynn paid the driver and took off running along the side fence of the warehouse. Mr. Holmes had told him to watch the crates. Right now, they were out of his sight. He ran faster. If he could get to the back, where the doors were open, he could see what was happening in there.

He reached the back. The smaller lorry was just coming out, and then turning left. He ran after it. He took a glance at the warehouse. The doors were closing up, with the bigger lorry still inside. He caught up to the smaller lorry and jumped onto the back, clawing with his fingertips and digging the toes of his boots into the space between the bare wood of the tailboard and the undercarriage. Peering through the rear window of the lorry he saw twelve crates neatly stacked inside. Labels on them said 'Royal Observatory.'

Not the luck he was hoping for, he thought, but at least he hadn't lost the crates. Or fallen off.

Chapter 10: Watson

We left the constable to keep watch at the Observatory and followed Becky to the location in the woods where Lucy had ordered her to flee. On the way, Becky told as much as she could recall of the incident: where the mysterious men in black had first shown themselves, what they said, and what they looked like.

Reaching the site, we found more of the rectangular prints, and also another scorch mark, this one on a yew tree. A bird lay dead on the ground, its feathers darkened with burn marks. From there Becky led us to where she and Lucy had parted company. There were footprints—ordinary prints of ordinary boots—in the leafy forest soil, showing where a scuffle had occurred. More footprints led away from the scene, and those, of two men and a woman, judging from the size, led straight to the paved road that ran alongside the park. There, alongside a fallen tree, the footprints ended.

Holmes crouched down for a long moment beside the fallen tree. I could not tell if he was studying the tree or pondering some implication that I myself failed to ascertain. Then he stood up, walked to the pavement, and turned to face us.

"She was placed into a cab here," Holmes said. "I had hoped to use a tracking dog, but that will be of no use to us if she was taken away in a vehicle."

"What happened, Mr. Holmes?" Becky was nearly sobbing.

"Lucy's abduction was not your fault in any way," Holmes replied. "And she has survived similar attempts. Now we must get back to the Observatory."

"Why?" Becky asked.

"We must telephone Jack." Holmes set out walking briskly. We followed, on a pathway that ran along the edge of the woods. I noted that Holmes was no longer watching for footprints or scorch marks on the ground.

A few minutes later we could see the Observatory. And the entry drive, where the body of the unfortunate Mr. Frazier had been found. And a small lorry, with the name 'Pike' emblazoned in red letters along its side, being slowly and laboriously drawn up the hill by a single horse. It passed us, heading for the entry gate.

And we could see that Flynn was clinging to the back of the lorry.

We went inside the Observatory to telephone Jack and wait for Flynn.

Chapter 11: Flynn

"Jack is away at a crime scene," Mr. Holmes said, emerging from the Observatory entrance. "He cannot be reached."

They were outside, because Mr. Holmes had wanted to keep their conversations out of the hearing of Observatory employees.

Flynn had already told Mr. Holmes what he'd seen at Lovejoy & Son, at the Pike warehouse, and during the ride from there to the Observatory. Mr. Holmes had nodded and said the information would be useful, and then gone into the Observatory to telephone Scotland Yard.

The wind off the river was cutting right through Flynn's navy pea-coat jacket. He wanted to do something. Get moving again. Anything but this standing around.

"Will Jack telephone here when he reports in?" Becky asked.

"I gave instructions for him to do that," Mr. Holmes said.

"What are we going to do now?" Becky looked as if she were about to cry. Flynn felt sorry for her. He felt worried about Lucy too, but he knew she'd been in dangerous situations before and managed to come out all right.

"Watson and I must remain here," Mr. Holmes said. "The almanacks have come in, and today is the important fundraising dinner event for the Observatory. I feel certain there is a connection with the death of Mr. Frazier last night."

"Do Flynn and I have to stay?"

"Where would you go?"

Becky took a deep breath and kept her eyes away from Flynn, and Flynn was sure he wasn't going to like whatever idea she'd come up with. But it had to be better than standing here freezing.

"To a dress-maker's shop." Becky said.

"Wot?" Flynn asked.

"It makes sense," Becky said. "Just let me explain. Mr. Holmes, I didn't have time to tell you about Mr. Frazier's mother. Lucy and I interviewed her this morning. She told us Mr. Frazier was sweet on a woman named Veronica who used to work with him here at the Observatory four years ago."

"And now she works at a dress-maker's shop?"

"Actually, Mrs. Frazier says Veronica owns the shop. Anyway, she came to visit Mr. Frazier a few days ago, but he wasn't home, and his mother thinks he may have been going to see her when he went out last night."

"So you think this Veronica may have information of value," Holmes said. "Do you have a plan for inducing her to tell you the truth?"

"I do," Becky said. With the I'm-sure-I'll-figure-something-out look in her eye that told Flynn she didn't. Then she added, "I'll need Flynn."

"Be careful," Mr. Holmes said.

Fine, Flynn thought. At least he would have something to do.

His eyes turned away, to the small lorry, which was coming towards them as it left the entrance. The horse was stepping more lively, now that the cargo of crates had been unloaded.

"Pike!" Becky almost screamed the word, pointing at the sign.

Mr. Holmes said, "Yes, Becky?"

Becky blushed. "I'm sorry. It's just—well, it may not be important, maybe it's just a coincidence—"
"Please tell us. But a bit more quietly."
"Mr. Frazier's mother. She said Mr. Frazier hoped a Mr. Pike would publish something he'd written."
Mr. Holmes was silent for a moment, and then he nodded, as if this all made sense to him. "Find out what you can," he said, "and report back here before the fundraising dinner begins at seven."

Chapter 12: Lucy

It was seldom that the words "pleasant surprise" and "abduction" occurred to me within the same sentence. But I had to admit that in this instance, the disagreeable experience for which I'd been bracing myself hadn't materialised.

True, Agent Wilson and the other man had tied my hands together, and true, I had been summarily bundled into a carriage whose doors were locked and whose windows were all painted black on the outside, so that I couldn't catch even a glimpse of where we were going. And the first thing they had done had been to take away my handbag, where my revolver was kept, which meant I was unarmed.

But my wrists had been tied in front of me, which was far more comfortable than behind, and I'd been alone inside the carriage. Agent Wilson and his companion had ridden on the driver's seat outside.

The ride had even been comparatively smooth, over what felt like well-paved roads, to judge by the lack of jolts and bumps. The drive had lasted for roughly half an hour, and then the carriage had drawn to a halt.

I'd half-formed plans of fighting when the men came to take me out. My hands were bound, but they'd left my feet untied. When the door opened and Agent Wilson appeared, though, his companion had stood a few feet behind him, with a gun trained steadily on me and a caution "not to try anything foolish."

Unexpectedly considerate these men might be, but they weren't stupid.

So I'd allowed Agent Wilson to pull me—still with an unexpected lack of brutality—out. I'd caught just a brief glimpse of an anonymous-looking brick building, of the sort common in London's warehouse district, before I was hurried in through a small side door, which led into a small, sparsely furnished office that probably belonged to the warehouse manager.

Now I was seated on a hard, wooden chair in the centre of the room. The second man stood guarding the doorway, still with the gun in his hand. But from a practical standpoint, the worst I had to complain of was the bright lamplight that was shining directly into my face and making it difficult for me to study the two men.

Agent Wilson, who seemed to be the designated spokesman, asked, "What do you know about the death of Emmett Frazier?"

"Less than you do, I would imagine. And you still haven't explained what possible interest our government could have in his murder."

Agent Wilson looked wooden. "Mr. Frazier was an employee of Her Majesty."

"I find it difficult to believe that a junior computer at the Royal Observatory warrants so much personal attention."

Agent Wilson and the other man exchanged a brief glance, and then Agent Wilson cleared his throat. "You're not a fool. I can see that. So I'll speak plainly. We—Thompson and myself—are agents of a government department that not many are familiar with. Not many people even know that our department exists. But we're tasked with investigating occurrences that are … strange. Otherworldly, so to speak." He spoke with slow emphasis on the words.

"Our government has a department dedicated to investigating the supernatural?"

"Is that so hard to believe?"

It actually wasn't entirely past the realm of belief. Thanks to Mycroft, I had some inside knowledge of the confusing, competing, and often contradictory departments that made up the government—from the War Office to the Foreign Office to the Ministry of Finance.

What I did doubt, however, was that these two men had ever been on the receiving end of a government pay stub in their lives. Although that didn't bring me any nearer to deciding who or what they were.

"You think there was something paranormal about the way that Emmett Frazier died, then?" I asked.

I raised my joined hands to shield my eyes, trying to see them better. Whoever they might be, government agents or otherwise, they weren't common London street toughs. For one thing, Agent Wilson, despite all his muscular bulk, spoke with the accent of an educated man. And for another, their clothes were much too high quality to belong to street thugs.

Although the dark suits didn't appear to have been made to fit either of them. Agent Wilson's jacket was too narrow in the shoulders, and the second man—Thompson's—sleeves were at least a quarter of an inch too short. There was a slight chalk mark—the kind that a tailor would make—on the cuff of his trouser leg, too, as though the trousers had been hurriedly hemmed, but whoever had done the alterations hadn't had enough time or material to let down the sleeves.

"Let me ask you this," Agent Wilson said. "What do you think the outcome would be if people learned that we're not alone in this galaxy of ours? If the average man on the street suddenly found out that the man whose death he read about in last week's newspaper wasn't killed by anything human, but by a visitor from another planet?"

I had to stop myself from staring at him blankly. If it hadn't been for the gun Thompson carried, this entire conversation would have felt as though we had just entered the realm of farce. A part of me still half expected Agent Wilson to burst into laughter and shout, "Joking! Only joking!"

He remained silent, though, staring at me with the same wooden expression.

"Well—"

"I'll tell you what would happen!" he interrupted. He struck one fist against the open palm of his hand. "There'd be a mass panic. Hysteria—rioting in the streets—looting—the end of law and order as we know it. For their own protection, we can't allow the population at large to learn the truth about what's out there beyond the stars. So, I ask you again: what did you learn about the death of Mr. Frazier this afternoon?"

I could refuse to talk, but that wouldn't gain me anything—and keeping Agent Wilson talking might lead him to reveal more information.

"I learned very little," I said slowly. The best lies included at least a portion of the truth—and in this case, that portion of truth was larger than usual; I honestly had found out almost nothing of real value from my conversation with Emmett's mother. Or I'd thought that I hadn't. In light of Agent Wilson's interest, it might be time to re-evaluate everything that Mrs. Frazier had told me. "His mother was quite bewildered by her son's murder. According to her, Emmett had no real enemies. Only a rather lukewarm romantic rivalry with another computer at the Observatory."

"Hmmph." Agent Wilson made a dismissive sound and jerked one shoulder. "We're not interested in Emmett's personal life."

"But surely," I said, "Emmett's personal life must have had some bearing at least on his death? If alien beings from another planet did conspire in his death, you don't believe that was at random, do you?"

As best I could, I watched Agent Wilson and Agent Thompson's faces. Agent Wilson's features were still rendered nearly invisible to me by the bright lamplight directly behind him. But Agent Thompson was standing at the door, a little off to one side, and his expression was easier to make out.

His nose was still swollen from the blow I'd given him, although he'd wiped the blood away at some point on our journey here. And as I spoke, I thought something shifted in his gaze, an indefinable look of—what? Satisfaction? Anger? sliding across his face.

"We're not at liberty to divulge any information about the presence of alien life forms on earth," Agent Wilson said.

"Of course not. But if he died simply because these Martian creatures want to take over our earth, they would hardly have confined themselves to killing just one man. So they must have had some reason for killing Emmett Frazier specifically. Maybe something to do with his work at the Observatory?"

"Did you find anything at Frazier's house to do with his Observatory work?" Agent Wilson asked.

Agent Thompson shifted his weight.

It was uneasiness, I realised with a jolt of shock. He was masking it fairly well, but something about this conversation was making him profoundly uneasy.

What, though?

Not our respective positions. With my hands bound together—and with him holding a weapon—there was practically no scenario in which I posed any kind of credible threat to him or Agent Wilson.

And yet still, Agent Thompson's shoulders were rigid, and his fingers kept tensing, as though he were fighting the urge to clasp and unclasp them, or fidget with the gun he was holding.

"I didn't really look through Mr. Frazier's work things," I said. "There were some star charts on the walls and some papers with mathematical calculations on them."

Agent Wilson was silent. I thought he seemed somewhat stymied, as though once again he was wishing he could consult a higher authority on how exactly to proceed. But he rallied and asked, "You saw nothing out of the ordinary about Frazier's place of residence?"

"Well—" a thought had occurred to me, a possibility about Agent Thompson and Agent Wilson. Although even if my guess were true, it really only opened up more questions about why I was here and what purpose lay behind their interest in Frazier's murder. "I didn't see anything at all to suggest the supernatural, if that's what you mean. Poor Mr. Frazier." I shook my head sadly. "We can only hope that after life's fitful fever he sleeps well. That's a quotation, of course," I added. "From the Scottish Play."

Agent Wilson grunted, then fixed me with a penetrating stare. "I don't believe you. I don't believe you've told us all you know."

I raised my shoulders, trying to ignore the electric charge

of confirmation that was buzzing through me. Wilson and Thompson might not be who they claimed, but I still had no idea how they had come to be involved in any of this or what their real motivation was. And they were still a potential threat. I didn't need either of them to realise that Agent Wilson had just given away more than he ought.

"I'm sorry." I widened my eyes and gave him my most sincere look. "But I really have told you everything that I can remember."

For answer, Agent Wilson only grunted again, then turned, abruptly dousing the lamp light, and plunging the room into near darkness.

He jerked his head at Agent Thompson, who—still keeping the gun trained on me—opened the door and slowly backed through it. Wilson followed.

"We'll be back," he said. "Maybe a few days alone in here will help to jog your memory."

Chapter 13: Becky

Flynn's brow furrowed as he eyed the storefront of Veronica Cowell's dressmaking shop in the Brompton Road. "You want to go in there?"

If Becky hadn't been so worried about Lucy, she might have smiled, because she'd heard him sound less horrified about stepping into a public house filled with murderers and thieves. But she *was* worried about Lucy. It felt like a stomach ache, except that it covered her entire body.

She kept feeling as though she should have done something else, found a way to stop those men from taking Lucy. Or at least stayed with her, even if running away was what Lucy herself had ordered her to do.

Crying only got you red eyes and a swollen nose, though. Becky had heard Flynn say that, and it was true. Right now, they had a job, which was to get Veronica Cowell to talk to them.

She'd told Mr. Holmes that she had a plan, and she hadn't exactly lied. She did have a plan—she just hadn't thought of it yet.

She studied the front of the shop, too, trying to think.

She couldn't really blame Flynn for wanting nothing to do with the place. The entire shop looked as though someone had set off a bomb—only instead of gunpowder, they'd used lace, ribbons, and pink and gold paint.

The front door was pink, with *Cowell's* painted in fancy gold script over the transom. The shop window was filled with spools and spools of frothy lace, white kid gloves, buttons, and all sorts of ribbons.

There was a dressmaker's model, too, showing off an evening gown—a *pink* evening gown—that had so many tiny crystals sewn into the bodice that it twinkled in the sunlight and would probably be so stiff to put on that it would feel like wearing wooden boards. Not that the ladies who wore that sort of thing seemed to care much about being comfortable. Or being able to move, for that matter. Whoever bought the pink gown wouldn't be able to walk more than about three steps without tripping over all the extra material in the train.

Through the window, Becky could see a superior-looking shop girl standing at a counter and talking to a large woman wearing a fur coat that had probably cost enough to feed an entire family in East End London for a year. She was carrying a pug dog that had on a diamond collar.

Becky blew out a breath. At this point, she was just stalling. "We'd better go in."

Flynn gave her a disbelieving look. "And you're going to stop them from throwing us straight back out again how?"

"It will be all right." Becky tried to sound more confident than she felt, but she wasn't sure she succeeded. This might help find Lucy, though, and that meant she was willing to lie down on the shop floor and refuse to move, if that was what it took to get Veronica Cowell to speak with them. "Just let me do the talking."

Flynn was still eying all the lace and satin in the window as though they were a nest of poisonous snakes. "No worries there."

Becky's heart was beating hard as she pushed open the door to the shop. She was dressed nicely enough. Not in her best clothes, but at least her sailor dress and patent leather boots weren't too dirty from running through the woods in Greenwich. And Flynn was cleaner than usual, even if that wasn't saying much.

The shop girl still gave a sniff and a disapproving look as they came in. She had blond hair and a narrow, pinched-up looking kind of face, her lips pursed as if she'd just tasted something nasty.

Becky would have bet an entire gold sovereign that she was on the verge of telling them to get out, but she didn't get the chance.

Becky gave both the shop girl and the large woman her sweetest smile and said, before either of them could speak a word, "Hello. Oh, I do hope that you can help us! We're here to buy an engagement gift for my sister."

Becky used her most posh accent, and she spoke quickly, because Lucy had once told her that people couldn't tell you were lying as easily if you sounded excited and out of breath.

"Our sister was at school with Miss Cowell, she's often talked about what good friends they were! And we've been saving all of our pocket money, and we thought wouldn't it be a perfect gift if we could find something from Miss Cowell's shop to give her as a present, now that she and the Duke are going to get married at last!"

If the shop girl or the customer asked her which Duke her make-believe sister was going to marry, Becky would be in trouble, because she didn't know the names of any real Dukes of marrying age.

But the woman actually smiled at them, and said, "How sweet."

"Thank you," Becky told her. "Is that your dog? He's beautiful!"

The dog poked his tongue out and panted as Becky scratched his head.

"Do you think we could talk to Miss Cowell?" Becky asked the shop girl. "So that she could suggest a present our sister might like?"

"Well." The shop girl sniffed and look disapproving again. "Really, I was just helping Madame with her order—"

"Oh, it's quite all right." The woman smiled again. "Go ahead and take them to Miss Cowell. It will give me a chance to look over some of these new laces from Brussels you've just unpacked."

Becky should have felt triumphant as the shop assistant led the way through the store—which was just as pink and gold and crowded as the window—and towards a door at the back. But her heart was beating in her throat and her stomach was in knots.

"Wait here," the assistant told them.

She tapped on the door and went in. Becky heard a murmur of voices, and then the shop girl came out again.

"You can go in now, Miss Cowell says that she'll see you."

Her tone of voice said that she would have been much happier if Miss Cowell had told her to shove them in the nearest gutter. But she stepped aside, and Becky walked into the office with Flynn following.

The room they stepped into was so different from the rest of the shop that it was almost like getting slapped in the face.

Surprisingly, the air smelled strongly of perfume: something with lavender and other flowers. But there was no pink, no gold, no frills or ribbons or anything fancy at all. Instead, it was all completely plain. Severe, even. Dark blue walls, dark wooden furniture all made with straight, simple lines. A plain wooden desk, with a young woman who must be Miss Veronica Cowell sitting behind it and frowning at them through a pair of gold-rimmed spectacles.

Miss Cowell had red hair that reminded Becky of a ginger cat, and she wore it piled on top of her head in the style of one of the Gibson girl magazine pictures. She looked a little bit like a cat, Becky thought, with a sharp, intelligent sort of face and green eyes.

Right now, she was looking from Flynn to Becky, her brow creased in puzzlement.

"You said that I went to school with your older sister?"

Becky's heart was pounding harder than ever, but she tried to stand up straight and meet Miss Cowell's gaze.

"I lied," she said. "We really just wanted to talk to you."

Miss Cowell's brows edged upwards. "I see. And what—"

Becky didn't give her the chance to finish. "All we're asking is that you listen to me for half of a minute. Then if you want to tell us to leave, we will."

Miss Cowell's eyebrows climbed still higher, but she put her head on one side, studying them, then seemed to come to a decision. "Very well. I must admit that this is far more intriguing than selling over-priced fripperies to a lot of over-indulged women. You have my attention for the next thirty seconds. Begin."

Becky took a breath. "Emmett Frazier is dead," she began.

She watched Veronica closely as she said it. Miss Cowell's eyes widened, her breath hitched, and the colour started to leach out of her face. "Emmett is dead? Was he … Was he taken ill?"

"No." Becky didn't know how to soften the news, so she just said it. "He was murdered. Someone killed him last night, while he was looking through a telescope outside the Observatory."

She didn't think Miss Cowell was quite ready to hear all of

the details about the green flash of light and the queer marks in the ground.

"But that's ... I didn't ..." Miss Cowell half rose from her chair. "I must—"

"Wait. Please," Becky added. "I still have another twenty-three seconds. Waiting that long surely can't make any difference."

Veronica must be a very self-controlled sort of person, Becky thought. Unless she was a very, very good actress—as good as Lucy—she was truly shocked to hear about Mr. Frazier's death. But she took a deep breath, shut her eyes for a second, then sat back down in her chair again.

"Very well."

"Thank you," Becky said. Even though it wasted another second or two of her allotted time. "Mr. Sherlock Holmes is investigating Mr. Frazier's murder. Probably the police will come to see you eventually, because you knew Mr. Frazier. But Mr. Holmes sent us to you now, because his daughter Lucy—she's married to my brother—has been kidnapped. And we're hoping that you might know something that will help us find her."

If Miss Cowell's eyebrows climbed up any higher, they would disappear into her hairline. "Sherlock Holmes sends children to do his investigating for him?"

Her face was still pale, but it looked harder somehow now, her jaw set and her lips pressed together. For a second, Becky thought that she was angry. But no, that wasn't it after all. She was trying hard to hide it, but Veronica Cowell wasn't angry, she was scared.

"Yes." She stood up straighter. "He does." Sometimes, she amended inside her own head. "He trusts us, even though most people don't think we could really find out anything or do anything useful, just because we aren't adults." She met Miss Cowell's gaze and added, "I wouldn't think that's so very different from being a woman computer at the Royal Observatory."

Veronica Cowell studied her another long moment, then suddenly smiled just a little. She looked a good deal nicer when she smiled—younger and not so hard. "You have that right, at any rate. They got rid of all female computers a few years ago—even though we were fully as competent as the men! But no, they thought only men could possibly understand the job, and they made us feel inadequate at every opportunity."

"Is that why …" Becky nodded towards the front of the shop, thinking of all the pink frilliness.

Veronica tilted her head. "That's rather insightful of you. And I suppose you're right. I decided that since all society seemed to expect me to understand was lace and ribbons and the latest fashions, I might as well do a thorough job of it." Her lips quirked again. "The irony, of course, is that I've been far more successful and made far more money with this shop than I ever did or would have at the Observatory."

She seemed to hesitate, then said, "You can both sit down."

"Thank you." Becky took one of the chairs in front of Miss Cowell's desk, and Flynn took the other. Becky saw him grimace; the lavender and flowers smell was stronger the closer you got to Miss Cowell.

Veronica looked at him with a glimmer of amusement. "I don't think your friend cares for the new line of hand lotions and face creams I'm supposed to be trying out." She indicated an array of bottles that sat on the edge of her desk. "To be honest, I don't much like it, either. These cosmetic companies are always sending me jars of beauty creams that they're hoping I'll sell to gullible older women as the fountain of youth. Usually they don't smell quite so overpowering, though." In a single brisk motion, she swept the jars and bottles into a top drawer of the desk and closed it with a thump. "There, that's better. Now. You said that your sister-in-law has been kidnapped?"

"Yes." Becky pressed her hands together, trying not to let the lump of cold fear inside her make her voice tremble. Lucy was smart and brave and strong. She would find a way to get free of the men who'd taken her. Or survive until Mr. Holmes could find her. "We had just spoken to Mr. Frazier's mother, and then two men appeared and said that they were government agents and that Lucy had to come with them. They had guns," she added.

Miss Cowell didn't move, and her expression didn't change, exactly. But her face still looked different somehow. Tighter and more drawn. She looked down at the papers on her desk, then finally said, "I'd like to help. Really, I would. But I don't see how I can."

She was still scared, Becky thought. Her own conscience was telling her she had to talk to them, which was lucky. But she was also frightened enough that she was hoping to end their conversation as fast as she possibly could without feeling guilty about it.

Which meant that Becky had to think very carefully about what she said next.

She hadn't missed the slight start Miss Cowell had given at the mention of Mrs. Frazier's name. But asking her about why she'd gone to see Frazier's mother? Becky didn't think that was a good idea.

She had been reading a book that Dr. Watson had leant to

her about surgery, and how careful a surgeon had to be not to accidentally cut a nerve or nick an artery. This conversation felt a bit like that: she needed to keep from saying the wrong thing, something that would lead Miss Cowell to stop talking altogether.

"You could tell us about Emmett Frazier," she suggested. "Did you meet him when you worked at the Observatory?"

Becky held her breath, waiting to see Miss Cowell's response. To her relief, Veronica's shoulders relaxed a fraction.

"Yes, poor Emmett. He has a brilliant mathematical mind. Had, rather." Her face clouded. "He could have been a professor or a true mathematician. He deserved better, anyway, than to be one of the Observatory's minions."

"You didn't like working at the Observatory?" Becky asked.

Veronica shrugged. "The work was all right. I like numbers—that's why my business here is a success. Account books and ledgers have always made sense to me. No, it was the … the atmosphere of the place I objected to. The elitism, the intellectual snobbery. They put out a useful enough almanac star guide, but now they go on, finding more and more stars with bigger and bigger telescopes, in the name of science. And what does it really matter, in the end? It's just more jobs and glory for them all, and a lot of useless work."

Becky thought that finding new stars—stars that might have planets circling around them, like earth's own sun—sounded interesting. But she wasn't going to say that out loud, either.

"Was Emmett working on any particular projects?"

"Well, I suppose there was his Mars obsession. Mars is the nearest planet to ours, you know—which he thought meant that travel there ought to be possible one day in the future. He was obsessed with learning everything about it that he could, in anticipation of that great day." Veronica gave a short half-laugh, then suddenly stopped. Something hard and guarded came down across her face, as though she'd just thought of something. Something unpleasant, because her lips pressed together tightly.

"I don't think—" she started to say.

Becky rushed to interrupt her, grabbing for a topic that would put them back on safer ground.

"Wasn't there a man called Brooks who worked at the Observatory, too?"

"Yes, that's right. Clyde." Veronica sounded calmer. "He sometimes hangs about here, hoping that I'll take an interest in him." Her lips quirked in a cynical half-smile. "It's funny how a woman who has money attracts men who don't."

"Did Mr. Brooks ever quarrel with Emmett?" Becky asked.

"Not over me, if that's what you're asking." Veronica looked mildly amused. "Not seriously, that is. They had a bit of a rivalry at one time—years ago. But as I said, I'm fairly sure that my chief attraction in Clyde's eyes is the fact that my business is earning me a good living. He wouldn't—" she stopped, the smile fading, leaving her tense and frightened-looking once more. "He wouldn't be at all the type to have murdered his romantic rival for the sake of love. And poor Emmett wasn't even that—a serious rival, I mean."

Becky drew in a breath. She'd been careful up until now, but there came a point where you couldn't talk in circles around the real question anymore.

"Miss Cowell," she began. "Why did you go to see Mr. Frazier a few days ago?"

Miss Cowell looked away. To the left, Becky noticed. That was the direction—according to Mr. Holmes—that people looked in when they were about to tell a lie.

"I don't think—that is, it wasn't anything important …" She began.

"His mother said that you'd come to their house, very upset, and wanting to talk to him," Becky said. "That doesn't sound as though it was nothing important."

Veronica's mouth opened and closed again. "I—"

Before she could finish, the telephone that was installed on the wall behind her desk suddenly rang. She jumped at the sound, then rose to answer it.

"Yes?"

Becky looked at Flynn, who grimaced and muttered, "Bad luck," under his breath.

It felt like worse than bad luck to Becky—it was as if the universe was conspiring against them.

She was at least sitting close enough that she could just make out the voice on the other end of the telephone line. The words were a little garbled, but she thought it said something about printing. Printing, and Miss Cowell needing to send a payment so that the handbills could be delivered.

"Yes, of course." Veronica pushed a hand distractedly through her hair, disarranging some of the perfect loops and waves. "I'll come over this afternoon, will that do?"

She hung up the speaking piece, turning back to Becky and Flynn. Becky's heart sank, even before she opened her mouth. Miss Cowell looked a bit pale, but brisk and capable and in command of herself once more.

"I'm afraid—" she began.

"Please," Becky interrupted. "Please tell us why you went to see Mr. Frazier? You liked him, didn't you—or at least you felt sorry for him. You surely don't want to see his murderer go unpunished?" She sat up straighter, feeling as though something had just snapped inside of her. "You still need to tell us the truth, because I need to find Lucy!"

For a moment, Miss Cowell just stared at them, her mouth dropped slightly open. Becky waited for her to throw them out of her office and out of the shop.

But instead she looked down at the desk again, and she appeared flushed, self-conscious and … embarrassed, Becky realised. She'd gone from scared to looking ashamed of herself.

"I'm sorry," Veronica muttered. "It's just that what happened … it's so unbelievable. Ridiculous, even, or I thought it was. After the first shock—after I tried to see Emmett—I just wanted to forget that it had ever happened. But now Emmett is dead, and I don't know what to think—"

She broke off, drawing in a steadying breath and looking as though she were trying to compose herself. "I'm sorry. I'm not making much sense, am I? But I will tell you exactly what occurred, and you can make of it whatever you want to." She seemed to think for a moment, then began again. "It was three—no, four days ago, now. A Sunday afternoon. The shop was closed, so I was here alone, in my office. I was sitting here, right at this desk, drinking a cup of tea and going over my account books. And then … then I wasn't anymore."

The words were so abrupt that Becky blinked. "What do you mean?"

"Just what I say. One moment I was sitting at my desk. And the next—" Veronica dropped her head into her hands, pressing her fingers into her temples. "This is the absurd, the unbelievable part. But I did promise that I would tell you the truth. The next moment, or so it seemed to me, I was … I can't remember all the details, just impressions, but it felt … it felt as though I were flying. Swooping, soaring through vast, empty space."

All the fine hairs on Becky's neck stood up. Flynn, who'd actually listened to her when she'd said to let her do the talking and had kept quiet until now, said, "Flying?"

Veronica looked at him with a brief ghost of her earlier smile. "So you can talk after all. I was beginning to wonder. Yes. Flying. It sounds insane, does it not? I would think that I was going quite mad—and maybe that is indeed the solution, except—"

"Except?" Becky prompted.

Veronica bit her lip. "Except that the next thing I remember—remember clearly, that is—is waking up in an empty, run-down warehouse, down by the docks. I thought at first that perhaps I'd had some sort of … of seizure, or brain-storm. Such things can happen, or so doctors say. But I hadn't walked there. It was raining hard that day, and I'd put on my galoshes to come here to the shop, then taken them off and put on shoes when I came inside. And when I awakened in the warehouse—" she took a breath. "When I was trying to determine what could have happened and how I'd come to be there, I looked down at my feet. My shoes were quite, quite clean. Not wet, not even damp, not a trace of mud on them. And my clothes weren't a bit wet, either."

The back of Becky's neck prickled again. If that was true, it meant that Veronica hadn't worn her shoes to walk to the docks. Anyone who had spent more than five minutes in London knew that you couldn't walk anywhere without getting your feet dirty, not even on a dry day, much less when it was pouring rain.

She stared at Veronica, trying to decide whether she was telling the truth or just spinning them a tale because they were children. But Veronica's cheeks were still a bit red, and she was looking at Becky with an odd mixture of embarrassment and defiance—as though just waiting for Becky to say that she was crazy.

Becky didn't think she was making up lies, as unbelievable as all of this sounded.

"Do you remember the address of the warehouse you woke up in?" she asked.

"Not the exact address, no. As soon as I came fully to my senses, all I wanted was to get away as fast as possible." Veronica shivered at the memory. "But I know … that is, I think it was on Cutler Street. That is the first street sign I remember seeing clearly as I ran away."

Becky pictured Veronica waking up, dazed and disoriented in the dark, with odd memories of flying, and then stumbling out into the street in a panic and running away. She supposed she couldn't blame her for not taking careful notes, but at the same time, just the name Cutler Street didn't help very much.

Mr. Holmes was having her study maps of London as part of her education, and she thought she remembered reading that the Cutler Street warehouses covered somewhere around 4 acres of ground.

"What was the warehouse like?" Flynn asked.

Veronica looked confused. "What do you mean?"

"I mean, did you smell anything? Tea or spices or anything like that? Or see anything? Bits of wool, pieces of cork, that sort of thing?"

Becky gave him a grateful nod. That was a good thought. If they could narrow down what sort of cargo shipments had been stored in the warehouse, they'd be at least that much closer to identifying it.

"I don't know, I wasn't really noticing …" Veronica screwed up her eyes, trying to remember, then abruptly opened them again. "Yes! There was one thing. The floor was sticky."

"Sticky?" Becky frowned.

"Yes. As though it had been covered with a layer of fresh tar. My feet stuck when I tried to walk. That tells you something?" she asked.

Flynn was nodding and looking triumphant. "Sugar. It leaks out of the casks they ship it in and gets on the floor."

Becky felt excitement race through her like one of the electrical currents Mr. Holmes had showed her in his laboratory. She might have studied the London Docks on maps—but Flynn would know all the empty and abandoned ones personally. He'd probably slept in half of them. It wasn't anything definite, but at least it gave them a place to start.

One last question was nagging at her, though.

"Miss Cowell," she began. "Thank you for telling us all of this. But there's one thing I don't understand. Why would you go to Mr. Frazier? His mother said that the two of you hadn't spoken in quite some time."

"I—" The flush of colour on Veronica's cheeks deepened again. "I suppose I lost my head. I couldn't explain what had happened to me—I still can't. But Emmett was always going on about that novel. Martian invaders and ray guns and …" She blew out a breath. "I don't remember anything clearly in between being here at my desk and waking up in the warehouse. As I told you, just a jumbled sense of flying—soaring in empty space. But the one other memory I do have … well." She stopped, and her mouth twisted in a wry quirk of a smile. "I don't know why

I'm having so much difficulty in coming to the point, when I've already risked sounding insane by telling you the rest of the story. But the fact is that the one other thing I do remember quite clearly is seeing a bright, blinding flash of green light."

Chapter 14: Watson

On the roof of the Observatory, I could feel the cold wind cutting through my coat. Forty feet below us at the gateway, the uniformed constable stamped his feet and swung his arms, hugging himself; he also obviously felt the chill. Holmes gave no signs of discomfort. He and I crept carefully sideways, close to the rooftop edge. We had a grand view, a wide panorama extending from the green lawn of the park down to the river and to the buildings of London beyond, and then to the blue sky, dotted with a few white clouds. But it did not do to dwell upon the scenery. The wind came in gusts, and I knew one of those, if we were caught off balance, could send us to a swift fall down to the hard pavement.

We both leaned into the outer wall of the dome, resisting the efforts of the wind to dislodge us as we made our way around its circumference. Our goal was a point directly across from the window of Harewell's office.

Finally, Holmes stopped. "There," he said. "Harewell was standing at that window."

I saw the tall window across from me. "When he saw the flash of green light?" I asked.

Holmes did not reply, for he crouched down, inching sideways and twisting his body so that he could make a close observation without endangering himself to a fatal fall.

Then I saw a coach and four pulling up to the entrance gate. The coach was turned sideways from me, and I could see a worn red painted crest with a faded white letter 'P' emblazoned on the door.

Holmes was examining the masonry around the edge of the roof, using his pocket knife to scrape something off the surface.

"A coach is coming, Holmes," I said.

"I see it." He quickly transferred the knife to a small envelope and tucked it into his coat. "We must go, Watson. Quickly and carefully."

* * *

"Ah, Mr. Holmes!" said the Astronomer Royal. "Please come in."

We were now at the doorway to Harewell's office, having made our way down from the roof of the great dome without incident. Once inside, we saw two more men in the room. The older man was standing near to Harewell's desk and the younger one farther away, by the window opposite the entrance.

Harewell said, "Mr. Holmes, please allow me to introduce you and Dr. Watson to our distinguished benefactor, Mr. Martin Pike."

He nodded in the direction of the elder man, a tall, lean, grey-haired gentleman with a grey beard cut in the van dyke style, and a white silk handkerchief in the breast pocket of his expensively tailored suit.

Mr. Pike regarded us with friendly blue eyes. "I am happy to meet you," he said, "and happier still that you may be able to clear up this unfortunate disturbance. Your reputation precedes you."

"Thank you."

"I hope you will be able to assure us that the Observatory is safe."

"Regrettably, all the facts are not yet in my possession," Holmes said.

The other man, a cherubic-faced, red-haired fellow, possibly thirty years old, spoke up from beside the window. "But surely you do not believe that this is a Martian invasion, Mr. Holmes?"

Harewell appeared annoyed at the interruption. He gestured towards the young man. "Gentlemen, this is Clyde Brooks. He was employed here as a computer and is now an assistant observer. Brooks, would you be good enough to leave us?"

Brooks pursed his lips, clearly offended at being put in his place in such a curt manner. But he turned and walked towards the office entrance. Then he stopped, directly facing me. His wide blue eyes had a troubled expression, almost as though they were about to brim with tears. "I knew poor Frazier, you see. I'm happy to tell you what information I possess." He paused and took a deep breath. "I only hope that it may be useful."

"Inspector Lestrade will want to participate," said Holmes. "Please remain on the premises."

Brooks nodded and left us, closing the door behind him.

"Now, Harewell," Pike said, "In view of Mr. Holmes's inability to assure us of our safety tonight, don't you think it would be best to call off the funders' dinner?"

"It's too important," Harewell said. "We need to show a united front. Our benefactors must see that our operation continues even when unfortunate events occur."

"I suppose," said Pike.

Harewell shook his head. "Come, Mr. Pike. I do need your support on this. Keeping unity on our board truly is a necessity. Just think. What would have happened six years ago, if we had broken ranks and cowered in fear of more anarchist bomber attacks?"

Pike looked unconvinced.

Harewell pressed his point more earnestly. "You remember that horrible day. We had no way of knowing if we would be safe. We might justifiably have called off that year's banquet. But had we done so, what supporters might have abandoned us? What great strides would we have failed to make? We might never have acquired the new great equatorial telescope, the new buildings, the new—"

Holmes held up his hand to interrupt Harewell's litany of achievements. "Pardon, Mr. Harewell, but we are all pressed for time. I wonder if anyone has a grudge against either you or the Observatory. A quarrel, perhaps, with the way you are operating things?"

Harewell gave a long sigh. He looked over at Pike.

Pike said, "You may as well tell him. We need his help, after all."

"Very well," Harewell replied. "There are some who, perhaps jealous of our success, have raised objections to the very achievements in which we take such pride. They say our expenditures are too high. They argue that the Observatory cannot sustain itself if it goes on spending at this rate. They will not admit that the scientific advancements—our very purpose for existing—far outweigh the costs, which represent only a temporary outlay. The new knowledge we have gained will benefit all mankind forever. Why, our expertise in spectroscopy, by which we can now detect the varying distances between Earth and our celestial neighbours—and our progress in photography—"

Once more Holmes interrupted. "Do your critics object to matters other than your budget? Your employment policies, for example?"

Harewell shook his head. "Some do criticise our employment policies. Are you referring to our employment of female computers?"

"If people objected."

"Well, then, yes, we did employ female computers a few years ago—an experimental program, done at my initiative, I must point out. But those young ladies did not succeed in their work, so the program was cancelled. Some persons opposed the initiation of the program, and others opposed its termination. I made both decisions and took full responsibility."

"No other opposition?"

Harewell shook his head again. "No other rational opposition. There are some irresponsible lack-wits who would relocate the Observatory to Oxford, on the grounds that the London fog and the vibrations caused by nearby maritime traffic interfere with our ability to make reliable, precise observations. But we have been here in London, on our little hill above the Thames, doing good, solid work for more than two centuries. And the cost to relocate would bring us to financial ruin. Not to mention the disruption in our work, the delays in our reports, which are crucial to the world's navigation—" He broke off and spread his palms. "Surely you can see that, Mr. Holmes."

Holmes nodded. "I presume you will be saying as much to the funders who attend the dinner here tonight."

Chapter 15: Lucy

I sat without moving, breathing through a knife-edged stab of panic as I heard a key turn in the lock on the other side of the door, and then the sound of Agent Thompson and Agent Wilson's footsteps walking away.

True, this afternoon had so far been much less unpleasant than it could have been. I wasn't hurt; I wasn't even tied to the chair on which I sat. But the rasp of the door being locked brought back memories of far less fortunate encounters, and at the moment my mind was unhelpfully calling up a vivid recollection of days I had spent chained up in a filthy underground cellar with a particularly ruthless murderer as a jailor.

Days. I was trying to ignore Agent Wilson's parting words, but they, too, kept echoing in my ears.

Maybe a few days alone in here will help to jog your memory.

There was no food or water in the room, and the air was unpleasantly damp and cold. It would be frigid—dangerously so—at night, when the outside temperature dropped below freezing.

I tensed against a shiver and pushed that thought, too, aside. Jack would find me. Becky would have run to find Watson and Holmes, and they would immediately start searching.

Unless there were more men in the Greenwich Park besides Agents Wilson and Thompson, and they caught Becky before she could reach Holmes.

Stop. All panicking ever accomplished was to make an already bad situation worse.

I stood up, turning in place to take stock of my temporary prison.

There was just the one door, and no windows. With the lamp extinguished, the only light came from a skylight in the roof overhead. It was a fairly large skylight. But—in the manner of warehouses—the ceiling was a solid twenty feet up above my head.

Even if I stood on the chair, I wouldn't be able to reach.

All right. There had to be other options.

The plaster walls were cracked, the paint peeling, but they looked depressingly solid, and the door, too, was a thick wooden panel of good quality, with a heavy lock of the type that requires an excellent set of lock picks to force, not just a simple hair pin. The floor was bare cement, and there was no other furniture in the room apart from the chair.

But there was a built-in cupboard set into one wall.

I crossed and opened it without much hope, then stopped, staring.

A battered metal tool box, the kind that a carpenter might use to keep his hammers and nails, sat on the dusty middle shelf. I tugged it out, awkward with my bound hands, but managed to flip open the latch.

I stared for a second time at the abundant array of chisels, screw drivers, pliers, and awls that met my gaze.

My brows edged upwards. If I couldn't find a way to break out of here with this degree of assistance, I *deserved* to be locked up here for days.

I should have been overwhelmingly relieved, but instead my skin was crawling with uneasiness.

Pleasant surprises were one thing. Strokes of luck that felt entirely too good to be true were another. Even the most incompetent of kidnappers surely wouldn't lock up their prisoner with an entire tool chest full of implements to help her get free—which made it seem as though this had to be some sort of trap.

I raised my head, listening, but there were no sounds at all from the warehouse beyond the door. Only the occasional squeak and rustling scamper of mice or rats that inevitably moved in to infest a place when the human tenants moved out.

Seconds ticked by.

Could it actually be considered a trap if I knew and was prepared to walk into it?

There was a hand saw at the bottom of the tool box. I could take care of the rope around my wrists, if nothing else. I fished it out, braced it against the side of the box, and moved my wrists to saw away at the ropes, all the while debating my options.

Holmes would be worried. Becky would be terrified—or else putting herself in danger to try and find me.

And Jack couldn't afford distractions right now, not when any day might bring danger to him, as well. And wasn't anything—even doing what the enemy expected of me—better than remaining stuck here?

The final strand of the rope around my wrists snapped and fell away.

Before I could change my mind, I picked up both the hammer and chisel, crossed to the door, and delivered a smashing blow to the wood just above the lock.

CHAPTER 16: WATSON

"Yes, it was my telescope," Brooks said.

We were in the computers' room on the first floor, a large, austere workplace barren of decoration, furnished only with wooden bookshelves, wooden work tables and uncomfortable wooden chairs. Brooks was sitting at one of the work tables, his hands clasped before him like a schoolboy. Lestrade, Holmes, and I stood across from him, along with one of Lestrade's constables.

Lestrade furrowed his brows in suspicion. Widening his stance, hands on his knees, he leaned forward to stare directly into the face of the younger man. "How did the telescope come to be found here, beside Frazier's body?" he asked.

Brooks did not appear at all frightened. "I don't really know. Frazier wanted to borrow it last night. I expect that's the explanation. He asked me to bring it for him when I came in to work yesterday, and so I did." Then he added, "By the way, Inspector, I understand you are merely doing your job when you stare at me the way you're doing now. However, it does not move me one way or the other—other than to make the situation more awkward than it needs to be. Could you please back away a bit to a more comfortable distance, there's a good chap?"

Lestrade backed away two small steps.

Holmes asked, "Did Frazier say why he wanted the telescope?"

Brooks nodded vigorously. "Oh, yes. Mars. He was somewhat obsessed with that particular planet. Turns out Mars is closest to Earth at this time of year, and since the weather was fair yesterday, he thought it might hold fair through the night and he might be able to observe the canals."

"Why was he interested in Mars?"

"He's been obsessed with it recently. I don't know why. Possibly because of Mr. Wells' book."

"Why didn't he use one of the larger telescopes inside the Observatory?"

"He wanted to keep his job, I suppose."

"Why would his job be in danger?"

"The staff is not allowed any personal use of Observatory equipment. That's the rule, and it's very strictly enforced, I might add. That is why I bought my own telescope."

Lestrade stepped forward again. "Where were you last night?"

"I stayed home. I only arrived this morning for work."

Lestrade turned to the constable. "Has this been verified?"

"We checked his employment record at the office here, sir," came the reply. "We made a visit to the address listed on his card and found it to be a boarding house. We interviewed the staff and several of the residents. No one there saw him leave or return before he took his breakfast this morning at his usual time."

"Checking up on me, eh?"

Holmes ignored the comment. "Are there other employees here who might have a motive to harm Mr. Frazier?"

Brooks stiffened. "I don't know of anyone here now."

"What about someone who was here before now?"

"Well, I don't like to get anyone in trouble."

Lestrade leaned forward. "Come, Mr. Brooks. We are

investigating a murder. You know there are penalties for withholding evidence from the police. I should advise you to speak up and be very forthright."

"Very well." Brooks sat back in his chair. "Since you insist. I don't say there was anything conclusive about this, but there was a woman employed here not too many years ago who Mr. Frazier courted. They had a falling out. I don't know the details, but, well, she left the Observatory soon after. And you know the sayings about those things."

"What sayings, exactly?"

Brooks squirmed a bit in his chair. "It's awkward. I really don't know who did the breaking up or any of that. But you know what people say about a woman being scorned, and still waters running deep, and revenge best eaten cold. Anyway, the woman was one of the computers here, back in the days when we had female computers."

"Her name?"

"Cowell, it was. Veronica Cowell."

"Do you have an address for her?"

Brooks pursed his lips and furrowed his brow. Then he spread his hands. "Maybe it's in the staff records?"

"I can get that for you, Mr. Holmes," said the constable.

He left the room with Brooks. Then Holmes turned to Lestrade. "Have you obtained the police patrolman's report from last night?"

Lestrade nodded. He pulled a page of paper from his breast pocket. "Here it is. But you won't find anything useful. It is quite perfunctory, and as regards the grounds of the Observatory, identical to the report from the night before and the night before that. Nothing happened there."

Holmes gave one of his little smiles.

Chapter 17: Lucy

It took me five blows with the hammer and chisel before the wood around the lock splintered enough that I could force the bolt open. With every crash, I fully expected Agent Wilson or Agent Thompson to step back through the door, ready to confiscate the tools at gunpoint.

Although if they tried it, at least I wouldn't be entirely unarmed. I would give myself at least a forty per cent chance of winning a fight, now that I had the hammer. Maybe more, depending on how experienced Agent Thompson really was with that gun of his.

But nothing at all happened.

The wood finally split, I wedged the side of the chisel into the crack to snap the bolt back, and the door swung open to reveal an empty, dusty, dimly lighted warehouse, nothing more.

I still hesitated.

I had once accused Holmes of a pessimistic outlook, to which he had responded, *And I have also thus far remained alive*.

It was true; ours was a profession that encouraged—even rewarded—a certain degree of paranoia and a willingness to assume the worst. Right now, I half expected the ground to give way under me the moment I set foot outside the office door.

I shook my head and took a step forward, then another, still clutching the hammer like a weapon. Still nothing happened.

I peered forwards, trying to see through the gloom to make out an outside exit. Night was falling outside, and since the only light came from a row of grime-smeared windows set high up close to the ceiling, it was getting increasingly difficult to—

Something metallic clanked in the darkness straight ahead of me, and then from out of the shadows came a near-blinding flash of green light, followed almost at once by a high, agonised scream.

Chapter 18: Watson

We remained in the computers' room after we had interviewed Brooks. Lestrade went to fetch Mr. Pike and returned with that gentleman soon after. Deferentially, Lestrade stepped aside to usher in the taller man.

Pike doffed his overcoat, slung it over a chair, and sat, giving each of us a pleasant nod.

"Thank you for returning, Mr. Pike," Holmes said. "We have a few questions. Purely routine, in a murder investigation. We hope you will understand."

Pike nodded amiably.

Lestrade, cleared his throat. "Well, to begin, Mr. Pike, where were you last night?"

"At my home in Mayfair."

"Can anyone attest to that?"

"My manservant will vouch for me."

"You came to the Observatory this afternoon."

"I did indeed."

"Weren't you bit early for the dinner? That doesn't start until six, I believe."

"I came to inspect the Observatory to be certain all is ready for the donors' tour."

"Wasn't that Harewell's responsibility?"

"Of course, but I have backed Harewell, you see, in the

board meetings. And important people are coming to the dinner. Anything that might go wrong would reflect badly on me as well. Also, I wanted to make sure the almanacks had been delivered. If they hadn't been, my reputation would truly have suffered. And as you know, Mr. Holmes, in business, reputation is a most essential asset."

Holmes sat forward. "I believe you own the company that printed the almanacks?"

"Quite so. I do own a controlling interest in Lovejoy & Son. One of my more rewarding investments."

"And you also own the Pike delivery company?"

"Yes. So I really couldn't afford for the almanacs to be delayed. I am a self-made man. I would have to take personal responsibility."

"Then your concern is quite understandable," Holmes said.

Pike fingered the tip of his beard. "But there is no point on dwelling on the past. Thankfully, Harewell has confirmed the books are here safe and sound."

"Speaking of your publishing business," Holmes said, "there appears to be a connection with you and the unfortunate Mr. Frazier."

Pike's eyelids flickered. "Oh?"

"According to Frazier's mother, you were thinking of publishing a book authored by him."

"More like the other way around, if you follow me." His features twisted in a wry smile. "He was hoping I would publish some twaddle he wrote about Mars."

"What happened?"

"A sad outcome from his point of view. From ours of course, it was a perfectly ordinary rejection—we turn away hundreds of worthless manuscripts sent to us every month. Frazier's, as I recall, was some dry-as-dust treatise on orbital paths. I did read it, because he was employed by Harewell and because H. G. Wells's book is so popular. But I sent it back straightaway. I couldn't understand one word in ten—and if I couldn't, then the great British public wasn't going to, either."

He paused and took a tarnished silver cigar case from his pocket. "I'm happy to support the Observatory as a donor, but it does no good for me to lose money on some gibberish from a lowly staffer. Lovejoy & Son needs to pay its own bills. Publishing is a business like any other, Mr. Holmes. Our aim is to make money, and we do that by giving the public what they want."

"And business is good?"

"We improve our results with every passing day. That is our objective, and we continually strive to attain it."

"Thank you, Mr. Pike," Holmes said. "Inspector Lestrade, have you any further questions?"

"Not at this time," Lestrade replied.

Mr. Pike put on his coat and left the room.

When he had gone, Lestrade shook his head ruefully. "Well, he wasn't much help, was he? And neither was Brooks."

"It would appear not," Holmes replied.

The little inspector eyed the floor, shoulders slumped, for a long moment. Then he straightened. "I must confess I don't see what I ought to do next. What are your intentions, Mr. Holmes?"

"Tonight's dinner appears to be the focal point for whatever is behind Frazier's murder. We can only attend and await further developments as they occur," Holmes said.

CHAPTER 19: BECKY

Becky liked going to the area around the docks, despite the strong smells of mud and tar and fish, and the fact that the air was always cloudy with black smoke that billowed from the stacks of the steam ships. But the streets were very interesting. All the shops were stocked with gear for sailors—quadrants and bright brass sextants and huge mariner's compasses; oil-skin hats and canvas trousers and fisherman's boots. Even the grocers' stores held the sort of provisions you would need for a sea voyage, like tinned meat and hard tack biscuits that would keep fresh on board a ship.

Today, though, she hadn't much attention to spare for it all—not even for the sailor who was striding along with a bright green and orange parrot on his shoulder. She was too preoccupied thinking about Lucy. What if she wasn't in the same place where Miss Cowell had been taken?

Now that Becky had the chance to think about it, there was nothing, really, to make it definite—or even likely—that Lucy would be there.

She wished now that after leaving Miss Cowell's she had thought to send a message to Mr. Holmes or Jack. Although Jack was probably still out on his investigation, and she didn't know how she could have sent Mr. Holmes a message when she couldn't even be sure that he and Dr. Watson were still at the Observatory. So maybe it wouldn't have made any difference if she had stopped to think.

At any rate, they were here now.

She turned to Flynn. "How are we going to find which warehouse Miss Cowell might have been taken to? Do you know all the empty ones that once had sugar stored in them?"

"Not all. But I'd say it'd have to be one of three," Flynn said.

They were walking along the quay, and he had to raise his voice to almost a shout to be heard over the din all around them. Sailors were singing boisterous songs from onboard an American ship just entering the docks. A cooper was hammering at some wooden casks with a steady rhythmic pounding. The chains of cranes for unloading the cargo ships rattled and clanked, ropes splashed in the water, a captain was shouting orders through his hands. Becky even caught the sound of a goat bleating from some ship in the basin.

"Most warehouses—even the empty ones—have a watchman on guard," Flynn went on. "Even the three I'm thinking of have watchmen who look in from time to time, make sure the windows aren't broken and the doors and windows are all locked, that sort of thing. We'd better have a plan for getting away if one of them spots us."

Becky nodded, although she wasn't really bothered about watchmen. "What did you think about Miss Cowell's flying story?"

"You mean, do I think she's a nutter?"

"Do you?"

Flynn considered. "No. She seemed straight all right—not

lying. And not crackers, either. I think something strange really happened to her." For the first time, he stopped walking and looked around them uneasily. "You reckon some of that stuff about men from Mars could be real?"

"They weren't men in the story," Becky said. "They were sort of slimy monsters—with tentacles and big eyes."

Flynn looked at her. "And that's supposed to make me feel better how?"

"It's supposed to make you feel better because I don't for a moment believe that if Martians landed here on earth, the first place they'd go would be the London Docks. Which makes the odds of our running into one approximately nil—oh."

Becky was the one to stop walking this time.

"What's the matter?" Flynn asked.

"I forgot! I completely forgot the paper that was tucked inside of Mr. Frazier's book! It fell out when Lucy and I were leaving his mother, and I picked it up, but then those two men came out and pointed guns at us—"

Becky still had *The War of the Worlds* tucked into her coat pocket. She tugged it out. "I slipped the paper back inside the front cover when I saw them, but then with Lucy missing I just didn't think of it, not even to tell Mr. Holmes."

The paper was exactly where she'd left it, tucked in between the cover and the first page.

"Let's have a look," Flynn said. "Anything important?"

"I don't know." Becky frowned at the series of dots and dashes that marched across the page in rows.

"Looks like Morse code," Flynn said. Mr. Holmes had given them a lesson on it a month or two ago, on the theory that one never knew when it might come in useful to be able to signal at a distance. "What'd Frazier want to go writing things down that way for? It's not much of a way of keeping it secret, if that's what he was trying for. Anyone can look up letters in Morse."

"I know. Do you remember enough to read it?" Becky knew that she for one didn't have the Morse Code alphabet well enough memorised to translate what the message said. She'd intended to study the sheets Mr. Holmes had given them, but the book on surgery and anatomy from Dr. Watson had been much more interesting.

"That word there." Flynn pointed at a series of dashes and dots. "Does that say, *Peace*?"

"I'm not sure." Becky stared at the paper, though this time she wasn't really seeing the markings. "I've just remembered something else about Mr. Frazier. His mother said that two weeks ago he was sleepwalking. He was leaning out of a window and when she called to him, he told her that he'd learned how to fly."

Flynn crinkled up his forehead. "You're saying whatever happened to Veronica could have happened to him, too? But he didn't go missing. Unless you think whatever picked Veronica up from out of her dress shop and dropped her off down here at an empty sugar warehouse somehow picked up Frazier, too—and maybe set him down hard enough to crack his head open?"

"No," Becky said absently. Something about Veronica's story was tugging at the back of her mind. "For one thing, I don't believe that anything can really make people fly like that. And for another, Mr. Holmes said it wasn't the fall that killed Mr. Frazier."

She frowned, trying to work out what part of Veronica's story had reminded her of something. Something about flying?

"This way," Flynn said, leading the way down a narrow passage between two of the warehouses that fronted the quay.

Night was falling, which was lucky for them, because it meant there were deep shadows that made it easier for them to pass through without anyone noticing.

"Did anything strike you about Veronica?" she asked.

Flynn considered. "She uses Lovejoy & Son for her printing," he said. "But that's probably not the kind of thing you mean."

"She does? How do you know?"

"She got that phone call about the handbills she was having printed, and she looked down at her desk while she was talking. So I looked, too, and I saw there was an invoice from Lovejoy & Son on top of a pile of papers. I saw their trademark all over the crates of books Mr. Holmes asked me to keep an eye on, so I know it was—" he stopped, tilting his head, then added in a whisper, "Hold on a second. There's a watchman or someone up ahead."

Becky listened, and heard heavy booted footfalls from close by. She held still, pressing herself next to Flynn against the side of the nearest building.

Frustration bit at her. But as long as she couldn't go anywhere, she could use the time to think.

Flynn was right, Lovejoy & Son billing Veronica for printing wasn't the kind of detail she'd been asking about, but at the same time it seemed like it might be important, if only she could work out how. Somehow, all of this fit together and made a pattern: Veronica's bill from Lovejoy & Son … the message written in Morse code in Mr. Frazier's book …

A rat squeaked and dashed across the ground right in front of them, followed closely by a black cat.

Becky drew a quick breath. "Witches!"

Flynn clamped a hand over her mouth. "Why don't you try

yelling again? I don't think the night watchman heard you that time," he hissed.

"I'm sorry." Becky peeled his fingers back and matched his whisper. "But I've just remembered! The black cat made me think of it: witches."

"You said that already." Flynn was looking at her like she was the one to sound crazy now. "Think maybe next you could get around to explaining what the dickens you're talking about?"

"I am explaining! I remember reading about it in one of the books on medicine that Dr. Watson lent me. It was talking about poisons that could be made from plants. Belladonna and atropine and things like that. And it said that if you took them orally—ate or drank them—they could make you sick and even kill you. But if you put them in an ointment and then rubbed them into your skin, they could give you all sorts of strange—"

Becky cut off speaking as the words—along with her breath—suddenly got stuck in her throat.

There was a window in one of the buildings up ahead, and through it a sudden flash of light had just blazed out: a brilliant apple green.

CHAPTER 20: WATSON

At the Observatory, Holmes and I waited just inside the doorway of what had been Harewell's spacious office. The area had been transformed since we had seen it this morning. It was now a banquet room, with white linen tablecloths on what had formerly been six long worktables. The guests were to arrive at 7 o'clock. Awaiting them were place settings with silver, china, and crystal goblets. At each place was a complimentary copy of the latest Nautical Almanac, personally inscribed by Harewell.

We had still received no word about Lucy. Nor had we heard from Jack, though Holmes had left a message for him at Scotland Yard. Holmes had not spoken more to me of Lucy's absence. However, his straight back and darting grey eyes revealed his tension.

We heard footsteps on the stairs leading up to the hallway outside where we stood. I consulted my watch. The time was exactly 7 o'clock.

A uniformed constable arrived. "We had them gather in the lobby as you instructed, Mr. Holmes," he said. "They are all behind me."

"Satisfactory," Holmes said. "Now, Watson, let us step back and watch Mr. Harewell greet his guests."

Harewell nodded effusively to Mr. Pike and to each guest as they entered, indicating that they should stand in a group to the side of the entrance. The guests were all resplendent in evening garb: the women in furs, the men in top hats. When all had clustered together, Harewell addressed them.

"Ladies and gentlemen," he said, "My profuse thanks to each and every one of you for attending our festive banquet. We will have no speeches here this evening; only a sumptuous meal." He made a sweeping gesture, taking in the room, where several liveried waiters had begun to file in from the other door, pushing champagne carts topped with silver ice-buckets.

"But before we begin our repast," he continued, "I propose we make a brief sojourn to the new building so that you can personally inspect the wonderful acquisition that has now been installed beneath the great dome of our Observatory. It is the largest telescope of its kind …"

Holmes whispered, "Downstairs, Watson," and stepped briskly to the exit, leaving the guests listening to Harewell's enthusiastic oration.

I followed.

On the staircase I asked, "Why, Holmes?"

"Brooks is not among either the guests or the staff," he said.

We reached the bottom of the stairs, where a staff member waited at the exit door, ready to escort the guests into the observatory. "Have you seen Mr. Brooks?" Holmes asked.

"A few minutes ago. He was going into the Observatory to make sure all was in order."

Holmes opened the door to the darkened courtyard. Cold air rushed in. We took the few steps across the courtyard to the Observatory. Another attendant stood at the entry door bearing a lit lantern. Holmes repeated his question about Brooks and received a similar answer.

"Prepare for the guests," Holmes told the attendant. "They will be down here momentarily."

The attendant stood aside for us to pass. Holmes opened the Observatory door.

The inside of the room was just as cold as the outside. Electric lights shone dimly on sconces around the walls of the circular enclosure. Their light revealed the great telescope, nearly thirty feet long and painted a greyish tan. The huge cylinder tilted sharply upwards towards the space high above us, where a cleft in the great onion dome allowed visual access to the night sky. From where I stood, the sky seemed only a curved swath of blackness.

"That is Brooks." Holmes said. "On the floor beneath the observer's chair."

I turned to stare at the crumpled figure beneath the great telescope, about a dozen feet from me. For a moment I felt a wave of dizziness, for I realised what a shock this would be for Hartwell and his guests and how utterly disastrous it would be for his planned festive event.

Then I was moving towards the inert figure. I thought, *I must do what I can for him.*

Holmes stood beside the body, his expression grim. He held a medicine bottle in his hand. "Chloral hydrate tablets," he said. "Sleeping pills. No way of determining how many Brooks may have taken." He gestured towards a work table beside the observation chair. "But it would appear he intended to take an overdose."

On the table lay a single page of notepaper. And on the paper, these words were printed in block letters:

I CONFESS TO POOR EMMETT'S MURDER.
I CAN NO LONGER LIVE WITH MY GUILT.

"Please do what you can for him," Holmes said. "I must keep the guests from seeing the spectacle."

But even as he spoke, two of the guests appeared in the doorway.

One of them was a woman.

She uttered a piercing scream.

Chapter 21: Becky

Becky stood stock-still, feeling as though her feet had got stuck in hardening concrete. The green light blazed out of the warehouse window—and then, as if that wasn't eerie enough, from somewhere inside, someone started screaming: high, thin yells that barely sounded like anything human.

Flynn snatched up the broken half of a brick that was lying on the ground and raised it, about to smash through the window.

"Wait—I'm not sure that's a good idea!" Becky said.

He gave her a look. "Oh, now you think maybe we shouldn't be here?"

Whoever was inside was still screaming though, sounding frantic—or maybe in pain?

Becky blew out a hard gust of air and nodded. "You're right. We need to get in."

Flynn smashed the pane of glass, using the brick to clear out the jagged bits along the bottom edge. Then he hoisted himself up and through the gap.

As she followed him, Becky thought about all the trouble they'd taken to avoid being seen by one of the night watchmen—and yet now just when she'd have been nothing but glad to see an adult coming to take charge, there didn't seem to be anyone within half of a mile, despite the green light and the amount of noise coming from inside.

Her dress caught on a shard of glass Flynn had missed and she tugged it free, then landed with a thump on the warehouse floor.

She stared. A man lay writhing on the ground a few feet away from her, his body engulfed in greenish flame.

Flynn jerked back, his eyes wider than Becky had ever seen them. "You said no Martians or heat-ray guns!"

Becky scarcely heard him, though. She had just caught sight of a second figure who was standing outlined in a doorway on the far side of the warehouse.

"Lucy!"

"Becky?" Lucy ran towards them, though she stopped when she came within a few feet of the man on the ground, who was still screaming and crying out.

"He's accidentally caught himself on fire!" Her voice was crisp, calm and commanding. "Step away or you'll get burned, too. But we need something to smother the flames."

They all looked around, and then Flynn said, "Here!"

There was a pile of old canvas in one corner—a sail from one of the ships on the quay, maybe, that had needed mending. Flynn caught hold of one corner and started to drag it over. Becky and Lucy ran to help, and together they dropped it over the burning man.

Lucy bent, slapping the canvas over the flames until they finally died down. The man had stopped screaming, but he must have fainted, because when the fire was finally out and his clothes stopped smouldering, he just lay motionless, his head lolling back.

Becky drew in a sharp breath as she looked more closely at his face. "That's—"

"Agent Thompson," Lucy finished for her. "Yes. Although

I'm certain that's not his real name. Whoever he is, he's going to need a doctor. Flynn?"

"A watchman could send for a doctor." Flynn looked down at the man on the ground and swallowed, his eyes still wide. "I'll try to find one. This is going to take some explaining."

"Just say that there was an accident with a lamp," Lucy said.

"A lamp?" Becky looked past the unconscious man and realised for the first time that there was a lantern knocked over on its side—one of the big brass maritime navigation lanterns she'd seen on board ships.

"That and the sodium borate he must have used to produce the green flames," Lucy said. "Likely his pockets were filled with the stuff. But there's no need to go into all of that, just fetch help. As quickly as you can."

Flynn nodded and took off at a run.

"What about sodium—" Becky started to ask, but Lucy cut her off by hugging her tightly.

"I'm so glad that you're safe! But what on earth are you doing here? How did you find me?"

"We went to see Veronica Cowell. Flynn and I." Becky told her everything—about their visit to Veronica's, and Veronica's strange story, and the message in Morse code that they had discovered inside the cover of *The War of the Worlds*.

"But I don't see how any of it makes sense," she finished at last.

Lucy shook her head. "It does, though." She didn't look anything like her father, not really. But when she'd got an idea about a case and her eyes sparked in a certain kind of excited way, she always reminded Becky of Sherlock Holmes. "It's actually all beginning to fit together at last. But as soon as Flynn comes back and we can hand Agent Thompson here over to someone who'll get him medical attention, we need to get back to the Observatory as fast as possible. Although I think—" she stopped, frowning. "Yes, I think it would be best if we made one short stop along the way."

Chapter 22: Watson

We had moved Brooks to a long table in the Observatory workroom. Fortunately, he still breathed. I had seen white powder around his lips and the corners of his mouth, and had done the best I could to expel it from his system by administering hot soapy water from a basin brought by one of the constables. Brooks expelled all the water into one of the champagne buckets from the banquet room, but I could not see the remains of any tablets.

His other affliction was a large swollen bump at the back of his skull. I had applied a wet towel, packed with ice from the champagne bucket. That towel now functioned as a pillow for Mr. Brooks, who lay on his back, stretched out on the table.

I stood on one side of the table, ready to stop him from rolling off if he suddenly awoke. A uniformed constable stood on the other side.

It had been nearly an hour since we had discovered him. His breath had grown deeper and more regular, which was a good sign. If his attacker had managed to hit him harder or get him to swallow any more of the sleeping pills, he would not have survived.

Now he moaned. I waited. Then he blinked rapidly and opened his eyes. He saw me. "What happened?" he asked in a hoarse whisper.

"You appear to be out of danger," I said. "What do you recall?"

He shook his head momentarily and winced at the pain. "Nothing," he said. "Nothing except getting into the observation chair of the great refractor."

"Why did you come to the telescope?"

"I knew Mr. Harewell and the others were all coming to see it before they went back for dinner."

"The donors, you mean?"

"Yes. I was hoping that I could get the eyepiece and focus worked out so that the most important donors could have a look for themselves. That would properly impress them, I thought."

"Then what happened?"

"I felt someone come up behind me. Then something hit the back of my skull. Then … well nothing, really. I woke up here and saw you."

"Do you recall writing a note?"

His eyebrows furrowed. "A note? What note?"

I hesitated. Holmes had the note. Or Lestrade might already have taken possession of what no doubt was important evidence. I wondered how much I ought to tell him while he lay there in his weakened condition.

"The note said you had murdered Emmett Frazier and could no longer bear your guilt."

His eyes widened. He tried to sit up. "I did no such thing! Let me see that note! I never wrote anything like that!"

"All in good time," I said.

"But it's all wrong! And it's not fair! I never—" He paused, as if recollecting something, and then drew himself up to a sitting position, elbows locked, palms at his sides, bracing himself. "It doesn't make any sense. Was I supposed to have tried to commit suicide by hitting myself on the head? You don't believe that, do you, Doctor?"

"There was a bottle of sleeping tablets beside you," I said. "You appeared to have taken an overdose."

"No, I didn't!" He paused, apparently thinking. "What time is it?"

"A few minutes past eight o'clock."

"In the evening?"

"Yes."

"And I'm awake. Not too alert, I suppose, but still awake. Would I be awake like this if I had really taken more than the prescribed amount?"

"That would be most unlikely. Though you clearly had ingested some of the sedative. Your heart rate was slow, and you took nearly an hour to wake."

"Then it means someone hit me and forced me to swallow whatever it was. Yes. Someone hit me and drugged me, and tried to blame me for murder!"

"That may indeed be the case," I said.

He turned his body and swung his legs over the edge of the table, preparing to get down and walk. But his legs buckled under his weight. He pulled himself up, with my help, and sat, legs dangling.

"So what happens now?" he asked.

"I will consult Sherlock Holmes. You will remain here. Constable, please ensure Mr. Brooks does not fall or otherwise injure himself."

* * *

A minute or two later I entered the Observatory banquet room and found Holmes and Lestrade interviewing the last of the guests. A constable stood behind them, writing in a notebook. Harewell stood at the doorway, awkwardly attempting to shake hands and mollify the still-shocked men and women as they completed their interviews and left the room. Most appeared simply anxious to get away. I noticed that the almanac books still remained on the tables along with the unused silverware and china.

When the last pair of guests had departed, Holmes turned to me. "Well?"

"Brooks is out of danger," I said. "If the murderer had managed to hit him harder or get him to swallow more of the sleeping pills, he would not be alive."

"So the dose he took was not fatal. Is he awake?"

"He is asking to see the note. He denies writing it. Says he doesn't remember."

"Can he walk?"

"If aided," I said. "A constable is with him."

Holmes turned to the Astronomer Royal. "Mr. Harewell, could you and the constable please go downstairs and bring Mr. Brooks up to this room?"

When Harewell and the constable had gone, Holmes took me to a desk that had been moved to the side of the room. "This desk belongs to Mr. Brooks." He opened the drawer. "And here is a jar of sodium borate hidden in his drawer. I found traces of the powder on the roof masonry. Those traces are in an envelope in my pocket."

Lestrade said, "Sodium borate?"

"It produced the interesting green flash of light that Mr. Harewell witnessed," Holmes said. "Sodium borate thrown on an open flame—such as in an oil lantern—would produce a flare of green flames which could then be quickly extinguished."

Lestrade said, "Which indicates Brooks may have been the murderer after all. He could have killed Frazier, tried to make it look like Martians, and panicked when he found that the police saw through the ruse. Then he made up that suicide note and took the sedative pills."

"And then coshed himself on the back of the head?" Holmes asked.

"It would be possible," Lestrade said.

Holmes nodded. "But you will note that we found no cosh. So I believe the explanation is not quite so simple as that."

He might have continued, but just at that moment, Lucy arrived with Becky and Flynn.

Chapter 23: Becky

When Becky arrived, she saw familiar people at the tables in the now nearly empty dining room. Mr. Holmes and Dr. Watson were seated at one table, while Mr. Harewell and a tall grey-haired man with a grey goatee sat at an adjoining one, along with Inspector Lestrade. Two uniformed constables stood at the door, guarding it so that no one could leave without getting past them.

Another man, young, red-haired, and round-faced, sat slumped a little off to one side. He looked exhausted and rather sick, his skin pasty white and his eyes slightly red-rimmed. He was rubbing his temples as though he had a headache.

"And you can remember nothing at all of the attack on you?" Mr. Holmes was asking him.

Becky felt a thrill of excitement slipping through her. She didn't know what, exactly, Mr. Holmes had in mind. But someone wasn't going to walk out of this room a free man, once Mr. Holmes had finished explaining.

That was why, when Lucy moved forward to sit beside Mr. Holmes and Dr. Watson, Becky had pulled Flynn to a table towards the back of the room. So long as they kept quiet, she thought, it would be easier for the adults to forget they were there. She didn't want anyone to tell them that they had to leave.

At the moment, though, she was regretting the choice, because she had to lean forward so that she could hear the young man answer Mr. Holmes.

"No. I'm afraid not, sir. I felt a terrific blow to the back of my head, and then—nothing. I'm sorry I can't be more help."

Mr. Holmes didn't look bothered by the lack of information. "It is only to be expected, Mr. Brooks. At least you are here with us still. I congratulate you."

So this was Mr. Brooks, Becky thought. Here was the man who had been sweet on Veronica Cowell, and a rival with poor Mr. Frazier for Veronica's affections.

"Indeed, sir." Mr. Brooks nodded, then winced as the movement probably made his headache worse. "I assure you, I consider myself to have had a very fortunate escape."

The man with the grey goatee didn't look as though he was likely to add to Mr. Holmes's congratulations. He looked to be in a very bad temper and wasn't bothering to hide it, either. "I demand some sort of explanation for all of this, Holmes," he growled. "Why are we still kept prisoner here instead of being allowed to leave with the rest?"

"And you shall receive your explanation, Mr. Pike, I assure you."

Becky's pulse quickened and her breath came a little faster. So this was Mr. Pike, the man who poor Mr. Frazier had hoped would publish his book, and who owned the company that delivered books to the Observatory that afternoon. How would he connect with the case? From the confident way Mr. Holmes spoke, Becky was sure she was about to find out.

Mr. Holmes turned. "Lucy. Would you care to begin?"

"Thank you."

Mr. Pike transferred his heavy-browed glower to Lucy for

a moment, then evidently dismissed her, because he turned back to Mr. Holmes. "I don't see why I should be forced to listen to some twittering female when I've not even been allowed to have my dinner yet!"

"I'm so sorry, Mr. Pike." Lucy gave him her sweetest smile, although seeing the look in her green eyes, Becky thought that if Mr. Pike had any sense, he would be worried. "But since I've been threatened at gunpoint, abducted, and held against my will today, I imagine that you might somehow bear up under the strain of delaying your evening meal. I promise to make the time well worth your while."

Mr. Pike made a wordless sound like, 'Hmph,' but subsided into his chair, arms crossed on his chest.

"To begin," Lucy said, "I suppose we must start with our murder victim's fascination with the planet Mars. And the fact that those who knew him reported that he had been excited about his important project, the details of which were a closely guarded secret. Unfortunately, an intruder broke into the house he shared with his mother and no doubt made away with the majority of the paperwork associated with the project. But they missed one small scrap. This."

She held up the sheet of paper that Becky had found inside *The War of the Worlds*.

"Since I'm endeavouring to be as brief as possible"—she glanced at Mr. Pike—"I'll spare you a reading of the entire thing. The messages are quite repetitive and not terribly imaginative, either, all about wishing to extend a hand of greeting in peace. Suffice it to say that Mr. Frazier believed he was receiving missives from the race of beings who inhabit Mars."

Mr. Harewell, the Astronomer Royal, startled. "But that's

outrageous—impossible!" he protested. "Frazier was a scholar and a man of science. He would never have believed such a preposterous hoax—"

"Not if he was in possession of all of his faculties, no," Lucy agreed. "The trouble was that poor Mr. Frazier was being subtly and systematically drugged. Not much, just enough to keep him off-balance and more readily credulous than he would otherwise have been."

"Drugged," Mr. Harewell repeated. "But what—how—"

"Becky was the one to first make the connection." Becky almost jumped when Lucy smiled at her from across the room. "She ought to be the one to tell of it."

If Mr. Pike didn't like having to pay attention to Lucy, he especially didn't like being forced to listen to an eleven-year-old girl. He looked like someone had made him take a drink of sour milk.

Becky stood up very straight. "Veronica Cowell talked about having a dream—a hallucination, rather—of flying through the air. It reminded me of a book I'd read about poisons and medieval witches. The author thought that maybe the witches confessed at their trials not because they were tortured but because they really did think that they could fly around on broomsticks and things like that."

Mr. Pike snorted.

Becky ignored him and kept going. "I don't mean that they could actually fly. But if you make an ointment out of certain herbs—Belladonna was one of them—it can make you hallucinate, sometimes about flying. I think that's what happened to Mr. Frazier. Mr. Holmes told me that he had a rash on his wrist. Nothing serious, but he had a jar of skin cream in his room. Lucy and I saw it. I think someone added Belladonna or some other drug to it. And I think the same thing happened to Miss Cowell. Someone had sent her samples of skin creams and perfumes and things. I think whoever did this mixed Belladonna into the skin cream—and maybe drugged her cup of tea on the day that she was abducted, too. She didn't actually say as much, but I think it's likely that she had a—" Becky looked at Mr. Pike's scowling face and faltered for a second. She'd thought Mr. Pike simply a bully up until now—a puffed-up rich man, the kind who thought himself much more important than he really was.

But the rage in his gaze now made her feel suddenly cold. "A delivery that afternoon," she finished.

"Yes," Lucy agreed.

Becky wasn't scared, not with Mr. Holmes and Lucy and everyone else here. But she still let out a small breath of relief when Lucy was the one to go on.

"Becky and Flynn tell me that you do all the printing for Miss Cowell's business, Mr. Pike. Handbills and sales circulars and such."

"What of it?" Mr. Pike bristled. "Lovejoy & Son has many business clients. Including the Royal Observatory."

"True. But not all of them are mixed up in murder cases or are mysteriously abducted by unseen forces." Lucy's voice was quite calm. "Do you know what I think, Mr. Pike? I saw the shoddy condition of your coach, which makes me think that Lovejoy & Son has been in difficult financial straits recently. You needed a way of earning money, and quickly. So, you thought up a scheme that would make one of your publications a bestseller. Did you plan Emmett Frazier's death from the first, or was he killed because he had started to suspect the truth?"

Mr. Pike had gone purple in the face. "Preposterous! Outrageous!" he spluttered.

"Is it, really?" Lucy, at least, wasn't the slightest bit intimidated by the hatred in his eyes. She leaned forward. "You and your accomplices managed to persuade poor deluded Emmett Frazier that he was receiving communications from another planet. Mirrors placed at just the right angles up on the Observatory tower would have made flashes of green show through the lens of his borrowed telescope. You had already, or so you thought, prepared him by drugging Veronica Cowell, too, so that she could be taken to an empty dockside warehouse—and then go running to Emmett with her strange story of what would appear to be a supernatural abduction. All of this was designed to make him ready to believe that there really were alien forces at work here. It was just bad luck that Emmett's mother didn't tell him of Veronica's visit, and so he never heard about the mysterious force that had brought her out of her own shop premises and down to the docks. At any rate, whether because he had begun to suspect the scheme or because it had been your intention to dispose of him all along, you killed him."

"Oh, I did, did I?" Mr. Pike was trying hard to sound careless—as though Lucy's accusation was too silly for him to even worry about. But he couldn't quite carry it off. A glistening of sweat had sprung up on his forehead. "And just how did I do that, eh?"

"As a primary benefactor of the Observatory, you had ready access. You knew the date of the funders' dinner. You knew the staff had been given the night off. I imagine that you lured him up to the Observation room, which you knew would be unoccupied. You induced him to look through the telescope, and then suffocated him. The black powder around the nostrils—coal dust, according to the preliminary report from the laboratory—disguised the bruising, but it was visible once you knew what to look for. Placing the body would have been tricky—but then, Emmett was killed long before Mr. Harewell actually found the body. That was why Dr. Watson thought the victim's muscles were unusually rigid and suspected poison. He had been dead long enough that rigor mortis had begun to set in. I imagine that sometime near midnight you and your confederates—likely the two men who abducted me—carried the body outside to the paved driveway where it was found, and lifted it with a tripod construction crane, like those used by timber mills to lift heavy logs. Such a crane is easily and quickly assembled, and its height can reach up to one hundred feet, high enough to produce a considerable impact on a falling body. You used a winch to raise the body up to the maximum height. You released the winch. The body plummeted to where it was found on the pavement. Then you and your confederates swept the pavement. Of course, you also had other work to do outside—the patches of scorched earth, the scorched trees, the odd marks in the ground, suggestive of a Martian tripod fighting machine. Although perhaps you staged all of that before Emmett arrived. At any rate, when everything was arranged, you ignited the flash of green light on the roof of the Observatory facing Mr. Harewell's window, using the sodium borate that we found in Mr. Brooks' desk."

"You haven't a shadow of proof!"

"Not yet. But Mr. Holmes did find a residue of sodium borate on the observatory roof, and Inspector Lestrade's constable saw a farmer's hay wagon pass through Greenwich Park below the Observatory early this morning. An odd occurrence, surely. This area isn't a particularly agricultural one. I doubt that your confederates drove the cart very far before hiding it in some convenient clump of woods further into the park. It shouldn't be hard to find it, and when we do, I would wager better than good odds that we find buried beneath the hay both the tripod and winch mechanism and the device you used for creating the three footprints of the Martian fighting machine."

Mr. Pike laughed. It was a very unconvincing laugh, high and strained-sounding. "And just why would I have carried out all of this … this tom-foolery?"

"For money, Mr. Pike," Lucy said. Her face was still calm, but there was something dangerous in her voice. "A great deal of money. Mr. H. G. Wells' story about a Martian invasion has sold a great many copies indeed. But how many more sales would come from an account of a true Martian invasion?"

Mr. Harewell sat bolt upright in his chair. "A true—"

"Indeed. In addition to all the mysterious evidence surrounding Mr. Frazier's death, there was my own abduction by a pair of shadowy government agents, supposedly charged with investigating occurrences that had no natural explanation. Or at least, that was what they claimed to be," Lucy said. "What they actually were, though, was a couple of out-of-work actors. I've worked in the theatre long enough to recognise their type when I see it. They were desperate enough for work to agree to play the parts of Agents Wilson and Thompson. But they were obviously nervous. Probably they hadn't been told that they were going to be mixed up in a murder case and it made them very uneasy. I did test the theory. While they were carrying out their so-called interrogation of me, I made a reference to The Scottish Play. You may not know it—not many people outside of the theatre world do—but actors consider it bad luck to ever reference Macbeth.

So much so that they won't even call the play by name. A pair of authentic government agents—or hired thugs—would have asked what I was talking about. Agents Wilson and Thompson knew exactly what the reference meant. They didn't hurt me or even try to, and they left me in a locked room that was so easy to escape from that it was almost laughable. That was another mistake—it made me realise that they intended for me to get out. That the entire purpose of abducting me in the guise of government agents sent to investigate a Martian attack was so that I *would* escape—and serve as one more impartial witness to the authenticity of Mr. Emmett Frazier's death by alien hands. They had even planned to stage another little performance for me once I did break out of the locked room—another mysterious flash of green light."

Lucy's voice hardened. "I hope you paid the man who called himself Agent Thompson well, Mr. Pike. He's going to need money to cover the medical expenses for treatment of burns over half his body. If he survives."

Mr. Pike passed his tongue across his lips. "You don't have a shadow of proof of that preposterous story either!"

"Oh, but that is exactly what I do have," Lucy said. "It may interest you to know that we paid a visit to your warehouse this evening on our way here. We found crates and crates of these." Lucy drew a book out from under the table and held it up, displaying the title. Becky had already seen it, but she still shivered a little all the same. *Messages from Mars* was written in bold gold lettering across the cover.

Mr. Pike's face wasn't purple anymore, it had gone all grey and splotchy. He tried to say something, but only a kind of hissing gurgle came out.

"Your sales would have been enormous," Lucy went on. "Especially if the Astronomer Royal could be counted on to provide a welcome to the crowds who would come flocking to see where Martians had first made contact with humanity. Human nature being what it is, I'm sure you could have done a brisk business in opening hotels and restaurants, selling refreshments and souvenirs—plaster casts of the supposed Martian footprints and little metal replicas of their fighting machines. The public loves a spectacle, especially one associated with violence. The Observatory might become as big an attraction as the Tower of London, which draws thousands of visitors every week."

"What?" Mr. Harewell was staring at her, clearly aghast. "I would never—"

"I don't mean that you would have permitted such a thing," Lucy said. She spoke more gently to Mr. Harewell than she did to Mr. Pike. "No, Mr. Pike would have needed to ensure the appointment of a new Astronomer Royal."

"A new …" Mr. Harewell sank back in his chair and mopped his forehead, looking dazed.

Mr. Holmes had been letting Lucy do the talking, but now he said, "Yes, Mr. Pike had already begun a concerted effort to discredit you. The first step of which lies at each place on the tables here in this room. I refer, of course, to these almanacks." He picked one up from the table nearest him. "Those intended for distribution at tonight's dinner—and indeed all the others that came to the Observatory—are counterfeit. And they are crammed with errors."

Harewell gasped and then recovered himself. "Impossible!" he said. "I inspected the galley proofs myself!"

"And those galley proofs would match the books that left

Lovejoy's this morning," Holmes said. "But the books that left Lovejoy's never reached the observatory."

"How can you say—"

"One of my agents observed the crates at Lovejoy & Son, being loaded onto the lorry owned by Mr. Pike's delivery company. The lorry drove into Mr. Pike's warehouse. Shortly afterward a smaller lorry emerged and then delivered twelve crates to the Observatory. But those were twelve different crates. During the period that my agent had them under observation, Mr. Pike's men never had time to transfer crates from the large lorry to the smaller one. That smaller lorry was already loaded and waiting with the crates that arrived here. Those crates contained the counterfeit almanacks. Those like this one." Holmes lifted the almanac in his hand, holding it out to the Astronomer Royal. "All intended to ruin your reputation, Mr. Harewell."

Harewell stared, mouth agape, at Pike.

"Well, Mr. Pike?" asked Holmes. "Have you anything to say? No? Well, perhaps we ought to try our luck with your co-conspirator."

Becky was watching Mr. Pike, and she saw his expression go from sullen to alarmed.

"Oh yes." Mr. Holmes didn't smile very often, but there was a faint curve to his lips now. "You didn't really believe that we were unaware of the identity of your partner in this enterprise, did you?"

He paused, letting the words hang in the air for a long moment. Then he suddenly swung around on Mr. Brooks, who was still huddled in his chair, looking ill and miserable.

"I refer, of course, to you, Mr. Brooks."

"I?" Mr. Brooks straightened up with a disbelieving sort of laugh and ran a hand through his hair. His laugh wasn't, Becky thought, any more convincing that Mr. Pike's had been. "What do you mean? I was attacked tonight—you yourselves were witness to it! I was attacked and poisoned! I might have died!"

"Hardly that, Mr. Brooks. Men very seldom die from a minor bump on the head and a mild dose of sleeping draught. Dr. Watson can testify that had you taken more of the chloral, you might well have perished. As it was, your life was in no danger. The staged attack was, however a clever way of diverting suspicion away from yourself. Two things gave you away, however. The first was Lucy's abduction. Only someone who worked at the Observatory could have overheard me speak of her visit to Frazier's mother, and ordered the false agents to intercept her upon her departure. And second, the involvement of Miss Cowell." Mr. Holmes's expression was stern with distaste. "That was unnecessary. It also smacked of pettiness and injured pride—exactly the sort of behaviour I would expect from a vain, shallow man whose romantic attentions to Miss Cowell had been spurned and who sought a way of getting even with the lady."

"It's not true!" Mr. Brooks mopped his forehead with the back of his hand. He was trembling, Becky saw. "None of this is—"

Mr. Holmes ignored him and kept talking as though Mr. Brooks hadn't even spoken.

"You thought to become the new Astronomer Royal, once Mr. Harewell was successfully disgraced and discredited. You managed to persuade Mr. Pike that you stood a good chance of being next in line for the posting. An ambition that, even if you were not a murderer, I feel sure would have failed. You lack both the brains and the scientific method to achieve such a position."

"That's a lie!" Mr. Brooks' face was flushed now, and had gone from scared to angry looking.

"Careful, Brooks," Mr. Pike growled. "Don't say anything!"

But Mr. Brooks kept on speaking as he stood up, glaring at Holmes. "It was a brilliant plan! We worked out every detail!"

"Be quiet!" With a roar of fury, Mr. Pike launched himself at Mr. Brooks, locking his hands around the younger man's throat and carrying him to the ground.

"I think that will do." Mr. Holmes regarded their struggling forms with a calm expression. "Lestrade?"

"Not quite a confession, but definitely incriminating." Lestrade said.

He nodded to his officers, and the two constables dragged Mr. Brooks and Mr. Pike apart, snapping handcuffs onto their wrists. As they turned Mr. Pike over, Becky noticed a bulge in the pocket of Mr. Pike's well-tailored suit. She signalled to Mr. Holmes, pointing first to Mr. Pike and then patting her own coat pocket.

"Lestrade, you might want to check Mr. Pike's pocket," Mr. Holmes said. "There may be a cosh in it."

CHAPTER 24: WATSON

Holmes and I were back in our sitting room, finishing a late supper kindly provided by Mrs. Hudson.

"I particularly enjoyed the way you goaded Brooks," I said.

Holmes dismissed my compliment with a wave of his hand. "It was necessary," he said. "We had good evidence that Pike *could* have committed the murder, but we did not have evidence that Pike actually did. Fortunately, Brooks was vain as well as emotional and incompetent. His own pride betrayed him. The subsequent scuffle with Pike gave Lestrade enough evidence to hold the pair, with the cosh in Pike's pocket being a bonus. Soon more evidence should be obtained."

"By finding what was hidden in the farmer's hay cart, you mean?"

"That and the testimony of Lucy's abductor, who is now in hospital. Assuming he survives. Or the testimony of the other man, the one who called himself Agent Wilson. Assuming we are able to locate him. Also, we shall investigate Pike's financial dealings." He took a pull at his pipe and exhaled a cloud of smoke. "Pike may have made investments in Oxford land, expecting the Observatory to move there. I will ask Mycroft to learn what he can. And finally, though perhaps this point bears more cause for concern than it does proof of Pike's villainy, we have the curious incident of the police patrolman's report."

"The police patrolman reported no activity."

"Yet the report, you recall, said that he made his rounds every half hour."

The realisation sunk in. "The erection of a hundred-foot-tall crane, the winching up and dropping of Frazier's body, the flames of the kerosene fire, the disassembly of the crane, and its being loaded onto a farmer's hay wagon—all of that could never have been done between the time the patrolman passed by once and then returned again a half hour later. And no patrolman with functioning eyes and ears could have failed to notice."

Holmes gave me a long, straight look. "Your conclusion?"

"That the report was falsified," I said.

"A cause for serious concern, you will agree."

Chapter 25: Lucy

The fire was burning low in our sitting room grate and rain pattered against the windows as I finished telling Jack about the day's events.

"So just as Lestrade was leading Brooks away, Becky suddenly came over and punched Brooks on the nose—for Veronica Cowell, she said, because Veronica wasn't there to do it herself."

Jack laughed. "Wish I'd been there to see it."

"I don't know who was more surprised—Lestrade or Mr. Brooks. I actually saw Lestrade trying to hide a smile afterwards, though, so it may be that he has a sense of humour after all." I paused, then asked, "How was your day?"

Jack had listened to my account of the case attentively, sitting on the couch beside me with all his usual still-muscled, coiled energy. But there was a grim shadow lurking at the back of his eyes.

"I—"

A knock at the door interrupted him. Instantly, Jack sprang up, his hand going to the regulation police club he'd set on the table when he'd taken off his uniform belt, and he stepped in front of me, putting himself between me and any potential danger.

He was even more on-edge than I'd realised.

He relaxed, if only partially, when the evening's post dropped through our letter box.

"Sorry." He stooped to pick up the envelopes.

I raised my eyebrows. "Do you think I can't defend myself?"

"Well …" Jack made a show of looking me over, head to toe.

"What are you doing?"

"Checking to see if you're still carrying a gun before I answer that." His smile faded in an instant, though, as someone knocked on the door. Jack jerked it open, then stopped in surprise.

"Nibbs."

Nibbs stood on the threshold, the brim of his stovepipe hat dripping from the rain that still fell outside.

"You'd better come in." Jack stepped back to allow him entrance, but Nibbs shook his head.

"No, I'm not stopping." He twisted long, thin hands together. "I … that is, I was just passing by, in a manner of speaking."

I stared, looking at Nibbs more closely. He had just turned down the opportunity to come inside and cadge a free meal. Something was badly wrong.

Jack's brows drew together. "What's happened?"

"I—" Nibbs swallowed visibly. I had never seen him look so shaken, his face pale and his eyes darting nervously from side to side. Cold crawled down my spine in anticipation of whatever it was he was about to say.

"Remember that mate of mine? The one I was telling you about, who got paid to act the jolly on the day that Inspector got himself shot?" he asked.

"I remember."

"Well." Nibbs gulped a lungful of air and started again. "The fact is, he decided to go to the police with wot he knew—or said he knew. I was against it! I told him, Nothing good ever comes of getting mixed up with the rozzers! But he thought as how there might be money in it for him, so he went along—"

"Yes, all right." Jack's voice was calm, but I could hear him working to keep the edge of impatience from his tone. "We understand. What happened?"

"Dunno." Nibbs' hands were shaking, now. "I dunno wot happened or wot he said to the rozzers—or them to him. Next thing I knew, he's turned up dead."

"Dead?" Jack repeated. His whole body had gone very still.

"S'right." Nibbs' head jerked in a nod. "He was found floating in the river not an hour ago. Thought you ought to know," he added.

"Nibbs, wait—" Jack began.

But Nibbs was already gone, not even bothering to close the door behind him before sliding off into the rain-drenched night.

"Are you going to go after him?" I asked.

Jack shook his head. "No point. He's too badly frightened to tell us anything more than he already has."

"So his friend was murdered, after telling the police he'd been present when Inspector Glenn was shot." I was liking this less and less. "It begs the question of exactly what story he gave the police."

"Or what story they'll say he told them," Jack said. "It's not like anyone can contradict any report they might have. Not now he's dead."

He was still holding the evening's post in one hand. He glanced down, saw the writing on the uppermost envelope, and tore it open.

"What is it?"

Jack looked up at me, his expression darkening. "Official notification that they're opening up an inquiry into Inspector Glenn's death. I'm to report to the Yard tomorrow morning for questioning."

The telephone rang. My heart was still thudding in my ears, but I went to answer it.

"Yes?"

Holmes' voice spoke on the other end of the line. "Mr. Pike and Mr. Brooks were questioned at Scotland Yard. Then they were to be transferred to Holloway prison tonight."

"Yes?"

"The police wagon transporting them was attacked, and both Pike and Brooks were killed by persons unknown."

THE END

Historical Notes

This is a work of fiction, and the authors make no claim whatsoever that any historical locations or historical figures who appear in this story were even remotely connected with the adventures recounted herein. However …

1. Photograph on the next page, contemporary to our story, shows where Mr. Frazier's body was found.

2. The Observatory remained in operation at Greenwich until 1948, when its telescopes and staff were moved to East Sussex due to the ever-worsening problem of air pollution. In 1990, the Observatory moved again, north to Cambridge, where it operated until its final closure in 1998.

3. The original Observatory buildings remain in Greenwich as part of the Royal Museums. Before the COVID epidemic they entertained and enlightened more than two million visitors every year. Learn more at https://www.rmg.co.uk/royal-observatory

4. In 1890 five women were hired to work as computers at the Royal Observatory by William Christie, the innovative and resourceful Astronomer Royal who inspired the character of Christopher Harewell in our story. The

women were paid monthly in amounts ranging between four and eight pounds. By the spring of 1892, three of the five women had left. The remaining two were gone by the end of 1895.

5. An anarchist bomber did detonate a dynamite bomb close to the Observatory, on February 15, 1894. The bomber was killed in the event, so his motives are unknown. Novelist Joseph Conrad drew inspiration from the incident for *The Secret Agent*, published in 1907 and now a classic.

Lucy James will return.

A Note of Thanks

Thank you for reading this collection of Sherlock and Lucy stories. We hope you've enjoyed it.

As you probably know, reviews make a big difference! So, we also hope you'll consider going back to the Amazon page where you bought the story and uploading a quick review. You can get to that page by going to this link on our website and scrolling down:

> sherlockandlucy.com/project/collection

You can also sign up for our mailing list to receive updates on new stories, special discounts, and 'free days' for some of our other books: www.SherlockandLucy.com

About the Authors

Anna Elliott is the author of the *Twilight of Avalon* trilogy, and *The Pride and Prejudice Chronicles*. She was delighted to lend a hand in giving the character of Lucy James her own voice, firstly because she loves Sherlock Holmes as much as her father, Charles Veley, and second because it almost never happens that someone with a dilemma shouts, "Quick, we need an author of historical fiction!" She lives in Pennsylvania with her husband and four children.

Charles Veley is the author of the first two books in this series of fresh Sherlock Holmes adventures. He is thrilled to be contributing Dr. Watson's chapters for the series, and delighted beyond words to be collaborating with Anna Elliott.

Printed in Poland
by Amazon Fulfillment
Poland Sp. z o.o., Wrocław
31 August 2023

18f21f26-fc8a-4553-a733-9244117358d9R01